Evil Above the Stars
Volume 2

The Power
of Seven

Evil Above the Stars
Volume 2

The Power of Seven

Peter R. Ellis

Elsewhen Press

To Alison

Map of Gwlad

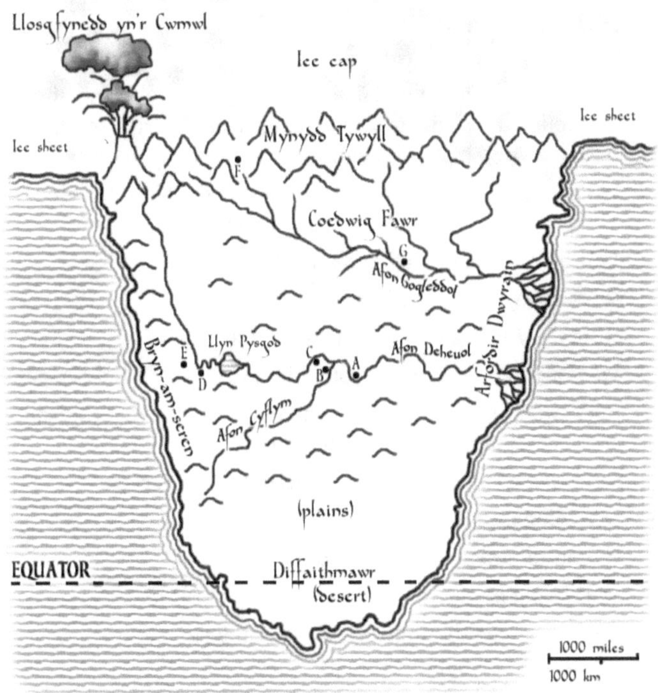

Towns and Villages:

A-Amaethaderyn

B-Abercyflym

C-Glanyrafon

D-Dwytrefrhaedr

E-Arsyllfa

F-Mwyngloddiau Dwfn

G-Trefyncoed

Pronunciation guide

The 'old tongue' used by the people of the Land is derived from Celtic languages such as Welsh. General guidelines on pronunciation are as follows.

'll' does not occur in English, in the glossary it is written as 'LL'. The sound is made by partly opening the mouth, pressing the tongue against the roof of the mouth and blowing gently.

'dd', written as 'TH' in the glossary, is the hard th sound in 'this' and 'that' but not as in 'path'.

'a' is always as in 'cat' and not as in 'ape'.

'e' is always as in 'pet'.

'f' is the v in 'van' while 'ff' is the f in 'fan'.

'c' is always the hard 'k' sound in 'kid'.

'ch' is similar to ck and pronounced as in the Scottish 'loch' and not the English 'church'.

'g' is always hard as in 'god' and not as in 'german'.

'o' is like in 'on' but not 'open'.

'i' and 'u' are pronounced 'ee'.

'r's should be rolled.

'si' is between the sh in 'shone' and the j of 'john'.

'w' is oo as in 'cool'.

'y' is sometimes the u sound in 'run', sometimes the i in 'bin' and occasionally the ee sound in 'been'.

'yw' is pronounced 'you'.

'ae', 'ai', 'au' and 'ei' are all pronounced 'eye'.

'eu' is the oy in 'boy'.

Glossary

Word	[Pronunciation] Meaning
Adarllwchgwin	[ad-ar-LL-ook-goo-in] giant eagle bearing red devil-like figures with tridents, air manifestations of the Malevolence
Adwyth	[ad-oo-eeth] The Malevolence, the evil from above the stars
Afon Deheuol	[a-von de-hoy-ol] Southern River, one of the great transport links of Gwlad
Afon Gogleddol	[a-von gog-leTH-ol] the great northern river
alcam	[al-kam] tin, a silver-grey malleable metal
Aldyth	[al-dith] a sword
Amaethaderyn	[am-eyeth-ad-er-in] Farm of birds, a village on the Afon Deheuol, the southern river
Arfordir Dwyrain	[ar-vord-eer doo-ee-rine] the coastal region on the east of Gwlad
arian	[ar-ee-an] silver, a rare silver metal
arianbyw	[ar-ee-an-byou] mercury, dense silver liquid metal
Arsyllfa	[ar-siLL-va] The observatory-cum-fortress in the Bryn am seren in the west of Gwlad
Aur	[eye-er] gold. A rare, maleable, yellow metal
Bryn-am-seren	[brin-am-ser-en] Hills of Stars, a range of low mountains in the west of Gwlad
carregmam	[kar-reg-mam] mother stone
Ceffyl dwr	[kef-ill doo-er] Water horse, a giant aggressive winged horse, a water manifestation of the Malevolence
Cemegwr	[kem-egg-oo-er] Creators, chemists, the Makers of everything
Cludydd	[klee-deeTH] bearer or wielder
Coblynau	[kob-lin-eye] dwarf-like creatures with rock crushing hands, earth manifestations of the Malevolence

Word	[Pronunciation] Meaning
Coedwig Fawr	[koy-doo-ig vow-er] The Great Forest south of the mountains
Cwn annwn	[koon ann-oon] fiery hounds, a fire manifestation of the Malevolence
Cyrhyraeth	[kir-hir-eyeth] a moaning, disease-bearing wind, an air-manifestation of the Malevolence
Cysylltiad	[Kuss-uLL-tee-ad] The Conjunction, the lining up of all the planets
Daear	[die-ar] Earth, the planet at the centre of the universe
Diffaithmawr	[dif-eyeth-ma-oo-er] The great desert at the southern end of Gwlad
Draig tân	[dry-g tarn] Fiery dragon, comet. A fire manifestation of the Malevolence
Dwytrefrhaedr	[doo-ee-trev-rheye-der] The two towns by the waterfall, on the River Deheuol
efyddyn	[e-vu-TH-in] copper, a malleable red metal
egwyddorpum	[egg-oo-eeTH-or- pim] the quintessence, the fifth element that forms the stars and the Maengolauseren
Glanyrafon	[glan-ur-avon] Village on the bank of the river Deheuol
Gwener	[goo-en-er] Venus, the 3rd planet from the Earth in the geo-centric system
Gwlad	[goo-lard] The Land – the occupied continent on Daear
Gwyllian	[goo-iLL-ee-an] old women, earth manifestations of the Malevolence
haearn	[heye-arn] iron, a hard grey metal
Haul	[h-eye-el] Sun, the 4th planet from the Earth in the geo-centric system
Iau	[ee-aye] Jupiter, the 6th planet from the Earth in the geo-centric system
Llamhigwyn y dwr	[LLam-heeg-oo-in u doo-er] giant flying frogs, a water manifestation of the Malevolence
Lleuad	[LL-eye-ad] Moon, the 1st 'planet' from the Earth in the geo-centric system

Word	[Pronunciation] Meaning
maengolauseren	[mine-gol-eye-ser-en] stone of starlight or starstone, the stone of power held by September
Malevolence	[mal-ev-o-lens] the power of evil from above the stars
Mawrth	[ma-oorth] Mars, the 5th planet from the Earth in the geocentric system
Mercher	[mer-ker] Mercury, the 2nd planet from the Earth in the geo-centric system
Mordeyrn	[mor-day-ern] Leader
Mynydd Tywyll	[mun-iTH tu-oo-iLL] the dark mountains in the north of Gwlad
plwm	[ploom] lead, a dense, soft grey metal
prif-	[preev] chief, head
Pwca	[Poo-ka] a shape-changer, an air manifestation of the Malevolence
Sadwrn	[sad-oo-ern] Saturn, the 7th planet from the Earth in the geo-centric system
seryddwr	[ser-iTH-oor] observer of the stars and planets
symudiad	[see-mud-ee-ad] the ability to transport instantly from one place to another
Toddfa Penbaladr	[To-TH-va Pen-bal-ader] The Alkahest or Universal Solvent. The liquid that dissolves and combines everything
Trefyncoed	[trev-in-koyd] Town in the trees on banks of the northern river
Tylwyth teg	[tul-oo-eeth teg] pale, fairy-like creatures, earth manifestations of the Malevolence

Dramatis Personae

Alawn	[ala-oon] young guide to Bryn-am-seren
Anarawd	[an-ar-owd] chief bearer of copper
Arianell	[a-ree-an-eLL] bearer of silver at Mwyngloddiau Dwfn

Arianrhod	[a-ree-an-rhod] Chief bearer of silver
Arianwen	[a-ree-an-oo-en] The cludydd o arian, silver-bearer, of Amaethaderyn
Aurddolen	[eye-er-TH-olen] chief bearer of gold and leader of the Land
Betrys	[bet-rees] Chief bearer of tin
Breuddwyd	[broy-TH-oo-id] September's mother
Cari	[kar-ee] bearer of copper at Mwyngloddiau Dwfn
Catrin	[kat-rin] The cludydd o efyddyn, copper-bearer, of Amaethaderyn
Collen	[ko-LL-en] elderly guide to Bryn-am-seren and cook
Cynhaearn	[kin-heye-arn] Chief bearer of iron
Cynddylig	[kin-THil-ig] older man, boatman and river guide
Cynwal	[kin-wal] Chief bearer of lead
Eluned	[e-lee-ned] The cludydd o arianbyw, mercury bearer, of Amaethaderyn
Elystan	[el-is-tan] young guide to Bryn-am-seren
Eryl	[er-ril] astronomer
Gwrion	[goo-ree-on] mature guide to Bryn-am-seren
Hedydd	[hed-eeTH] astronomer's apprentice
Heini	[High-nee] Chief bearer of mercury
Heulfryn	[hoyl-vrin] bearer of gold at Mwyngloddiau Dwfn
Heulwen	[hoyl-oo-en] daughter of Aurddolen
Heulyn	[hoyl-in] chief bearer of gold and leader of the land at the last conjunction
Ilar	[ill-ar] bearer of tin at Mwyngloddiau Dwfn
Iorwerth	[ee-or-oo-er-th] The cludydd o haearn, iron-bearer of Amaethaderyn
Isfoel	[is-voy-el] bearer of mercury at Mwyngloddiau Dwfn
Maerwen	[my-er-oo-en] the name given to Malice by her mother
Malice	twin sister of September
September	The Cludydd o Maengolauseren
Sieffre	[jef-re] young man, lead guide to the Bryn-am-seren
Tudfwlch	[teed-voolk] young warrior and ironsmith, apprentice to Iorwerth

Previously... in Seventh Child

Part 1 ~ Arrival

Looking at the stars through a glassy stone September has found she is transported to the world of her dreams. She is greeted by the Mordeyrn Aurddolen, a bearer of gold, as the Cluddydd o Maengolauseren, the wielder of the starstone, who will save the people of Gwlad from the Malevolence, the "evil from above the stars". September is told that she has this position of responsibility and power because she is the seventh child. September is confused because she only has four sisters and a brother but nevertheless when she helps Aurddolen resist an attack by a Draig tân, a fire dragon, she discovers that the starstone does indeed have miraculous properties.

September returns home till the time when the threat of the Malevolence will be reaching its peak. At school she is bullied because of her flab, white hair and silly name and is considered lazy and dim but she finds some answers to the questions her brief visit to Gwlad has posed. On her sixteenth birthday she learns that she had a twin sister who died at birth and that she is indeed the seventh child of her mother. In the evening she looks through the stone at the stars and is again transported to Gwlad.

Her arrival in the village of Amaethaderyn is welcomed by the bearers of the other six metals but they tell her that she must embark on a long journey following Aurddolen to the fortress-observatory, the Arsyllfa. During the preparations for her departure the village is attacked a number of times by manifestations of the Malevolence and September realises that she is the focus for the attention of the evil.

Previously... in Seventh Child

Part 2 ~ Journey

The metal bearers give her gifts of silver, copper, iron, mercury, tin and lead imbued with the powers of the six planets which, together with the Sun, orbit the stationary world of which Gwlad is part. She sets off on the river in a gold-powered boat accompanied by Tudfwlch, an apprentice warrior/blacksmith and Cynddilig a boatman/guide. During the weeks that follow September learns more about her task but they are attacked by various manifestations. The starstone will protect September but only when she is truly afraid.

Tudfwlch and Cynddilig are killed and September is rescued by Heulwen, the daughter of Aurddolen. She is taken to Dwytrefrhaedr, the twin towns by the waterfall. From there, September and Heulwen, assisted by warrior/guide Sieffre and four other guards, set off on the final stage of the journey, on foot, across the range of hills known as the Bryn am Seren. Climbing the highest peak with the Arsyllfa at its summit they have to fight through hordes of manifestations. At last they reach the great doors of the fortress but September is hailed by a woman in black who appears to be directing the besieging monsters. She has white hair and a face that September recognises as her own. The woman warns September that the Arsyllfa will become her prison and then unleashes her forces. September steps through the doors of the fortress, her journey complete, but her task barely begun.

Part 3

~

Conjunction

1

September looked up and saw Nisien's dark, lined face. She was resting in his arms, facing the closed iron doors of the Arsyllfa. This was her destination, the culmination of a month's journey, but she felt drained and more frightened than at any time since she had been summoned to Gwlad. What was the apparition that she had just seen? It looked like a version of her, a shadow of herself; could it really be her unborn twin? What did it mean?

"Are you hurt, Cludydd?" The deep, mellow voice of the Mordeyrn was familiar and the warmth in his tone so reviving. The burning in her birthmark on her hip was gone and although she was exhausted she discovered that she was actually unharmed. She pushed herself onto her feet and thanked Nisien.

"No, I'm okay," she said, seeing the entrance hall of the Arsyllfa for the first time. In contrast to the dull brown of the exterior, the inside was light. The floor and the columns that held the ceiling were of white marble, veined with gold. The walls were also white, and the ceiling high overhead was translucent. Despite the evil fog that had surrounded the peak, light streamed in from above.

"In that case, Cludydd o Maengolauseren, welcome to the Arsyllfa."

"Mordeyrn!" September ran forward and fell into his open arms. He hugged her to his white-robed chest. There was something about his father-like authority that made the Mordeyrn special to her. Perhaps it was his dedication to her; the fact that he was the first person she had met when she had first been called to the Land and the only connection with Amaethaderyn, the village that had welcomed her arrival.

"Please, call me Aurddolen."

"Did you see what I saw?"

"Now, just before you came through the doors?"

"Yes, the woman in the cloud, dressed in black."

"I did but I do not understand. She did not appear to be another Pwca or any other of the Malevolence's familiar manifestations."

"No, she wasn't. She was me."

"She bore a resemblance. An attempt at imitation perhaps."

"No, I mean, she wasn't me but like me. My twin. The twin that died."

"Ah, I begin to comprehend. We have much to discuss you and me, but first we must welcome you properly to the Arsyllfa, make you comfortable and let you rest."

The great doors resounded to an impact. September turned, suddenly fearful that the doors would come crashing open. Aurddolen held her tight.

"Do not fear. The doors will hold. The Malevolence does not have the power to break through the doors or the walls. Yet." He put an arm around her shoulder and guided her into the fortress with Nisien behind them.

They left the high, spacious hall and entered a more intimate room furnished with chairs and wooden tables. Heulwen was already handing out orders to men and women who scurried around. She saw them enter.

"Ah, father and Cludydd, there you are. I am trying to get some order here. Nisien, go and help in the kitchen."

Sieffre had been keeping quiet, standing with his back to a wall. He spoke.

"I think, Heulwen, it would be advisable if Nisien and myself cleaned up before assisting the preparation of food. We both carry the sweat of battle."

September looked from Sieffre to Nisien and it suddenly came to her that of the six men who had set out from Dwytrefrhaedr with her, only these two survived. A sob welled up in her throat.

"What is the matter my dear?" Aurddolen asked.

"I've just realised. I don't know how I could forget really, but four of our guides didn't make it here. Alawn, Elystan, Gwrion, Collen, they've all been killed by the monsters. I only knew them for a few days." She cried. Aurddolen took her into his arms.

"Brave men they were too. I knew them well. They would be pleased to know that you are here safe."

"That's it. It's all about me isn't it? All these people getting killed trying to help me and I've got no idea what I'm supposed to be doing."

Aurddolen caressed her head.

"Now, now, my girl. You have done a tremendous amount just getting here and without any guidance in bearing the Maengolauseren. Come, let us go to my study and talk things over." He guided September through the room, pausing to speak to Heulwen, "Oh, daughter, let Sieffre and Nisien get cleaned up and let the people get on with their jobs. I am sure you need to rest too."

Heulwen was speechless and stared angrily at her father.

Aurddolen led September along a corridor and up a spiral staircase until they were far above the entrance floor of the Arsyllfa, then along another corridor. At last he stopped at a door and pushed it open. They stepped into a small study with a table, a chair, a more comfortable easy chair and a bookcase. The books caught September's eye immediately: large leather-bound books. She hadn't seen any reading material since she had arrived in the Land and she wondered what was in them.

"Sit down my dear. Make yourself comfortable. You must be exhausted after your climb. Oh, and you can take the cloak off now. You won't need concealment here."

September slipped the metallic silver cloak from her shoulders. It felt strange taking it off after the weeks of wrapping it around her.

"May I look at it?" The Mordeyrn asked.

"Yes, of course." September handed it over then sank into the softly furnished chair. It felt delightful to be sitting comfortably. The fatigue oozed from her legs.

"It is a work of great skill and beauty," Aurddolen said, examining the minute links made of the tin-lead alloy.

"It is and I think it worked well except that I had to get the stone out so many times," September said.

"Yes, you met more opposition than I expected. The Malevolence has grown more powerful very quickly, and it has been surprising."

"Surprising?"

"Yes, its attacks have seemed to have had more purpose, more direction than I expected from the old stories."

"What do you mean?"

"Well, the stories tell that on previous occasions when the evil has risen, the attacks have been spread across the Land, random, unfocussed, meaningless. That is until the Cludydd and the Maengolauseren drew them. But on this occasion the manifestations have been concentrated around the route you were expected to travel, and the concentrated siege of this building over the last three days is unheard of. The Malevolence should not have the wit to maintain such an onslaught."

"But, I've been told that the Arsyllfa wasn't even built the last time and you have said yourself that it is pretty special with all the iron, tin, lead and gold in its walls."

"You are correct of course, September, but nevertheless I am worried that the Malevolence seems to have acquired some intelligence."

"Such as my twin sister?"

"Ah, now there you have it." The Mordeyrn scratched his chin while sitting down in the other chair. "That is indeed an unexpected factor. A soul that failed to achieve life cast out beyond the stars and yet bound to the Cludydd o Maengolauseren by the womb."

"She spoke. She knew who I was, my real name I mean, and she threatened me."

"Yes, there is knowledge, intelligence and power there; something that the evil has never had before. Its blind hate has been sufficient in the past to wreak havoc until the Cludydd banished it from the Land. But with your twin to influence it our task may be more difficult than I anticipated. Hmm." He pondered silently and September watched his furrowed forehead.

"I think," he said at last, "we must make a start on your training at the earliest opportunity. When you have developed control over the powers of the Maengolauseren you will have the strength and resilience to probe this link with your sister." September didn't like the sound of that. "But first, I must act the good host and show you to your accommodation, get you fed, and acquaint you with the other guests of the Arsyllfa." He stood, placed the cloak over his arm and held out a hand to September. Reluctantly she relinquished the comfort of the chair.

They left the Mordeyrn's office but only went as far as the next doorway on the corridor. Aurddolen pushed the door open and stood aside.

"Enter, please, my lady. This is your accommodation while you are with us here."

September took a step inside and then stopped. The room was much bigger than the Mordeyrn's simple study. The marble floor and walls had brightly coloured rugs and hangings that made it warm and welcoming. There were lights in the ceiling but September could not see the source of the illumination. Oil lamps and candles had been the only artificial light she had experienced on her journey but these seemed brighter and more like electric lamps. The furnishings too were unlike anything she had seen previously. There was a bed, larger and more comfortable even than the one that she had briefly lain on in Dywtrefrhaedr, and there was a table and chairs, a sofa, cupboards and shelves.

Aurddolen strode across the room to a large wardrobe. He flung the door open.

"I knew you would not be bringing much luggage, so I had these clothes prepared for you," he said. He hung the metal cloak over an empty coat hanger. September saw gowns and dresses in a variety of colours and textiles hanging there.

"This is all just for me"?"

"Of course. You are our most noble guest, the one for whom the Arsyllfa has waited since it was constructed. This suite was built at the heart of the fortress to provide a safe dwelling for you." Aurddolen moved to another door, and opened it revealing a bathroom as well equipped as any September had seen at home.

"Everyone is of course eager to meet you, hear about your journey and discuss the battles that lie ahead, but you should not feel that you have to hurry. Take your time to rest and join us for a meal when you are ready."

"Everyone?"

"The Prif-cludyddau; assembled here to plan our defence

against the Malevolence at the Cysylltiad."

"Prif-cludyddau?"

"The senior bearers of all the metals. The Council of Gwlad, if you like."

"They are here to meet me?"

"They are here at my bidding to face the greatest threat to our existence since the last Cysylltiad and you are the focus of all our effort."

"I see." What September did see was a lot of people expecting a lot of her.

"How will I find you?"

Aurddolen indicated a thick rope beside the bed.

"Pull the bell cord and someone will come to your aid or to guide you. Now I will leave you and hope to see you shortly, but only when you are ready."

September guessed that in fact they would like to meet her immediately but that their good manners prevented them from insisting that she join them at once.

"Thank you, Aurddolen. I'll join you as soon as I can."

Aurddolen bowed and retreated to the door, closing it behind himself.

September walked around the room. The plush comfort seemed unbelievable after the hardships of the last few weeks. With relief she unbuckled the belt from her waist and laid the sword, knife and pouch attached to it on the table. She went into the bathroom and turned the bronze taps over the bath. Hot and cold water poured out. She had thought to wash briefly and re-join the Mordeyrn but the filling bath tempted her. She tore off the soiled and threadbare clothes she had worn for the last three days and stepped gingerly into the steaming water. It was delicious to immerse herself. She lay in the hot water for some minutes just revelling in the fatigue and fingering the phial of mercury and the starstone in its clasp that lay against her breastbone. Sleep may have come to her there and then but conscience pricked her. Soap and a sponge were placed handily on the side of the bath so she gave her whole body a thorough scrub. Then she pulled the plug and stood up to let the water run off her. She looked around for something to dry herself with and saw a pile of soft, fluffy towels on a wooden stand. She stepped out of the bath dripping water on the marble floor and flung a towel around herself.

I really am dreaming, she thought, this is like staying in a five star hotel. The contrast with the hovels at Amaethaderyn and the hardships of her journey across the Land seemed incredible. She investigated the toilet and found it as sophisticated in its flushing qualities as any that she had experienced at home.

She returned to the bedroom and looked in the wardrobe. The variety astounded her but she decided that she did not want to wear anything too ostentatious. She'd leave that to Heulwen. There was a simple white gown, not of the heavy linen that the women of Amaethaderyn wore, but neither was it expensive silk. At home it would have clung to her bulges but here it fitted her toned body perfectly. At the bottom of the wardrobe she found simple sandals. She removed the tube of mercury and laid it on the table next to her other possessions. Now, just the Maengolauseren in its silver case rested between her breasts. There was no mirror to check her appearance so she just hoped that she looked respectable. She ran her fingers through her white hair which had grown considerably in the last few weeks and now rested on her shoulders. A brush would be useful but she could not see one anywhere. That would have to wait. There was nothing now to stop her from joining the waiting throng, but she was worried. She had never been someone that people looked to expecting something of her, not even her group of friends. She was that silly girl September, talentless, brainless and despite the distinctive white hair definitely not good looking. Facing a whole crowd of people each with their skills at manipulating metals was scary. Nevertheless, she couldn't keep them waiting for ever.

She tugged on the bell rope. There was a distant, faint, sound of a bell. She sat on the sofa and composed herself for a wait, but just moments passed before there was a tap on the door.

"Come in," September called uncertainly, trying to find the correct tone of voice to use. She was not used to giving orders. The door opened and Sieffre entered. He too had washed and changed into clean clothes.

"May I help you, my lady?" he said, bowing slightly.

"Oh, please call me September. I'm no-one's lady."

A smile flickered across his face.

"Oh, I think you are, but I understand what you mean. What do you wish, September?"

"Aurddolen said there was food and a whole bunch of people waiting to see me."

"That's right. They are trying not to look impatient."

"Well, you had better guide me to them then."

"I will be delighted. Come with me."

They walked along corridors and down stairs until September was thoroughly disorientated. At last they came to a pair of tall doors. Sieffre stepped forward, pulled both doors open then stood to the side. He signalled for September to pass through. She entered a huge room with a large table laid for a formal dinner. The diners had been sitting but now they rose, some more swiftly and athletically than the others. It was difficult for September to take it all in at first. She saw Aurddolen at one end of the table, Heulwen sitting between two middle-aged men and about ten other men and women sitting around the table. There was one empty place at the end opposite to Aurddolen.

"Welcome, Cludydd. We have kept your place for you. Please join us." Aurddolen pointed to the unoccupied chair. September realised that it was a place of honour and she felt nervous, not used to being treated as someone special. Nevertheless she made her way to her place and was pleased that Sieffre, having closed the doors, followed her. She placed her bottom on the chair and everyone sat down. Immediately more men and women entered the room from other doors carrying plates and trays and bowls. Food was laid in front of her and a goblet filled with liquid. September discovered that she felt ravenous and quickly joined the other dinner guests in tucking into the cooked meats and vegetables with spicy sauces. September was surprised to see people serving others because she had come to believe that in Gwlad no-one was above another except in talent. Yet here the guests seemed to be treated as special people. She noticed, however, that the servers didn't retreat or stand aside as servants were accustomed to do but they also took plates and bowls and sat at smaller tables around the room eating, drinking and chatting.

Once September had consumed a few mouthfuls of food she remembered to take a closer look at the dinner guests, starting with the pair closest to her. On her left was a man. He looked to be over seventy years of age with white hair and wrinkled face and hands. To her right was a woman who could have been the mother of Arianwen, the silver-bearer of Amaethaderyn. She too was silver-haired and sat with her back straight but her age and experience were obvious in her lined face. Having filled her mouth again September smiled at her two neighbours. They seemed to have been waiting for her to notice them.

"We are delighted that you have arrived safely, Cludydd," the man said, "let me introduce myself. I am Heini, Prif-cludydd o arian byw."

"Arian byw? Oh that's mercury, Eluned's metal."

"Eluned?"

"She gave me some mercury which helped me find the stone when it was lost." The elderly man looked confused. "I'll explain some time." He looked relieved.

"And this is Arianrhod, the Prif-cludydd o arian."

"Ah, silver. You remind me of Arianwen at Amaethaderyn."

The woman smiled.

"She is my daughter. I visited her at Amaethaderyn once. A charming place. That was where you were summoned I gather."

"Near there. On a hill across the river from the village. That was where I, um, arrived."

"Aurddolen's adopted home. He seemed to sense that that was where he could make the link to you in your world."

"But you're not from there?"

"No. My home is on the Afon Gogleddol, the other great river, north of Amaethaderyn. That is where Arianwen was born."

September turned to Heini.

"And where is your home?"

"A village on the eastern coast between the two rivers. I

wish I was there now. The cold winds in these hills freeze my bones."

"And these other people are also Prif-cludydd?"

"That or mordeyrn of their region," Heini said, "Aurddolen called everyone here to discuss how we can defeat the Malevolence. I must admit we did not expect to be besieged in the Arsyllfa."

"But we are grateful for the forethought of Heulyn in designing such an impregnable fortress against the powers of evil," Arianrhod went on.

"This Heulyn seems to have been a great man."

"He was," Heini nodded emphatically, "Defeating the Malevolence at the last Conjunction was only part of it. He made preparations for the next rise of the evil."

"Tudfwlch told me the story of the last bearer of the starstone."

"Tudfwlch? Who is he?" Heini asked.

"He was my companion from Amaethaderyn. He died."

"Oh, I am sorry," Arianrhod said her face full of sympathy, "Was he a victim of the Malevolence?"

"Yes," September's voice croaked and she felt a tear run down her cheek.

"Oh, my dear," Arianrhod said, "we heard that you have had a troubled journey beset by the manifestations. I am sorry if this is difficult for you."

September wiped her eyes.

"I'm being silly. Aurddolen says that they gave their lives willingly to get me here but it seems such a waste and I don't know whether I deserve such help."

"You certainly do, Cludydd," Heini said firmly, "you are the hope of all of us in the Land."

"Now, Heini, can't you see that the Cludydd is just a young girl not used to such responsibility? Telling her that it's up to her to save us all is hardly going to cheer her up is it?"

"Yes, but..."

"Now, Cludydd, or may we call you September?"

"Please, I'd like that," September sniffed and took a sip of the drink in the goblet. It was the same sharp, refreshing liquid she had drunk at Dwytrefrhaedr.

"Would you like to tell us about your journey and these

brave friends that you had, or is that too painful?" Arianrhod asked.

"No, I'd like to. I want to remember what they were like." September began to tell her story from the moment she arrived in Gwlad. It took a lot of telling in between eating the wonderful fresh food. She had barely started on the journey up the river when the room fell silent and she looked up to see the Mordeyrn rising to his feet, a goblet in his hand.

"I want to welcome the Cludydd o Maengolauseren, the latest bearer of the starstone. She barely understands the purpose of her calling but knows that we have great faith in her. But faith is not sufficient to defeat the Malevolence, so we must also thank the brave people who have supported the Cludydd on her arrival amongst us and on her journey, and especially we remember those who gave their lives to give us hope." Aurddolen paused and there were murmurs of approval from the guests, then he continued, "But enough of solemnity. Thank you all for your company this evening, and," he said casting his eyes away from the main table, "all of you who are working so hard to maintain this observatory and look after its guests. I am pleased to report that the Malevolence has ceased its siege of the Arsyllfa, at least for the time being. The sulphurous mists have lifted and our view of the heavens is once again as clear as it should be. Night has fallen while we ate and so I suggest we climb to the observatory itself and show the Cludydd a little of the purpose of this institution, fortress and refuge. First however, let us drain our cups and be cheered that we are together," he urged, raising his goblet, "To our hopes for times to come."

The Mordeyrn sat down amongst echoes of his toast, and excited chatter. People got up and started to clear away dishes or to talk to someone other than their neighbour. September was about to continue eating and resume her conversation with Heini and Arianrhod, when she was greeted by Heulwen. September looked up to see the girl flanked by two large dark-skinned men.

"Oh, hi, Heulwen," September said.

"I want you to meet Cynhaearn and Cynwal," Heulwen said. The two men nodded their heads to September.

"Hello. You are…?" September looked from one tall,

stocky man to the other.

"Cynhaearn is prif-cludydd o haearn and Mordeyrn of Mynydd Tywyll," Heulwen said. The slightly taller of the men nodded again. Both looked to be middle-aged with grey in their short hair, although Cynwal was the greyer of the two.

"That's the mountain region with the metal mines, isn't it?" September said.

"Yes, we produce all the metals used in the Land," Cynhaearn said proudly, "and Cynwal is my fellow miner and Prif-cludydd o plwm." His companion nodded.

"Oh, I know that one. That's lead," September said, relieved that she was getting the hang of the metals although Cynhaearn's accent was difficult to understand.

"We are very pleased to meet you, Cludydd," Cynwal said in an equally broad accent.

"It's nice to meet you too. I haven't met anyone from the mountains before."

Before September could get into further conversation, Heulwen pulled on the two powerful men's arms.

"Let's go and check the Arsyllfa's walls, shall we." Cynhaearn and Cynwal reluctantly allowed themselves to be lead away.

September turned back to Heini and Arianrhod.

"Cynhaearn and Cynwal are responsible for the Arsyllfa's defences," Arianrhod explained, "but I think Heulwen likes to keep the two of them to herself."

September could see the attraction of the strong men even though they were considerably older than Heulwen.

"And Heulwen does like to think she plays a part in protecting us all in here," Heini added with a wink.

"Shall we guide you to the Observatory?" Arianrhod said, "It is quite a climb and I'm afraid I am rather slow these days so you may prefer to go with one of the young people."

September looked around and saw that most of the dinner guests, particularly the younger ones, had already left. Aurddolen was deep in conversation with a frail old man and a young woman. They left the dining hall together.

"No, I'll come with you," September said and stood just as they were approached by two women, one tall and thin with auburn hair and the other, short and a little stout. Both were past middle-age. The tall one spoke.

"Cludydd, we are so delighted to speak to you at last. I am Anarawd, bearer of copper. I am sure you understand that better than 'Prif-cludydd o efyddyn'. The old language is so obscure."

"Oh, thank you. Copper, yes, the metal that my strange phone is made of," September said.

"Phone?" Anarawd looked confused.

"Um, speaking thing," September tried to explain.

"Ah, yes, you have a horn for communicating over great distances."

"That's right. It was given to me by the cludydd at Amaethaderyn; her name is Catrin."

"Can I get a word in do you think?" the plump lady said light-heartedly.

"Of course, my dear," Anarawd said, "This is Betrys, the bearer of tin and bringer of joy."

"That's right, that's what my name means," Betrys said, "and as Anarawd has said we are so happy to see you, my dear. You have given us all hope, as well as an opportunity for a lovely dinner." She giggled.

"She may look dizzy," Anarawd said, "but don't be fooled, she is also mordeyrn of Arfordir Dwyrain."

"Where's that?" September asked.

"My home, the eastern coastal region," Heini spoke up.

"Thank you Heini," Betrys replied, "yes, we're both from the other side of Gwlad. Now we had better get up to the observatory and see what Aurddolen has got for us."

They left the dining hall through the large doors by which September had entered and walked down wide corridors until they came to a spiral staircase. The marble steps wound around a stone pillar. September began to climb and soon left her four companions behind. Before long she caught up the ancient old man accompanying Aurddolen and the younger woman. She slowed down until they reached a landing where Aurddolen and the woman were waiting. The old man paused, wheezing.

"Ah, September," Aurddolen said, "This is a good moment to introduce Eryl the Seryddwr and custodian of the

Arsyllfa."

"Seryddwr?" September asked.

"I observe the stars and the bodies that wander across the sky," the frail old man whispered between breaths.

"And Hedydd is his apprentice or perhaps I should say his deputy," Aurddolen continued.

"Oh, I will always be Eryl's apprentice," the fair, young woman said cheerfully, "Shall we climb the stairs and leave these old ones to follow us, Cludydd?"

"Is there much further?"

"Oh yes, the observatory is at the top of the tallest tower of the Arsyllfa." Hedydd led September up the steps, leaving the Mordeyrn and the astronomer to make their slow ascent.

The two of them climbed quickly but even September was beginning to feel the strain on her thighs. Cold gusts blew down on them and she began to regret wearing just the thin dress. At last they reached the final step and a small landing.

"Put a coat on," Hedydd said, taking a thick woollen jacket from a hook beside the door, "it's cold outside."

September needed no persuading so chose an oversized jacket and wrapped it around herself. When Hedydd pushed the door open a blast of freezing air hit her, but she stepped out on to the smooth black floor of the observatory full of wonder. The sky was clear and filled with stars. Each star seemed like a tiny lantern that she could reach out and grab. She wondered at being exposed at the very top of the building on the tallest hill but as her eyes adjusted to the night-time light she saw the skeleton of a dome curving above her head. It was the dull grey of iron inlaid with silver-coloured metal and wound around with a thin gold thread.

Hedydd saw her tracing the semi-circles of the framework.

"We are still in the protection of the Arsyllfa," she reassured September, "The dome is made of haearn, plwm, alcam and aur, but its structure allows us to see all of the sky."

The dome covered the whole top of the tower, a considerable area, occupied by the dinner guests and some strange pieces of equipment. Some were long straight wooden rods fixed to tripods, but in the centre of the floor stood an instrument that looked to September like a giant protractor. It too was made of dark wood standing on a circle of copper inlaid into the floor and engraved with radiating lines and numbers. She realised that they marked out the degrees of a circle and that the protractor was similarly marked. A rod some six or seven metres long was fixed to the centre of the protractor with what looked like gun-sights at each end.

"These, um, instruments, what are they for?" September asked.

"They assist our observations and allow us to record the positions and movement of the planets and the stars," Hedydd replied.

"But I don't see a telescope," September said, looking again around the observatory.

"Telescope?" Hedydd asked.

"You look through it and it makes things look bigger."

"I have no knowledge of such a thing, Cludydd. How does it work?"

That stopped September. How does a telescope work, she wondered.

"Well it's a tube which has lenses at each end, or I think you can use mirrors instead."

"I do not understand you, I am sorry. You have these instruments in your world?"

"Yes, astronomers have used them for ages to look into space." September vaguely recalled that Galileo had something to do with the invention of the telescope. Now how many hundreds of years ago did he live? It seemed that astronomy in the Land was stuck in the Middle Ages. "Have you been observing for long? You said you were Eryl's apprentice."

"I have been here since I was a child, over twenty five years. Eryl has taught me much but I fear that he still has things to show me although he nears the end of his life."

"He seems pretty old. Are there no other astronomers? Is this whole fortress just for the two of you?"

"The Mordeyrn has suggested that more be trained and half a dozen children have been brought here to learn. It is my job to teach them. But Eryl is the Seryddwr and I am his pupil."

The other Prif-cludyddau were arriving puffing and panting

from their climb, their breath forming a mist around their heads. Finally, Aurddolen came supporting Eryl. He closed the door to the stairs shutting out the light. Now the rooftop was completely dark but for the light of the stars. The guests gathered around Aurddolen and Eryl next to the big protractor.

"Friends, I have brought you up here into the cold of the mountain night for a number of reasons. First of all, because we can. The besiegers have left, for the time being at least, and the obscuring stench of the Malevolence has blown away. We have fresh air and a clear view of the sphere of stars revolving around us and the planets moving across the sky." There was a murmur of agreement and sighs of relief. Aurddolen went on.

"I also brought you here to remind you that this is why the Arysllfa exists; Heulyn's life's work; the means by which we plan for the resurgence of the Malevolence. Eryl and the Seryddwr before him have, over the centuries, recorded the wanderings of the planets and noted signs of disturbance amongst the stars. This enables us to predict the time of the next Cysylltiad when the planets, the Moon and the Sun will be together in the sky. Their protecting influence will be reduced almost to nothing and we will be exposed to the full power of the evil above the stars. We have known for a lifetime that the time was approaching. For years we have known that it is soon. The successful summoning of the Cludydd o Maengolauseren confirmed that the evil is descending in greater and greater power. I thought it fitting, now that the Cludydd is with us, to announce to you the final conclusions of Eryl's calculations, here where he has laboured night and day throughout his long life. We now know the time and the place where our destiny awaits us."

The hushed silence of the throng told September that the others anticipated the Mordeyrn's words as much if not more than she did. They had lived their lives waiting for the moment they would discover when their greatest battle would take place. Aurddolen took a deep breath and spoke slowly but powerfully.

"The time is sooner than we expected, sooner perhaps than we hoped. The Conjunction is just two months away. It will take place at the close of this year, on the day of the winter solstice." There were gasps and cries from the assembled cludydds.

"We cannot be ready," someone called out.

"So soon!" another exclaimed.

Aurddolen ignored the rising murmur of disquiet. "On the shortest day, the Land will be at its most vulnerable to the Malevolence. The focus of the evil power will be where the Sun will not rise, in the frozen wastes beyond the Mynydd Tywyll. There we must meet with the forces of the Malevolence and, with all the energy and skill at our service, fling it back beyond the stars. Already Iau and Sadwrn are gone from the night sky, hidden by the brilliance of the Sun as they revolve around us together. In the coming weeks the other planets will also disappear from view and on that night Lleuad will be invisible. The time is almost upon us but we have the Cludydd o Maengolauseren and my symbol of the power of gold will be restored. The people of Mynydd Tywyll are gathering together all that we need for our expedition into the ice. Very soon we must journey to join them."

Many of the audience began talking urgently to each other. September wasn't sure that she had understood everything that he had said but gathered that the climax to her mission in the Land was just a few weeks away, somewhere in the Arctic north, thousands of kilometres away. There was a cold hard lump in her stomach. She didn't want to face the journey, the cold or the Malevolence but she could think of no way of getting out of any of it. Her hip started to itch. Memory flickered. She reached inside the thick jacket for the pendant. Her thumb pressed the catch and she stared at the dimly glowing stone within.

"But it is so far. How can you get there in time?" September could not see who had spoken.

"It is true that the place is distant from us," Aurddolen answered, "We shall have to travel as fast as boat and steed will allow us, but we..."

"Draig tân! Due west!" Hedydd, standing by September's side, shouted and pointed. Everyone turned to look in the direction she indicated. There, unmistakably, was a bright star with a curving tail.

"So the Malevolence has not given us much time of respite," Aurddolen said, "Do not fear, the Arsyllfa will protect us."

"Another one, to the north!" Eryl shrieked, his shaky voice causing all eyes to turn ninety degrees to see where his finger pointed. September marvelled at how his aged sight could pick out the point of light amongst all the other stars, but it was there all right.

"And another, coming from the south!" another voice called.

"And from the east!" cried another.

September span around looking for each of the comets at the four points of the compass. Already it was possible to see that the comets were approaching, the points becoming discs. There was none of the panic she had witnessed at the previous appearances of Draig tân, but the Prif-cludyddau were agitated.

"Four, at once!"

"Never have we seen so many!"

"The directions are so precise. It's unheard of!"

September turned to face Hedydd.

"Have you seen one of these things before?"

"No, there have been none here. We presumed that our defences deflected them."

"Well something has attracted them, and it's probably me." She looked at the Maengolauseren, now glowing more brightly, and rubbed her hip where the itch was becoming a burn.

"But I know this is remarkable," Hedydd continued.

"Why?"

"A coordinated attack from the four corners of the Land. It shows pre-meditation that the Malevolence is not supposed to possess."

"You know all about it?"

"Oh, yes, I have studied all the tales and reports of the evil over thousands of years. There has never been anything like this before. The attacks, even when drawn to a cludydd, are always random, uncoordinated, unplanned."

"Something has changed."

"Yes, and I don't like it."

The Mordeyrn strode to the edge of the floor, standing by the low parapet.

"We will withstand this unprecedented onslaught," he said, "Our power will prevail." He grabbed hold of one of the spars of the dome. A glow spread from his hand along the gold thread entwined around the iron bar. The golden illumination spread over their heads until every part of the framework was radiating yellow light. Cynhaearn, Cynwal and Betrys joined him and took hold of the metal rods.

"The power of Haearn is with us," Cynhaearn shouted.

"Plwm too!" "And Alcam!" Cynwal and Betrys added their voices.

Red light sprang from Cynhaearn's hand and white from Cynwal and Betrys. Their energy spread and mixed with Aurddolen's golden gleam so that a tracery of shining light was formed in a hemisphere over them.

The night sky was still visible between the strips of light and the four comets were growing rapidly and coming straight towards the tower of the Arsyllfa.

"I'm sure the power of the metals can protect us," Hedydd said to September, "but the Arsyllfa's defences have never been tested like this."

September gripped the Maengolauseren in her right hand and stretched out her arm.

"The starstone knows what to do. It's destroyed comets before, but I haven't dealt with four at once." Its violet glow was weak compared to the brilliance of the dome over the observatory. September still felt neither fear nor anger. This was merely a spectacle to watch. The other guests however were beginning to have second thoughts about confronting the approaching fire dragons. They edged towards the wall on the south side of the tower and the doors to the staircase. The four metal wielders stood resolutely gripping the spars and Hedydd remained by September's side.

All four comets had grown to the size of the full Moon, their discs a roiling mass of flame, and their tails curled across the sky. Now September could sense their movement. The four fireballs were coming to her. She was the target, not the Arsyllfa itself. What if the protection of the metals should fail? What if the starstone did not respond? A tickle of apprehension crept up her spine. Her birthmark was burning too. She stretched her arm higher still.

The discs of fire and the streamers of light that trailed behind them grew until their combined intensities banished the stars from view. Their heat stirred up a wind which, blowing from all four directions, created a vortex that swirled around them catching at September's dress. Hedydd staggered, the whirlwind threatening to blow her off her feet.

"Go," September told her, "get inside." The woman dropped to her knees and crawled to the doorway, her hair blown upwards. The four Prif-cludydd clung to the metal bars with both hands, screaming unintelligible incantations at the heavens. The skeletal dome shone but now the globes of fire were brighter than anything in the sky and filled the view.

September was scared. She wanted to follow Hedydd, to hide away from the Malevolence but was frozen to the spot. What if Aurddolen or one of the others lost their grip and were blown from the top of the tower? Could the magic of the metals withstand four of the comets? The wind swirled around her but she didn't feel the buffeting. She gripped the stone firmly and shouted,

"Stop!"

The violet light of the stone grew in intensity and expanded from her raised fist. It filled the dome of the observatory; and stopped. The Draig tân stopped in their paths, suspended in the sky.

September was surrounded by a translucent white haze which obscured her view. She was looking straight up and saw, descending towards her, a figure. The white hair and black dress identified her immediately as her twin even before she could make out her features. The figure got closer until she floated down to stand in front of September.

"You did this, didn't you?" September said.

Her twin looked around at the four indistinct glowing globes hanging motionless in the foggy sky.

"These? Yes they're mine. I thought it would be an interesting test of your skill with the starstone."

"Aurddolen thought he and the others could defend the

observatory alone."

"Perhaps they can. But the stone and metals of this puny tower are not my target. I don't think they can protect you. Only that pebble that you carry may have the power to do that. As you can see you have the power to stop time."

September realised that the fireballs were hanging in the sky unmoving and their flames were frozen.

"Why?"

"Why what?"

"Why do you attack me?"

"You are my enemy. Throughout the history of this universe the Maengolauseren and its bearer have opposed the Malevolence."

"But that history is not yours. You and I grew together in Mother's womb. We are, or rather I am, just sixteen years of age."

"In your world perhaps. Time is different here. Above the stars there is no time, the past, the now and what is yet to come do not exist. I have no experience of life in your world. My knowledge, my experience, my memory is of the cosmos of the Malevolence, and its eternal fight with the powers of Daear and its guardians."

"I don't understand. What are these powers? It's different in our world. The Malevolence doesn't exist there."

"What do you mean 'our world'? Have you forgotten? I never lived there. I died before I became me and my soul was flung beyond the stars. The Malevolence gave me succour, gave me knowledge, and I shall repay it by ensuring its victory at last over you and these insignificant people."

September was confused but knew that she could not, would not let her twin succeed.

"I won't let you."

"You will. Give me the stone."

Her twin leapt for the Maengolauseren which September had kept raised above her head. The girl's hand closed around her own and tried to pull it down. September shook her hand trying to loosen her twin's grip but without success. She lashed out with her right foot striking her sister in the stomach. Her twin winced and let her grip slip but then flung herself at September, her hands groping for her neck.

September ducked and twisted, evading the clutching hands. The stone now was wrapped in her hand and she swung her arm. Her fist struck the side of her twin's head. A blast of violet light sent the young woman sprawling away from her.

Her sister slowly picked herself up and stood facing her again. She rubbed the side of her head.

"You have some power over the stone, but it is uncontrolled. You don't know what you are doing." She raised a hand towards one of the Draig tân fixed in the sky. Her hand seemed to grasp it and fling it at September. Instinctively September raised the stone to ward off the fiery ball. The violet beam shot out and met the globe in its flight. It exploded in a blast of blue light.

"You're right," September said, "I don't know how to use it properly, but I will and I will be ready to fight the Malevolence and everything it can do. But we are sisters; we don't have to be enemies."

"Don't we? It's the law of the universe, this universe," her sister said, flinging another comet at her, "We were born together. It was luck which of us was the seventh." September fended the comet off with another blast of violet light.

"It could have been, should have been, me that is the bearer," the twin continued sending the third comet blazing towards September, "It's you who should have died."

September held the stone firmly and again the blue beam stopped the missile in a shower of violet.

"But I didn't" she said, "Things happened as they happened."

Her twin reached for the final comet somehow holding it in her outstretched hand.

"But they may not have done. We are bound by that possibility, and so I, who never lived, and you, who inherited the powers of the Maengolauseren, are forever destined to struggle for victory." She threw the final comet towards September with all her force. It sped towards September. Calmly she held the stone in front of her and waited for the blue beam to shoot out. The ball of fire came closer and closer and still nothing happened. The comet was almost upon her when September felt a stab of fear. Immediately blue fire exploded from the stone, blasting the comet from the sky.

"You see," her twin cackled, "the stone only reacts to your emotions. Only when you are threatened does it protect you. That's why so many of your companions perished. You are only concerned for your own safety."

"It's not true," September cried, "I didn't want Tudfwlch or Cynddylig to die, or the others."

"But you let them."

"No, you're wrong," September was angry. She raised the stone towards her twin, about to will the blue light to destroy her sister. She wanted to see her sister blasted into oblivion. Her sister.

She lowered her arm.

"I don't want to fight you," she said.

"You will. When I bring destruction on all who inhabit the Land, you will wish me dead all over again. It is a race between us. As you learn the powers of the stone you wield so the strength of the Malevolence will grow as the Conjunction approaches. Before my coming the Malevolence had no guiding intelligence to overcome the Maengolauseren but now it has me to direct its energy. This time we will win."

Her twin started to walk away, retreating into the mist.

"Wait," September called, "What do you call yourself? Do you know the name Mother gave you?"

"The Malevolence is my mother now and I am called Malice."

Her voice faded into the enveloping clouds.

September called after her, "No, your name is Mairwen."

September was back on the dark floor of the observatory, the white glow gone, her hand still raised up, but the Draig tân had disappeared and the sky was filled merely with stars. The wind had calmed.

Aurddolen and the other three Prif-cludyddau stared at the sky with bewilderment.

"What happened there?" Cynhaearn said.

"I don't know," Betrys replied, "The Draig tân were almost upon us and then they weren't."

Aurddolen faced September.

"Do you know what happened, Cludydd?"

September lowered the starstone, its light gone out and the fire in her hip just a memory.

"I don't know. I shouted 'stop' and everything did. My twin appeared, we argued and fought and then she went away."

"Your twin sister summoned the Draig tân?"

"That's what she said. She is directing the Malevolence. She tried to kill me to get the stone."

Aurddolen released his grip on the dome and the others did the same. The illumination died. He came to September and folded his arms around her.

"This is not good news. It is a development that we have not planned for. We will need to discuss what it means."

"And I need some answers. Although I'm not sure what the questions are. I'm confused." There were tears in September's eyes.

"Let's get back downstairs. I think you need a good rest and then we can try to find answers to those questions whatever they might be." He guided September to the stairwell, with Cynhaearn, Cynwal and Betrys close behind.

2

September stirred in bed. She felt so comfortable that she didn't want to wake up. Just a bit longer of snug warmth before getting up to say good morning to Mother, Father, her sisters and perhaps even Gus, and then her day would begin. Her first day of being sixteen. She half-opened her eyes and had a shock. The bed may have been comfortable but it wasn't her bunk; it was a wide divan. The room wasn't her small bedroom, but a huge suite. The light that illuminated the room wasn't from the sun she was familiar with; it came from the minute bright lamps in the ceiling. It all came back to her. Her birthday had been weeks ago and she had travelled hundreds of kilometres across the Land, seen amazing sights, fought fierce monsters, lost good friends. She was overwhelmed with fear and sadness and a sob made catch her breath. She was choking; the air wouldn't enter her lungs. Her arms waved involuntarily and a hand hit the bell rope. She grabbed it and pulled.

Instantly the door opened and Sieffre entered. He saw her gasping for breath. He ran to her, scooped her up in his arms and hugged her. The shock of the movement did something because September felt cool air rush down her throat. She took a deep breath and felt the air fill her chest. Her heartbeat began to slow. Sieffre kept hold of her but loosened his grip.

"What is the matter, Cludydd? Were you attacked?" He looked around the room.

September found that she had the breath to speak.

"No, it was just the shock. I'm alright now, thank you."

Sieffre released her but stood beside the bed.

"The shock?"

"I woke up thinking I was at home and then everything came back to me in a rush."

"Ah, I see. The sleep of the night banishes memories but the light of day brings them back."

"Something like that. Actually I think it was the bed."

"The bed?"

"It's the first time I've had a comfortable night since I got here."

Sieffre grinned.

"I understand. You slept well."

"Well, no, not really, not for a long time. I was restless because I could not get things out of my head. But then I suppose, I was just too tired, and the bed so soft I eventually fell asleep but when I woke up it felt like I was at home."

"I don't suppose any of us realise what you have been through, thrust into our world from a place we have no knowledge of, and given a task that not one of us could take on."

"So you people say, but thank you for calming me down."

"My pleasure, my lady."

"I've told you before. I'm not your lady. I'm September." Something flashed into September's mind prompting her to ask, "How did you come in so quickly? You were outside in the corridor, weren't you?"

"Yes, September."

"On guard?"

"Yes, September."

"Not all night?"

"No. Nisien took the first watch."

"Why?"

"To protect you and in case you had need of something."

"I'm not used to being waited on, or needing protection." No, she was just stupid September, the snow-haired fatty; loved by her parents but hardly noticed by anybody else.

"Aurddolen thought you needed both."

Another tremor of fear and trepidation gripped September. She shivered.

"Are you alright, Cludydd?" Sieffre asked.

The moment passed. September smiled.

"September, please. And yes, I'm okay. I suppose I had better get up and meet everyone again. Is it late?"

"I imagine everyone will have breakfasted by now; the morning is well on, but everyone understands that you need rest, September."

"I wish Mother was so understanding." An image of her mother shaking her awake gave her another brief pang of homesickness. "Right, I'll move." She swung her legs off the bed and Sieffre stepped back hurriedly.

"I'll wait outside until you need me again," he said, backing away to the door.

September couldn't resist making use of the marvellous plumbing again. She soaked in the bath then wrapped herself in the soft towels. Rummaging through the huge wardrobe she looked for something to wear. There were dresses of all colours, fabrics and styles, all long, but nothing like a pair of jeans or cut-offs for knocking around in. She sighed and finally pulled out a pale blue cotton dress that only came down to her calf. At least she could move without tripping up. She pulled it on, ran her hands through her frizzy white hair and pulled the door to the corridor open.

Sieffre was there, relaxed but alert. He escorted her down to the dining room which was empty but food and drink was awaiting her; far more than she could eat herself, although she was hungry. Sieffre left her to eat alone.

As she was biting into a pear, Aurddolen came in.

"Good morning, Cludydd. Sieffre said you were breakfasting."

"'Morning. This fruit is so good."

"Do you feel well? Sieffre said you awoke in something of a panic."

"I'm fine," September said jauntily. It was her nature to be bright and cheerful. It was the only way to be in a large family. Then she realised that actually she wasn't alright, that the events of the past weeks were pressing on her, that the thought of what lay ahead was daunting, and the plans of her twin terrified her.

"Well, actually I'm not. I'm scared silly and I've got no idea how I'm supposed to do whatever I have to do."

"I understand," Aurddolen said, as he sat down beside her, "You have seen and done so much since you arrived amongst us, with so little help or explanation. Defeating the Malevolence was always going to be a tremendous quest and now with your twin directing the evil I am not sure how that affects the plans we have set in motion. But it is time that we talked. When you have finished we will go to my room and I will try to answer your questions."

September looked at the remains of the pear in her hand. She laid it down on her plate.

"I'm ready."

They climbed the stairs to the Mordeyrn's small study. He sat her down in the most comfortable chair and pulled up the lighter, wooden chair to be close to her.

"I thought you would be busy preparing for the journey," September said. The Mordeyrn smiled.

"Preparations are indeed being made for our departure, but there is much to be done before we set off."

"Last night people seemed to think there was a long way to travel in the time left."

"There is indeed," Aurddolen sighed, "I do wish that Eryl had been able to calculate the exact time sooner, but we have no control on when the Conjunction occurs and we had to await your arrival."

"Can we get to the place in time?"

"It is a long distance and travelling, particularly over the ice, will be difficult, but I am confident that it can be done."

"Shouldn't we get started as soon as possible?"

Aurddolen gave September an expression that hinted of unspoken thoughts.

"There are things to be done before we leave the safety of the Arsyllfa. The most important being helping you."

"Me?"

"Yes. You are the one who must face the Malevolence at the Conjunction."

"But, I don't know what I have to do." September felt her task weighing on her like a heavy burden.

"Exactly," he said, "now where shall we start?"

September's mind was blank. So much had happened to her, so many people had spoken of their hope in her, but she was confused.

"I don't know. Everything is so different here compared to my home, my world. It's all a mystery. I'm not even sure whether this is Earth, although you talk about the Sun and the

Moon and the planets – well, as far as Saturn."

"Yes, I understand. Well, I think I do." Aurddolen stood up and went to his bookcase. He lifted down a large, heavy book. "You heard the story of the last descent of the Malevolence and how your mother, Breuddwyd, the Cludydd, defeated it."

"Yes. Tudfwlch," she replied, hardly able to say his name without it catching in her throat, "told me the story of how she fought the Malevolence in the southern desert."

"That's right. Tudfwlch told you the version that has been handed down from generation to generation by cludyddau across the Land."

September detected a strange tone in Aurddolen's voice.

"Is the story true?"

"Oh, yes. Breuddwyd and the Maengolauseren cast the Malevolence beyond the stars where it comes from. But Heulyn was careful to ensure that only a special version of the story got spread around the people. This is the full version." Aurddolen tapped the leather bound book.

"What does it say?"

"Heulyn describes the confusion Breuddwyd felt on her arrival, her struggle to understand what was required of her, her temper and depression when she felt cut off from her home, her determination to master the starstone and the difficulties she faced in doing so. All that she said and did is recorded because Heulyn realised that one day there would be another Cludydd and we would need all the information we could get to help her through her ordeal."

Aurddolen placed the book in September's hands. It was very heavy. She turned the thick, hard cover and the first few pages of stiff, rough paper. The book was written in ink by hand. The writing was small and the shape of the letters strange but by concentrating hard she could make out the words and the sentences.

"Don't read it now. You may take it with you and read it whenever you wish," Aurddolen said.

"Oh, thank you." September closed the book and held it against her chest. It was a link with Mother and home. "Do you have another copy here?"

"There are no copies. This is the book written by Heulyn,

hundreds of years ago. There is one passage I would like you to read soon. It describes how the Cludydd Breuddwyd learnt how to control the Maengolauseren."

September was excited. Could Mother teach her what to do? To protect others in addition to herself? Her twin's taunts had hurt her but she realised now that so far the stone had only responded to her basic need for survival.

"But not now," Aurddolen continued, "First I will try to explain why you are here." He got up and drew another heavy tome from the bookshelf. "This is a collection of the writings of mordeyrns and Prif-cludyddau through the history of the Land. It describes what we know about Daear…"

"Daear?"

"The earth on which we live."

"You mean planet Earth."

"Daear is not a planet. It does not wander. It is fixed at the centre of the universe." Aurddolen tapped the book, "The book tells of how six thousand years ago the universe was a seething ferment of energy, good and bad. Then the good came together, separate from the evil and the universe as we know it was formed. Daear at the centre with its seven guardian planets on spheres revolving around it. Haul the greatest amongst the planets giving us light and warmth."

Again, September was reminded of how different this world was to everything she had learnt about the Sun and the planets.

"What about the stars?" she asked.

"Ah, the stars, the beacons that mark the boundary between good and evil; lights fixed to the outer sphere that encircles us."

September had an image of something like a light shade pricked with tiny holes surrounding a light bulb.

"So all the stars are the same distance from us?"

"That is correct."

Another marked difference with her own world, September reflected. At home the stars and galaxies, billions of them, extended far into space while here there was just Daear and its guardian planets and sphere of stars. What other differences were there for her to discover?

"What's beyond the stars?"

"Chaos, evil, the realm of the Malevolence. We do not know what is there but it is from there that everything bad and sick and corrupting originates."

"And it's where my sister went."

"Yes, the souls of the unborn, untouched by the good of Daear, ascend to the sphere of stars and become merged in the maelstrom of evil."

"But not my sister. She still has her own personality."

"Yes. I do not fully understand what has become of her. Something like this has never occurred before. It must be because as the child of your mother she is partly of this world and of yours and as your twin she has retained a separate existence. Somehow she has influence over the Malevolence and is able to direct, at least in part, its evil fury."

September did not feel enlightened but she guessed that she would have to confront her sister again before her task in the Land was completed. The Mordeyrn did not however have all the answers.

"What part do the Cemegwr play?"

"The Cemegwr?" The Mordeyrn seemed mystified by her question but surely he knew the stories of the mysterious creators of the universe that she had been told of.

"Didn't they make this world?"

"So say the tales that old folk tell," Aurddolen agreed.

"But I have been told that they are still around. Perhaps they have a part to play."

September saw a dark cloud cover the Mordeyrn's face.

"Utter nonsense," he roared, "there is no evidence that such beings ever existed let alone that they walk amongst us now, unseen. Their existence is a myth that mothers use to soothe their children's fears. Do not consider the Cemegwr or the stories that are bandied around concerning them." Aurddolen turned away from her, struggling to calm his outburst.

September decided to change the subject.

"Where do the metals and the cludydds come into all this?"

The Mordeyrn turned back to face her, his breathing normal again.

"Ah, metals. The greatest gift that we are given. All that exists within our universe is made from the four elements, earth, air, fire and water. Have you heard of them?"

"Um, I think so." But her hazy recollection of chemistry was telling her that an element was something else and there were more than four, "I've been told that the, what do you call them, 'manifestations' of the Malevolence come from each of the elements."

"That is correct. Malevolence corrupts the elements to its own will. The metals are of course formed from the four elements, each in its own proportion but each is also imbued with the power of the heavens. The seven metals grow from the depths of the earth and are drawn upwards by the powers of their respective planets. They embody the goodness at the heart of Daear and rise close to the surface where our miners can find them."

It was meaningless mumbo-jumbo as far as September could follow it.

"What about the Maengolauseren? Where does that come from?"

"It is the material from which the stars were made that was formed at the very centre of the universe."

"The centre? From what you say the Earth or Daear is at the centre."

"That is correct. The Maengolauseren was forged at the very centre of Daear."

"But how have I got it? I just seemed to find it."

"It found you, my dear. The Maengolauseren is linked to the Cludydd by some attraction that we do not understand. It can cross from one world to another and as you found out it carries the Cludydd with it."

"How do you know it was formed at the centre of the Earth?"

"In the very deepest shafts, the miners occasionally find tiny fragments of starstone, mere specks. They have the same appearance as the Maengolauseren but on a smaller scale and like it, embody the energy of the stars."

"Oh, what do they do?"

"Just glow, I'm afraid. When night falls and in darkness they light up, but that is all. We have never found a way of invoking the energy of the stars in the way that the Cludydd and the Maengolauseren can. We just use the fragments to illuminate the Arsyllfa."

September recalled the lights in the ceiling of her room. She looked at the stone in its locket. It seemed like a rough glass pebble, dull at the moment, but she knew its power.

"So that's it, is it? The good Earth and the Sun, Moon and planets battle to keep out the bad with just the metals and the starstone to help." She decided not to add the Cemegwr to the list.

Aurddolen smiled, "You have summed it up quite well."

"What does that huge book have to say then?"

Aurddolen tapped the cover of the book on his lap.

"It recounts all that has happened in the Land since the last descent of the Malevolence, records the movements of the planets, the recovery of metals, the names of cludyddau across every region. There is not just this one book, this is just the latest. There are many more." He pointed to the packed bookshelves.

"And these books have told you what to do when the Malevolence came again?"

Aurddolen looked desperately miserable.

"I realise now that I committed the sin of complacency. I thought the records gave us everything we needed to cope with this onslaught of evil. The astronomer would forecast the exact time of the Conjunction when Daear would be most exposed to the forces of evil. I successfully summoned you and you have proved a worthy successor to your mother. The date and place of the confrontation is set and I had no doubt that you would overcome the Malevolence and all its manifestations."

"But?"

"The arrival of your twin is not something I either planned for or expected. The Malevolence has never had direction before. Its destructive power has been indiscriminate and widespread. But with her commanding the legions of evil, I do not know. What is she called?"

"Apparently my mother had the dead baby christened Mairwen, but she doesn't seem to know that. She calls herself Malice."

"Ahh," Aurddolen nodded, "We must find out how much power she does indeed wield over the manifestations."

"The manifestations, the monsters that have attacked me?"

"Yes. You may have been a particular focus, but there are reports of increased attacks across the Land."

"How do they form? You said the Earth and the planets are good. How can the Malevolence turn air and water into monsters?"

"Ah, this is something you need to understand," Aurddolen leant forward earnestly before continuing "When the Malevolence can reach through the sphere of stars it can corrupt the fabric of our universe; not the metals, or the Maengolauseren, for they are protected by the power of the planets and the stars, but the ordinary fire, air, water and earth that make up the rocks, the rivers and lakes, the air we breathe. They are all vulnerable to the Malevolence's corrupting influence. Surely you know that good can turn bad. A firm, shiny apple decays into a loathsome, poisonous pus. Each element can be turned against us."

"I remember Cynddylig and others saying that one monster was an air thing and another was water and so on."

"That's it. The Draig tân are conjured from fire, the Adarllwchgwin from air, like the Pwca and Cyhyraeth; Ceffyl dwr are summoned from water; Gwyllian and Tylwyth teg from earth."

"Tylwyth teg?"

"You seem to have escaped them so far. They are more often sent to torment the miners in the depths. There are Coblynau too. I hope you escape their nasty attentions."

"So do I." September didn't need any description to want to avoid further monsters.

"When a manifestation is destroyed its matter reverts to its original element and finds its own place."

September recalled the Adarllwchgwin exploding into air when they were destroyed, the Ceffyl dwr becoming a deluge of water and Gwyllian falling into heaps of dust.

"You said the Malevolence cannot corrupt metals or the starstone, but why did Tudfwlch want it when he was under the evil spell?"

"Yes, that surprised me but now I think I understand. Perhaps Tudfwlch's actions were being guided by Malice."

"She tried to grab the stone from me last night."

"Did she?"

"But what can she do with it?"

"Well, apart from depriving you of it, and hence weakening our defence, perhaps she thinks she could wield its power and become a sort of Cludydd."

"That's what she said. She thinks it was luck that made me the Cludydd while she died. She thinks that if she had been born after me our positions would have been reversed."

"Chance is a narrow line between what is and what may have been."

"Perhaps she feels that she could use the energy of the stone for evil purposes and increase her power over the Malevolence still further."

Aurddolen didn't reply but stood and put the book on the table. He began to pace around the small room. There was silence for many moments. September grew a little impatient.

"Aurddolen?"

He stopped and looked at her as if noticing her for the first time.

"I'm sorry. What you said made me think. I have never had to contemplate the Maengolauseren falling under the power of the Malevolence. Previously it seemed unthinkable but now with Malice or Mairwen growing in dominance I have to include that thought in my plans."

"Do you want me to leave?"

"As I have considerably more thinking to do perhaps that would be for the best. Take the time to relax and recover from your journey and trials."

September hauled herself out of the comfy chair, lugging the big book.

"And read this," she said.

Aurddolen smiled.

"Read what you can. I will help you."

As September walked to the door she noticed that Aurddolen was already far away in his thoughts.

3

September went to her room next door and flung herself and the book on the bed. Her head was spinning from all that Aurddolen had told her. She had been in Gwlad for long enough to accept that she was not dreaming and that her surroundings were real, but she had experienced so many strange, wonderful and terrifying things that she felt overwhelmed. Was all that Aurddolen had told her correct, at least in this universe? There was so much more for her to learn particularly about the role that had been thrust upon her.

She opened the thick cover of the book, and started to read. The formation of the letters was strange and many of the words were unfamiliar, but the writer had taken care that this handwriting would be legible for a long time. She ran a finger along the lines reading one word and then the next like she had when she learnt to read. Slowly she got used to the shapes of the letters. It was like reading some fancy font on the computer that one of her friends had decided to use for artistic effect. Gradually her reading sped up although there was still a great deal that made no sense.

The first few pages recounted Heulyn's summoning of Breuddwyd and her arrival in the forest. Her mother seemed more confused than she had been and Heulyn reported her rambling about God and heaven and angels in white robes. September could perhaps make more sense of that than Heulyn since she knew that Mother must have imagined that she had been carried off into some Biblical dream. It took Heulyn quite a few days and pages of diary before he managed to get Breuddwyd to accept that she was not dreaming or dead and in some kind of hell, by which time they were already under attack by the Malevolence.

There was a light tap on the door. September looked up as Sieffre peered around the door.

"Ah, September you are here. I wondered if you would like

some food. The mid-day meal has been served."

September felt reluctant to have to meet all the other guests of the Arsyllfa.

"Do I have to come to the dining room? Could I have something here?"

"Of course," Sieffre replied, noticing the book, "I see you are busy. Is that the Book of the Maengolauseren?"

"If you mean is it the book about my mother, the last Cludydd, then, yes it is."

Sieffre was wide-eyed with awe.

"The book is always kept in the Mordeyrn's study. No-one but him may read it."

"He gave it to me to read. He thinks it may help me find out what I'm supposed to do with the stone."

"Ah, yes. Those of us who know of the book's existence would like to know what secrets it tells. We know that the last visitation of the Malevolence cannot have been quite as the popular tales tell."

"How's that?"

"Well, the tale is that she appeared as a great warrior and leader who immediately took control of the war against evil. But those of us who have worked here know that it was Heulyn who guided the Cludydd and who left instructions as to what to expect of her when next the Malevolence came upon us."

"You're right. Aurddolen told me that there is more in this book than has been let on to the people outside. I can tell already that Heulyn had problems getting across to Mother what had happened to her."

"Perhaps it is for the best that only the Mordeyrn and the Cludydd should know what really happened. I will leave you to your reading and go and get some food for you."

"Thank you Sieffre. You're very kind."

"It is my pleasure."

Sieffre left and September returned to the book. She could read lines quite quickly now and get the gist of Heulyn's account. She turned the pages, hoping for accounts of what she really wanted to know. How did Breuddwyd learn to use the Maengolauseren? What powers did it have? How did she defeat the Malevolence?

There were no immediate answers to her questions in the pages that she read. Heulyn recorded attacks by the manifestations of the Malevolence and Breuddwyd's involuntary use of the Maengolauseren to defend herself just as September had done. Heulyn had to protect himself and his followers with the power of gold when Breuddwyd's wild responses left them exposed. Heulyn also reported her mother's prayers and oaths to God and Jesus and all the saints she could name which seemed to mystify him as they had no effect. September recognised her mother from Heulyn's description; she still appealed to the saints whenever she needed help or advice. Gradually however, as Breuddwyd's time in the Land lengthened, her experiences forced her to a realisation that she had a role to perform and that Heulyn and not God would have to be her guide.

A knock on the door brought September back to her own situation. She sat up on the edge of the bed.

"Come in," she called. The door opened and Sieffre entered bearing a tray of food. He laid it on the table.

"There you are, September. Don't forget to eat while you study Heulyn's book."

"Thank you. What is everyone else doing? Do they think me rude for not joining them?"

"Not at all," Sieffre reassured her, "everyone knows that you have a great deal to learn about your task. They all have their own duties and of course there is the preparation for the long journey that must start soon for those who will accompany you to the Cysylltiad. Of course, Heulwen is giving her orders to those that aren't Prif-cludyddau or mordeyrn. She says that we must review our defences now that we have your sister guiding the evil descending on us."

"How is she suggesting that we fight Malice?"

"Malice?"

"That's what my sister calls herself. Mairwen was her real name but she died before it was given to her."

"Ah, I see. You have talked to her?"

"Last night, on the roof, when she sent the comets."

"Which you defeated."

"It was just a trial. She wanted to see what I could do. She knows I can use the stone to defend myself but I don't know how to stop the Malevolence from attacking the Land. She said I let my friends die to save myself."

"That's not true. You saved us from the Cyhyraeth and again when we fought our way to the Arsyllfa."

September shook her head. Malice's taunts had bitten her hard.

"No, Malice was right. I saved myself but I couldn't stop Gwrion, Elystan, Alawn, or Collen from being killed." Tears rolled down her cheeks. Sieffre knelt beside the bed and looked up into her tear-stained face.

"September, listen to me. Each of us knew we would be in danger. As it happened the attack by the Malevolence on the Arsyllfa was much worse than anyone anticipated. It was only through your power that any of us made it. Collen, Alawn, Elystan and Gwrion were all my friends and I grieve for them, but I know you did all you could to save us as well as protect yourself. None of us, not even the Mordeyrn could wield the power of the Maengolauseren as you have done, but one thing we all know from Heulyn's record is that the Cludydd has a lot to learn before she can dismiss the evil from the whole of Gwlad."

September sniffed and smiled weakly.

"Thank you, Sieffre, you're so kind."

"It is not just kindness, September. Since we met I have come to like you a great deal. I don't just want you to succeed in your task; I want you to be happy that you came to the Land."

His face was so close to hers. She leant forward and kissed his cheek. He pulled back and raised a hand to caress the place she had touched. Then he leant forward again and his lips touched hers. She felt a tingle which rippled down her spine.

He rocked back on his knees and stood up. September felt a twinge of regret.

"I must leave you to continue your study," he said.

"Of course," she replied, wondering what would happen if she asked him to stay, "but don't leave me alone for too long."

"I'll stay close and make sure you are not disturbed. That will stop Heulwen sending me on a fool's errand." He backed to the door.

September sat still for a moment considering what had just passed between them. Did Sieffre fancy her? She wasn't used to men or boys being attracted to her; boys usually hurled insults at her. Did she fancy him? The kiss had given her a tingle of pleasure but she didn't know what she should do. Sieffre was quite a bit older than her but still a young man, pretty fit and more mature than Tudfwlch. Why did she think of the young warrior? Was it just because he was another young man she had begun to get close to, and then lost? Could she afford to get close to Sieffre when he could fall to the Malevolence at any time? She shuddered. It was up to her. She must learn how to control the Maengolauseren and protect not just herself but Sieffre and everyone else. She turned back to the book, forgetting the food that Sieffre had delivered.

She read page after page of Heulyn's account of their slow journey through the forest heading south towards their encounter with the Malevolence. Day after day passed and more and more people joined them. The attacks by manifestations became more frequent and violent. September recognised descriptions of Adarllwchgwin and Pwca and Ceffyl dwr. There was a devastating visitation by a Cyhyraeth that killed many of Heulyn's followers. There were descriptions of monsters that September had yet to meet; Cwn annwn, ghostly dogs that attacked during the heat of the day, and Llamhigwyn y dwr, giant, winged froglike creatures that rose from rivers and lakes. The travellers came to villages where the people had turned to evil and fought with them. Each time she was threatened, Breuddwyd drove off the attacks but seemed to have no more influence over the starstone than September had.

Then the party reached a town on the banks of the Afon Gogleddol. There Heulyn organised the townspeople to defend themselves while Breuddwyd and the other followers rested. There were sporadic attacks by various manifestations but nothing like the concerted attacks that September had experienced here at the Arsyllfa. According to Heulyn, Breuddwyd experienced a crisis and shut herself inside a building. She wasn't seen for three days, would not respond to Heulyn's appeals nor did she seek food or water. When at last the door to her room opened, Heulyn and everyone else was astounded by the change in the Cludydd. She glowed with an inner light the colour of the Maengolauseren and her talents had been transformed. She seemed to embody the skills of the cludyddau of all the metals – she healed the sick as did the cludydd o arian; where before she had shunned contact with Heulyn's followers now she encouraged them like a cludydd o alcam; she stood beside Heulyn radiating goodness and power like a cludydd o aur; she imbued the simple weapons of haearn wielded by the townspeople with the power to defeat the manifestations of the Malevolence like a cludydd o haearn; when next they were attacked by a Draig tân she absorbed the fires like a cludydd o plwm; she changed into a river dolphin to race to fight a Ceffyl dwr like a cludydd o arian byw; and finally she communicated with the people across the Land like a cludydd o efyddyn.

September read of Breuddwyd's exploits with growing excitement. What had happened to the Cludydd during the three days she was locked away? Heulyn was unable to report what had occurred as all Breuddwyd would say was that she had been amongst the stars. From that time on Breuddwyd was transformed. She and Heulyn together organised the growing army as it travelled on southwards, but Heulyn's account of the journey itself seemed not to include the Cludydd. She reappeared whenever the party was in danger but at other times seemed to be absent and Heulyn recorded tales of her performing great deeds all across the Land. Gradually however, the growing size of Heulyn's force began to draw the majority of the attacks and Breuddwyd spent more and more time with Heulyn fighting off the manifestations and the bands of humans turned to evil. They had reached the southern river when September paused in her reading.

She was excited. Could she become transformed as Breuddwyd had been? How did Breuddwyd achieve the change in herself? What had happened to her locked inside the hut?

She heard a frantic knocking on her door.

"Come in," she said. As she had hoped, it was Sieffre. When he saw the untouched tray of food he frowned.

"You have not eaten, September. Hours have passed since I brought it to you. I thought you may be ready to eat again and perhaps come out and speak to people."

"I'm sorry, Sieffre. I was so involved in Heulyn's story that I forgot the time and didn't feel hungry." Enclosed in the windowless room with specks of starstone providing a uniform light, she had not noticed that night had fallen.

"But you must eat, September. You have just completed a long and difficult journey and soon you will have to set off again."

"Set off again?"

"The Conjunction. The meeting with the Malevolence beyond the mountains."

"Oh, yes," September didn't want to think about that part of her task.

"The Mordeyrn is already talking about travelling to the Mynydd Tywyll to meet the miners providing him with the aur to replace his plate."

September knew she wasn't ready for another long trek and that she wouldn't be until she had transformed like Breuddwyd had done.

"And what of the others?"

"The other Prif-cludydd will travel with him and the mordeyrns from the regions will return to their peoples and help them prepare."

"What is Heulwen going to do? I bet she has plans."

"She is talking of staying by your side to help the 'fight between the twins' as she calls it."

"I wonder?"

"Wonder what, September?"

"Which twin she will help."

"You cannot mean it."

"What?"

"That Heulwen may be on the side of Malice."

"No, I suppose not, but she seems too fond of giving her own orders than actually supporting me."

"She just wants to be at the centre of things, to earn her father's approval."

"Yes, you're right, I'm being a bitch."

"A what?"

"Not a nice person."

"I do understand. Heulwen does not always bring out the good in a person. But now, what about you? Are you coming to the dining hall to eat or do you want me to bring some fresh food?"

September thought about what she had read and of the expectant crowd of people awaiting her below.

"No, I'm not ready to meet everyone. The book has shown me what I must do."

Sieffre looked excited.

"You have learnt how to wield all the powers of the Maengolauseren?"

September was reluctant to dash his hopes.

"No, not yet, but I have read enough to know what I must do, I think."

"What is that?"

"Well, not meeting with everyone else is one thing."

"Yes."

"And I must stay alone, undisturbed for as long as I need."

"Undisturbed?"

"Yes, I must lock myself away here, so no one can get in until I am ready to come out."

"Ah, now I understand."

"What?"

"Why this room, of all the rooms in the Arsyllfa, has bolts on the inside of its door, and no other way in." Sieffre crossed the room and pointed out the heavy iron bolts around the door.

"When these are shut no-one will be able to enter, not even a cludydd o haearn. They were put in place by Heulyn himself."

"That was foresighted of him."

"And now I understand what the Mordeyrn said when he instructed me to watch over you."

"What was that?"

"He told me to do whatever you asked even if it seemed strange, such as if you were wanting to hide from me and everyone else."

"I don't want to hide from you, just keep apart until I have done what I can. Aurddolen has read the book and understands."

"So when I leave you will lock the door?"

September was certain that she must copy Breuddwyd and close herself away, although the thought of being locked up scared her.

"Yes, that's it."

"In that case let me replace your food so that you have some sustenance during your ordeal, whatever it may be."

"Thank you, but do not tell anyone but Aurddolen what I am doing, or let anyone come banging on the door."

"I will do as you ask, September." Sieffre picked up the tray of food and hurried from the room. September closed the door behind him and began to push the heavy bolts across. She had decided that she was not going to await Sieffre's return. According to Heulyn's record Breuddwyd had not had food during her vigil. September decided to be as much like her mother as she could be. She lay flat on the bed, her legs stretched out, her arms by her side, looking up at the ceiling.

What now, she thought, do I just wait for a miracle to happen? I'll probably just fall asleep, and then wake up in the morning feeling silly. She stared at the ceiling and the little glowing lights, listening to her breathing and the blood rushing through her ears.

There was a knock on the door and the handle rattled but the door did not move. She heard Sieffre's muffled voice through the thick heavy wood. His words were indistinct but she knew he would be anxious and annoyed that she had locked the door before he had returned with her supper. September had to resist the temptation to let him in. She covered her ears with her hands so she couldn't hear a thing. After a few moments she tentatively dropped her hands. There were no sounds from outside the door. Had Sieffre gone or was he resuming his watch in the corridor?

She lay quietly again. What did Breuddwyd do when she was alone? How were they similar? Breuddwyd had been locked in a hut by the river while she was here at the top of the mountain. They had both been on difficult journeys but in different directions in different regions of the Land. They were both scared and confused and bewildered by the task that lay in front of them. They both had the Maengolauseren. Of course, that was the one thing that linked them across the years both here and at home.

September removed the silver chain from around her neck and flicked open the locket. The stone was clear and dark. She held it up and looked through it to the ceiling. She could see a few of the glowing lights, their pattern distorted by the curvature of the stone so that they resembled the stars in the night sky. She moved the stone a little. The specks of light grew in number but the space between them became darker. It was like looking up into space, as if the ceiling and roof of the Arsyllfa had melted away. She drew the stone closer to her eye. The blackness of space wrapped around her, the sphere of stars surrounding her. The bed and the room had gone. She was floating in space.

4

September looked around herself. She couldn't really believe it but she was definitely in space. The stars shone all around her in numbers greater than she had ever seen but between them there was darkness blacker than the sky could ever be on Earth; and yet she could breathe – or rather, she wasn't struggling to draw breath. She was still holding the starstone in her hand but it was no longer in its silver casing. A thin haze of bright pale blue surrounded her arms and legs and body but she could not feel the dress against her skin anymore. She was clothed in light. Was it somehow protecting her from the hard vacuum of space? She looked down at her feet and there, way below, was the planet Earth, or Daear, looking just like it did in those NASA pictures. Its blue and white looked so beautiful but she couldn't make out the shapes of the continents beneath the clouds. It was so far away, the size of a football at her feet. As she looked she realised that the Earth was getting smaller, receding. She was travelling through space but totally unaware of movement. She twisted her head around and there above her was the Sun, an unbearably bright, golden white sphere and to the left a thin crescent moon, already bigger than the Earth and growing visibly larger as she watched.

Was she dreaming? A month or so ago she would have been certain of it but after weeks of living in the dream, or nightmare, of her journey across Gwlad she was prepared to accept almost any experience as real. So here she was, travelling at great speed through the emptiness of space and feeling quite comfortable.

The Moon appeared to turn as it grew so that soon she was heading towards the fully lit sphere. The Moon shone with silver light. There were darker patches as seen from Earth but now they appeared to be just shadows over the silver surface. September wriggled until she turned herself to face her destination. The Moon grew so that it filled her field of vision. For a moment she did feel that she was falling. She closed her eyes.

She opened them again to find herself standing on the silver surface of the Moon. It didn't look at all like the pictures of the Apollo astronauts. The surface was smooth and polished; there were no mountains or craters to be seen just the perfect curve of an horizon which seemed very close. Directly overhead was the brilliant Sun in a black sky. Stars were visible away from the dazzling brightness. Still September felt comfortable and had no trouble breathing. She was surrounded by a glow that was bluer than the reflected light of the Moon.

What happens now? She thought. I'm here, on the Moon, but why? As the questions passed through her head she noticed figures approaching her from the horizon all around her. They were pale translucent beings, almost impossible to see against the silver light of the Moon. As they got closer September saw that they were people; women to be precise. They looked very similar to each other. All had long flowing silver hair, silver skin and they each wore a long silver dress. Their facial features differed slightly. One face was familiar; it was the face of Arianwen. Then she saw Arianrhod, the other silver bearer she had met. They were at the head of a crowd of ghosts that clustered around her.

"Welcome, Cludydd o Maengolauseren," the spirit that resembled Arianrhod said.

"Hello. Who are you?" September replied.

"We are the spirits of all the cludydd o arian, living or who have ever lived. We are the essence of their characters, their link with the power of Lleuad." September looked around the throng of thousands, perhaps millions of figures. Perhaps, she thought, the ones at the front are the ones still alive on Earth, including Arianrhod and Arianwen.

"Why have you brought me here?"

"We did not summon you. You travelled here by your own power, the power of the Maengolauseren, but we were expecting you."

"I was just looking through the stone and trying to work out how I can become a real Cludydd and carry out the task that everyone says I must do," September said, feeling confused.

"We understand," Arianrhod said, "You were summoned to banish the Malevolence from within the sphere of stars. You have faced many dangers and the Maengolauseren has protected you but to accomplish your task you must learn to control its powers and those of the other bodies within the universe."

"That's right. That's what Heulyn's book said; but how?" September asked.

"The Maengolauseren will show you the way. That's why it has brought you to us."

"The stone brought me here?"

"As it brought you to the Land."

"What for?"

"To learn how to wield the power of arian."

"Oh, how do I do that?"

"By performing a task."

"What task?"

The circle of spirits around her took each others' hands. The faces of each one looked at her.

The scene changed. September staggered at the sudden shift. One moment she was standing on the silver Moon and then, well, where was she? She heard the groans before she took in the sights around her. She was in a large tent. There were beds on which men and women and children lay moaning and crying with pain. The floor between the beds was filled with more tormented people, some lying on blankets, others on bare earth. The cries of agony hurt September's ears and when she looked at the nearest patients she was filled with revulsion. Each had grotesque open wounds or missing limbs which oozed blood and puss. There was a stink of rotting flesh. September felt that she was going to be sick, that she may even faint, except that there was nowhere to fall other than across one of the hideously wounded people.

"Why am I here?" September cried, trying to hide the scene from her eyes but unable to shut out the wailing or the stench. What had the spirit of Arianrhod meant by saying she had a task to perform? How was this hellish scene connected to the serene, clean Moon? Then she remembered when Tudfwlch was wounded and how she used the silver of her locket to heal him and how Arianwen had used her silver bracelet to heal Eluned. Of course, silver was the metal of healing. Was that her task? To heal all these people? But she had no silver. She only had the Maengolauseren in her hand. What had Arianrhod said? The Maengolauseren will show her the way. The starstone was her link to the energy of the universe. Perhaps it would do her bidding and help her to heal them She felt a wave of sympathy and pity wash through her. She wanted to help. She raised her hand holding the stone. Blue mist swirled within it. What now? Perhaps she should say something. It came to her.

"Be healed," September shouted. At once blue light flowed from the stone down her arm and body and legs and spread out across the floor of the tent. It covered the bodies of the people on the floor then over the beds, submerging all the wounded in the blue glow. It spread out to fill the tent as far as she could see. The cries of the sick and wounded died away. A breeze of clean air blew away the noxious smells of decay. The blue light slowly sank into the ground revealing the patients. Their wounds had disappeared, their bodies were made whole, the skin, white and brown and yellow, smooth and unmarked. The men, women and children stood and began to express their thanks to their healer.

September was back within the circle of silver wraiths, again standing on the surface of the silver Moon. The spirit of Arianrhod stepped forward.

"Well done, Cludydd. You have tapped the power of Lleuad and arian, the healer."

"But I just waved the stone and asked for all those people to be made well."

"Exactly. You used the Maengolauseren to do good. You could have taken yourself away, swept the wounded from your sight. You may have seen the people as servants of the Malevolence and commanded the Maengolauseren to destroy them. You could have just saved yourself. Instead you showed pity and used your power to heal. You fulfilled your task. Now you know you can call on the energy of Lleuad and the power of arian at any time. We know you will use the skill for the good of all."

"Um, thank you," September murmured, trying to take in what had happened and what Arianrhod had said. The starstone would do anything she wanted, if she made the correct choice of action. Despite her revulsion she had acted to help the people out of sympathy and compassion instead of simply protecting herself, and in her response she had drawn the power of the Moon through the starstone.

"Goodbye and good luck with your task," Arianrhod said, "we trust that you will push back the Evil and restore goodness throughout the universe." All the spirits raised a hand to wave to September. She wanted to ask more but she felt herself rising from the surface, leaving the Moon behind her.

She was in space again, the Moon receding beneath her feet. She looked up and saw the Sun above her, but she did not seem to be heading exactly towards it. She strained her neck to see where her trajectory was taking her. She saw a small, pale white disk that grew rapidly. Where was she heading now?

The Earth and Moon became tiny dots while the white planet became larger until it filled her sight, with the Sun, now over her shoulder, also larger and brighter. I'm travelling through the Solar System towards the Sun, September thought, so the next planet must be Venus. She had learnt that the planet was a fiercely hot world covered in an atmosphere of carbon dioxide and sulfuric acid but she descended to a shining, smooth ocean of silver liquid with no hint of atmosphere to hide the Sun. Her feet touched the surface of the liquid but did not sink into it. It looks more like mercury, September thought.

As on the Moon, she was soon surrounded by spirits to the horizon but these were men and women glowing with a silver coloured light. They were unfamiliar but then September recognised a face; it was Eluned, and next to her was Heini. Both of them were cludydd o arian byw. This must be the planet Mercury.

"Hello, September," the spirit of Eluned said. September

was delighted to see Eluned looking, at least in spirit form, fit and well. It seemed so long since she had last seen her lying injured on a bed in Amaethaderyn. Nevertheless she was confused.

"It's lovely to see you Eluned but I thought I was coming to Venus not Mercury."

"Mercher is the next planet closest to Daear after Lleuad," Eluned replied.

September was quite sure it wasn't the same at home, but she was getting used to things being different here.

"You look well, Eluned, or am I just seeing some kind of ghost of you?"

"This is my planetary spirit, September. I still live on Daear, but it is a true reflection. I am fully recovered from my injury."

"That's great. I've been worried about you. You saved me from the Ceffyl dwr."

"No, you saved me, September, by wielding the Maengolauseren."

"Well, I did something, I'm not sure how."

"That is why you are with us now; to learn how to wield the power that lies within you."

"That is what the spirits said on the Moon. They gave me a task which showed how I can use the stone to heal like the silver that Arianwen has."

"Yes, and here you will discover the power of arian byw."

"I already have. The mercury you gave me helped me find the stone when it was lost at the bottom of a lake. It turned me into a mermaid."

"I'm glad my gift was of use, but its powers were limited. With control of the Maengolauseren you will be able to call on the power of Mercher directly."

"You have a task for me like the Moon people had?"

"Yes. It will lead you to an understanding of the secrets of arian byw. Good luck Cludydd."

She was back on what looked like Earth. A grass-covered plain stretched ahead of and around her. In the distance was a hazy, purple range of mountains. The sky was blue with fluffy white clouds. She felt warm although she appeared to be only clothed in the blue white light of the Maengolauseren. The place was unknown to her and could have been her home, Earth, or the Land, or indeed somewhere else entirely. There was just one other feature. A path stretched in front of her, a sandy coloured line that snaked across the green plain until it was lost in the distant haze.

September looked around. She was alone. What was her task? She looked at the starstone that she still gripped in her left hand. It was clear and dark but offered no clues. For want of anything else to do she started to walk along the path. She tried to think. What were the special qualities of mercury, or arian byw as Eluned preferred to call it? In her first task she had needed to show sympathy and then the healing power of silver was channelled through the stone. There was a clue there. An emotion triggered the reaction of the stone. Previously when she had used the starstone it was because she had experienced fear and anxiety. So what emotion would enable her to use the power of mercury? The metal had the property of changing its shape; it was liquid, and hence it gave its bearers, such as Eluned, the ability to change their shape, or the shape of other things. She remembered the shock of seeing Eluned change into the dolphin and, before that, appearing as a tiger. Her abilities were unexpected, surprising. That is it! September danced with glee. The emotion I'm looking for is surprise. Eluned used the surprise appearance of the Adarllwchgwin and the Ceffyl dwr to change her shape. The shock of the loss of the Maengolauseren had enabled her to use Eluned's gift to become the mermaid. The power of arian byw was to react to the unexpected, to change oneself or one's surroundings.

She had been walking for some time while thinking, just following the path across the endless plain. She had no idea how much time had passed. The sun did not appear to have moved. The mountains, she decided, must be miles and miles away because they did not appear any closer than when she had arrived. There seemed little chance of a surprise here; the more she walked the less change there appeared to be. The landscape was featureless and nothing could creep up on her. If anything unexpected was going to happen it was going to be due to her. Then she understood. The trigger was to do something different, unpredictable, unexpected. But what? She had been a rather unimaginative child, had always done as she was told, a bit boring really. How could she suddenly do something different?

She stopped. Why was she following this track? It didn't seem to lead anywhere. She was just plodding along it because it was there. That was what paths were for. As always, she was following convention; keeping to the path laid out for her. She made up her mind. September stepped off the path and walked across the grass. She felt the starstone come alive in her hand. It felt hot. She ran and skipped.

"I want to fly," she shouted at the top of her voice.

She was swooping through the air, skimming across the plain at speed with great cobalt blue wings stretched out beside her. A flap of her arms and her wings scooped the air and she rose. Her nose and mouth felt strange; she had a beak. She wiggled her bottom and her tail wagged. She was a bird, flying; yes, she really was flying. Soaring up into the sky she headed for the mountains. They appeared closer. Snowy peaks, craggy cliffs and deep valleys appeared. She banked and swept down a cleft between sheer rock faces then, climbing, she headed for the summit of the highest mountain.

She was back on the silver-white plain of Mercury with the spirits of the cludyddau around her.

"Well done, Cludydd," Heini said.

"Yes, September. We knew you could do it," Eluned added, clapping her hands excitedly. Murmurs of approval came from the other spirits.

"I think I'm getting the hang of these tasks now," September said, feeling proud of herself, "I have to find the right emotion to trigger the action I want. It took me a bit of time. I'm just not good at puzzles; never have been"

"But you were excellent September. You soon realised that with arian byw you have to be ready for the unexpected," Eluned said.

"Now you can go on to your next appointment," Heini said.

Already September felt herself lifting off the ground.

"Goodbye, and thank you!" September called as the crowd of spirits receded, each individual waving.

In moments she was back in the blackness of space, the planet Mercury dropping away from her. She felt buoyed up by her success at solving the riddle of the task and filled now with the power of silver and mercury she looked forward to her next encounter. Surely it must be Venus next. She looked up. There was the Sun, still a little off to her right but ahead, growing quickly, was an orange disc.

A hot world with a poisonous, corrosive atmosphere; that was what she remembered about Venus. But that was in her universe. Neither the Moon nor Mercury resembled what she had learnt in school so Venus too would be different. Which metal was connected with Venus? She wracked her brain to recall; it was so long since that first meeting with the Mordeyrn when he had presented the metals and their bearers to her. It would not be long before she found out as the disc grew quickly to fill the sky.

She was standing on an orange plain and approaching her was the expected throng of spirits. This time they shared the orange hue of their planet. She remembered – copper, of course, and there was Catrin, who had given her the little speaking horn, and Anarawd together at the forefront to greet her.

"Welcome, Cludydd, to Gwener," Anarawd said.

"Thank you, this tour is fun. It's nice to see you again Catrin, so I can thank you again for my present. It saved me after Cynddylig drowned and the boat sank."

"I am pleased, Cludydd," Catrin replied, "it was given to you to be of use."

"Now the Maengolauseren is teaching you its power," Anarawd said.

"Yes, I've learnt how to control the powers of silver and mercury. Now I will have to find the emotion that gives me the power of copper."

"That is true. Efyddyn draws its energy from Gwener and our task will show you how," Anarawd continued.

"You have all the love we can give you," Catrin said.

She was nowhere. She felt as though she was standing on a white floor with whiteness all around her. Were there walls and ceiling or did the whiteness just go on and on? There was light but it had no source; it surrounded her. She was alone, simply clothed in the blue haze of the starstone.

"Hello. Is anybody there?" she called, but her voice even sounded faint to her own ears so obviously it didn't carry. She felt isolated, far more so than on the vast plain of the previous task. At least on Mercury there had been colour and perspective. She sat down, crossed her legs and wrapped her arms around herself. She had to think.

What were the skills of the bearer of copper? The little horn that Catrin had given her allowed her to speak to Aurddolen across hundreds of miles, and she had seen Catrin wield a pole that captured electricity from the air to fire a bolt of lightning at the Gwyllian. That meant that copper somehow allowed communication and channelled electricity. The bearers of copper must provide a link between the widely spread communities across the Land and the conduction of electricity gave them a useful weapon against the Malevolence. But what emotion was needed to trigger it?

September rocked and tapped her hand against her forehead. Something Catrin said was a clue, she knew it was. What did she say? "You have all the love we can give you." Of course! How could she be so dumb? Venus was the goddess of love. Love was the emotion. It was love for her people that enabled Catrin to create the communication links, love for her fellow villagers that enabled her to protect them by blasting the Malevolence's monsters to dust. So, September had to feel love in order to draw the power of copper from the Maengolauseren. There was only one problem, she couldn't think of who she loved.

The starstone was gripped in her left hand. She unfolded her fingers and looked at the dark, lifeless pebble. Perhaps love of her mother and father would do it. Did she love them? Of course she did, they had brought her up, looked after her, protected her when people called her names. The stone remained cool and unmoved. That love was not strong enough. What about love for her sisters and brother? Gus was usually annoying but her sisters were pleasant to her; she must love them. The starstone did not respond. She had girl friends but she couldn't honestly say she loved them. No boy had ever shown any interest in her so that was a non-starter. Hold on though. What about Tudfwlch? They had got on well and she had grown to like him until he was injured. Having to kill the monster he had become still hurt her. She felt grief, but it wasn't love and the stone remained dark. Sieffre had shown a lot of concern for her and she liked him. They had even kissed. The starstone remained resolutely unchanged. That was all; there was no-one else she could feel love for.

She was stuck; trapped in this white prison because she did not feel enough love for anybody. She might be imprisoned here forever if she couldn't find the key to love. She felt sorry for herself. Herself? Did she love herself? Most of her life she had been disappointed with herself. She was slow to learn, no good at anything, fed up most of the time because everything she tried failed. She was useless at every sport she attempted, she couldn't even catch a ball; clumsy when Mother showed her how to sew and cook, and when she'd picked up Julie's clarinet she couldn't even get a sound out of it. Whenever she gave up something, she ate to make herself happy and then was disgusted when she put on weight and looked fat. There it was – she didn't love herself. That was why the Maengolauseren was lying in her hand lifeless. She was going to be stuck here forever.

Catrin's last words went around her head, "You have all the love we can give you". Catrin thought she deserved her love and the love of the other copper bearers. She remembered the joy of the spirits of the Moon and Mercury when she succeeded at their tasks. They loved her. She had solved their problems. She recalled how Aurddolen, Berddig, Sieffre and all the others had congratulated her each time she had driven off the manifestations of the Malevolence. They thought she would succeed. Here, she was a success and she was learning new skills with the starstone.

September stood up, stretched her back, felt the strong taut muscles in her body. She loved the body she had here. Yes, love. She did love herself. The stone in her hand suddenly felt hot. She looked at it. It was glowing. She clasped it in her hand and raised her arm and shouted out,

"I love myself and I love everyone. Listen to me. I am here, the Cludydd o Maengolauseren and I will defeat the Malevolence."

Her voice was strong. A sheet of lightning flashed out from the starstone. The white prison was gone and she was standing again amongst the orange band of the cludyddau o efyddyn. They clapped loudly.

"We hear your message, Cludydd," Anarawd said over the din, "and so does every person in the universe."

"You found your love for yourself," Catrin said.

"Yes," September cried, filled with satisfaction, "thanks to you. I don't think I have ever really loved myself before but now I do and I love you all."

"Now you have the power of Gwener at your disposal, you can communicate with anyone in our universe whenever you wish," Anarawd explained.

"But I don't have the copper horn with me."

"You no longer need it. The Maengolauseren is your link to the network of efyddyn that is in and around every living thing. You can also summon electric energy from the earth, air, fire and water that make up the substance of the universe, reinforcing the energy that the stone draws from the stars."

"Thank you, Anarawd, for explaining it to me."

"Now you have added the essence of efyddyn to your skills, your time with us is at an end," Catrin said sadly, "we hope you will return to us some time, but now you must travel on."

Once again there were farewells as she rose from the planet's surface. September looked up and saw the Sun directly ahead.

5

The Sun was a great golden ball in front of her. As she got closer September expected the heat to become intolerable. After all, it was the Sun that warmed the Earth. How would she survive?

She wasn't burned to a cinder. Although the growing Sun became brighter, making the stars invisible to her eyes, she didn't feel heat. Was the blue glow that surrounded her protecting her? Now that the Sun filled her field of vision she realised that, like the Moon and the planets she had already visited, it didn't look like what she might have expected. She recalled films showing huge flames leaping off the face of the Sun and a mottled, boiling appearance. Here the Sun was a uniform golden sphere.

She was on the surface. Well not exactly. She was floating a centimetre above the incandescent material that was the Sun. Even the air or gas around her glowed brightly, making it difficult to see far. She didn't see the approaching spirits until they were close enough to speak. Their wraith-like bodies were luminous like the Sun itself and they had hair that varied from the yellow of daffodils to pale straw. There at the forefront was the spirit of Aurddolen, smiling warmly. September felt a spurt of happiness at seeing him.

"Welcome, Cludydd. You have travelled far and have a long way still to go but we are pleased because your arrival here shows that you have been successful in your first three tasks." Aurddolen's voice was formal but friendly.

"I think I am beginning to understand how things work," September said, "I have to use my emotions to control the Maengolauseren and your tasks are teaching me the feelings I need."

"That is correct, September. Only by drawing on the energy of the seven planets as well as the stars will you be powerful enough to overcome the Malevolence."

"And Malice?"

"We have no knowledge of a spirit with that title."

September was confused but before she could enquire further she noticed one of the most aged spirits stepping forward.

"I am Heulyn, Cludydd," he said.

"The one who built the Arsyllfa?" This must be the cludydd o aur she had first heard of in Tudfwlch's stories, who Aurddolen had told her about, whose book had set her on this trek through the solar system.

"That is correct."

"The Mordeyrn who knew my mother?" He was ancient in appearance but still retained a power.

"I was honoured to accompany the Cludydd Breuddwyd. You are very alike. You and she are worthy bearers of the stone."

"But she didn't have a twin to make things worse."

Heulyn ignored September's comment as if he was reciting a recorded statement. "After Breuddwyd banished the Malevolence I devoted my life to preparing for the next Cysylltiad expecting it to follow the same pattern as before. All the cludyddau o aur that followed me including Aurddolen, continued my work."

"You must complete your awakening, September," Aurddolen said, "so that we can develop our plans."

"So you have a task for me?"

"Of course. We are sure you will find the key to access the power of Haul."

The noise was deafening; people shouting and screaming, the crash of stone pulverising stone, the roar of fires. A stench of burning wood and something else filled the air. Was it meat or human flesh? September felt dizzy. Where was she? It felt like she was on Earth or in the Land again. She rested a hand against a rough wall to steady herself. Men and women ran past, seeing her but taking no notice of her. She peered through the billowing clouds of dust and smoke that obscured her view. She seemed to be in a village or town. There were buildings of stone and wood although most now seemed to be in ruins. It was not a place she recognised.

She followed the people, picking her way over the debris of fallen stone and half-burned timbers that filled the streets and alleyways. There was a line of people ahead of her, their backs to her. They were kneeling or crouched down. A few held bows with arrows poised to fire, some grasped short swords, but most held rocks in their hands, ready to throw. September could see over their heads to hilltops and realised that the town was also on top of a hill. The people seemed to be gathered at the edge, looking down at something.

She edged forward until she was standing in the row of men and women waiting behind a low parapet. Then she saw what they were waiting for. Climbing the rough hillside, grasping at shrubs and outcrops of rock was an army, a motley, dusty, undisciplined army but a determined one. She couldn't count their numbers but everywhere she looked she saw another figure, scrambling up the steep slope. They grasped all sorts of weapons in their hands – swords, knives, axes, scythes, burning torches, or simply heavy sticks. Some were close enough to see their faces. September recognised those faces. They were the same as she had seen at Glanyrafon, the faces of the servants of the Malevolence, faces that were distorted with hate. These people were driven with just one purpose – to do the bidding of the evil, to kill and destroy.

Beyond the attackers, lower down the hillside, September could see the reason for the town being a burning ruin. There were dozens of war machines. Each was different but each was designed to throw missiles of one sort or another. Even to September's untrained eye they seemed makeshift and hastily lashed together from misshapen pieces of wood but they were effective. As she watched, one lobbed a boulder into the sky. It ripped through the air over her head and crashed into the unprotected town. Another fired a bundle of burning wood that passed over them dripping sparks and cinders.

"Get down, or you'll get your head knocked off!" The man next to her tugged on the grubby gown that covered her body. He held a sling for flinging small rocks and looked to be in his fifties. "It won't be long now before they're at us."

September saw the desperate look in his eyes. These

people, these few people, were defending themselves against the hordes of the Malevolence with the rubble of their own homes and a few real weapons.

"Where are the cludydds?" she asked, wondering who was in charge.

"What are you on about? You know we have no cludyddau here."

Not one cludydd, so there was no one to wield the power of iron or copper or lead or gold to defend these people from the power of the Malevolence. They were relying on their own strength and courage to repel the hate-driven attackers. September wondered why she was here. The noise, the smells, the eye-smarting smoke, seemed real but, she remembered, it was a test for her. What did the spirits of the Sun intend her to do?

She needed to pause to think, but the chaos around her, the missiles flying overhead and the knowledge that the army of the Malevolence was getting closer with every moment made her head spin. The starstone was still in her hand. She looked at it. It was cold and dark. What did she know about the power of gold? She had seen Aurddolen draw on its power to destroy the first Draig tân and a speck of gold powered the motor that drove her boat. Gold was a conduit for the energy of the Sun but it also seemed to imbue its bearers with the skills of leadership. Everyone looked to Aurddolen to guide the Land through the Conjunction and the invasion by the Malevolence as Heulyn had done before.

There was no gold here and no cludydd o aur. Very soon the townspeople would be fighting for their lives and their identities against the overwhelming numbers of the mindless attackers.

"Do you think you can defeat them?" September asked of the man beside her.

"How can we win against the Malevolence? We do not have the power." A few of the defenders let fly with arrows. Each found its mark and the attackers fell but the vast numbers remaining took no notice and continued their advance.

"Why are you here then?"

The man showed surprise that she should ask such a

question but answered her nevertheless. "There is no way of escape. We are surrounded. I will fight and die rather than become like them." He nodded at the approaching horde now barely forty metres away.   September recalled how the people of Glanyrafon had been turned to evil.

"They were ordinary people once."

"That is true and some of our own folk have already been turned to evil in the same way. They killed their friends and families as well as destroying their own homes."

"Is there no way they can be stopped?"

"A visitation from the Cludydd o Maengolauseren perhaps? Some hope."

Hope. As he said it, September realised that was what Aurddolen and the other cludyddau o aur had within them. They radiated optimism and hope while the people trusted in them and had hope themselves. Wherever there was a cludydd o aur to plan and guide, the people were filled with the hope that they would succeed against the Malevolence. With the power of the Sun behind them, of course there was hope.

September felt the stone getting hot in her hand. She leapt to her feet raising her hand high. The dusty gown that had covered her dissolved into the air and she was clothed once again in royal blue.

"Cludydd?" the man cried out. Others surrounding her looked towards her, recognition dawning on their faces.

September took a deep breath and shouted, "Have hope!"

She was back on the Sun facing Aurddolen, Heulyn and the others. Her heart was thumping with the thrill of discovering how hope could defeat the enemy. She lowered her hand and gripped the starstone tightly again.

"Well done, Cludydd," Heulyn said, "You discovered hope."

"Yes, now I understand how you can prepare for a battle against something that seems impossible to destroy."

"We know we cannot destroy the Malevolence, but you are correct, hope gives us the strength to stand against it and banish it from our world." Heulyn said.

"Was I really there defending that town?"

"It was a vision of what could be," Aurddolen said, "There are many places across Daear that have little defence against the manifestations and servants of evil other than what the people can provide themselves. They face pain, death or perhaps conversion to evil but yet they persevere. With the powers that you are acquiring you will be able to help them and give them hope."

"Can't you?"

"If I was there I could, but I cannot be everywhere and there are few cludyddau o aur." September looked at the assembled spirits. There were many of them but she remembered that this included all the past cludyddau like Heulyn. Aurddolen was the only living one she had met or heard of. Then she noticed for the first time that they were all men.

"Are there no women gold bearers?"

"Aur and arian are the husband and wife of metals. The Sun and Moon determine who can become a cludydd. The Moon always chooses women, the Sun, men."

"But your daughter, Heulwen, she carries gold and says she is your apprentice."

Aurddolen looked sad.

"Heulwen certainly has a little aptitude for wielding gold and she has had a dream that Haul for whom she is named, will select her despite the rules."

"Rules can be broken or changed."

"Perhaps rule is the wrong word. It is a law of our universe that cannot be altered."

"So Heulwen is wrong."

"She is misguided. Her mother died when she was just a baby. As a child I taught her some simple ways of drawing energy from gold, barely more than anyone using an engine powered by gold can do. Then I had to leave her at the Arsyllfa while I toured the Land to spread the message of hope. I was absent for years during which Heulwen became convinced that she was my apprentice and would assist me in the struggle against the Malevolence. I have been unable to shake this belief."

"She's bananas."

"I don't understand."

"She's mad."

"I hope not. Somewhat overconfident I feel."

September didn't say anything more as she felt that Aurddolen, or his spirit, had a rose-tinted view of his daughter. The opportunity passed as she felt herself lifting off from the Sun.

"Farewell, Cludydd," called Heulyn, "Take our hopes with you for the rest of your journey."

While Heulyn was smiling warmly, September saw that there was a frown on Aurddolen's face. Perhaps his daughter is yet another worry for him, September wondered. Further thoughts about Heulwen slipped from her mind as the Sun diminished behind her. Now she was heading into the outer solar system; next stop, Mars. The planet was a red dot in front of her but it grew rapidly. A variety of vague but conflicting ideas about Mars flashed through her mind. Mars was the god of war but the planet was a dead, cold world covered in red rust. There was a link. There were three bearers of iron that she had met: Iorwerth, Iddig and Cynhaearn. They were also warriors as Tudfwlch had been.

The three cludyddau were at the front of the crowd of crimson spirits welcoming her as September's feet touched the surface of the planet but she could not see the youthful features of Tudfwlch among them. The bright spot of the Sun, high in the sky, did not seem to dispel the ruddy gloom. September looked at the assembled cludyddau. There were women as well as men but they all looked strong and muscular and suited to wielding heavy tools and weapons too.

"Welcome, Cludydd," Cynhaearn said, "We are eager for your presence among us."

"Have you been waiting long?"

"Time has little meaning for us. The spheres of the planets continue on their endless rotation around Daear and the incursions of the Malevolence grow stronger but we do not measure hours or days. We knew the Cludydd o Maengolauseren would join us in the battle and we are delighted that you are here."

"I am interested in what I have to learn here but first I

wonder if Tudfwlch is with you?"

"I am sorry, he is not," Iorwerth said, "News reached us that he had fallen to the Malevolence."

"Then shouldn't he be here?"

"Alas, Tudfwlch was an apprentice and not a cludydd. He hadn't established the full connection with Mawrth that would have brought his spirit to us. It is a sad loss as I am sure he would have been a fine cludydd o haearn."

"What happened to him when he died?"

"The spirits of the good return to the soil of Daear but those of servants of the Malevolence ascend above the stars." Iorwerth said, "Do you know what death befell him?"

"I killed him – twice. First with the knife you gave me and then with the starstone. He was infected by the evil and attacked me."

"Ah, that is a sad end. His spirit will now be full of hate and is merged with the Malevolence. You must remember his fate as you take the test that Mawrth has set."

Again, September stood on ground somewhere in the Land. She was beside a river in a broad valley surrounded by snow-capped mountains. There were even patches of snow on the thin, sparse grass of the flood plain. This isn't the Bryn am Seren, September thought, the mountains are far too tall. I must be in the Mynydd Tywyll. She noticed activity by the river a couple of hundred metres away. A party of people were climbing over a tangled heap of iron girders. September decided to join them. As she was again clad in luminous dark blue the people soon saw her and stopped their work in order to greet her. One man stepped forward. He seemed the oldest among the crowd.

"You are the Cludydd o Maengolauseren?" he asked.

"I am. What are you doing?"

"We have been attacked by the Malevolence. A Draig tân destroyed our bridge." He indicated the wreckage. "It is haearn but our cludydd o haearn was killed by Llamhigwyn y dwr so we are unable to rebuild it."

"Lam… what? That is a manifestation of the Malevolence I've heard mentioned but I haven't met them."

"You are lucky, Cludydd. They are immense creatures that

have heads shaped like those of frogs, wings of skin like bats and tails of a lizard that carry a fierce sting. They arose from the river as the Draig tân struck the bridge. The cludydd attacked them with his great sword but one of the stings struck him down."

September didn't like the image she had of the Llamhigwyn y dwr.

"I see. The cludydd would have repaired your bridge, I suppose."

"Yes. Our flocks graze on the other side of the river and the current is too strong for us to cross so the bridge is essential to our village. Without the cludydd we cannot rebuild the bridge. We have the cludydd's tools but not his skill in manipulating haearn." The old man struggled to lift a heavy hammer such as she could imagine Iorwerth wielding.

September was at a loss. How could she rebuild the iron bridge as the people expected? The Maengolauseren was useful for despatching manifestations and servants of the Malevolence, but how could it be used for manipulating iron? Of course, this was the task set by the cludyddau of Mars so she had to find a way. She had learnt how to wield the power of silver, mercury, copper and gold through the starstone, now it was the turn of iron. But as in each other task she had to find the correct emotion. She had seen Iorwerth brandishing his great sword, Aldyth, to kill the Adarllwchgwin. Iddig had shaken his sword at the Draig tân and Cynhaearn had made the iron framework of the Arsyllfa glow to withstand the attack lead by Malice. Each had bellowed oaths and imprecations against the attackers. But there was another side of the cludydd o haearn's power. She recalled Tudfwlch telling of how he had been chosen as an apprentice after watching Iorwerth hammer red-hot iron into intricate shapes. How could they be both warriors and craftsmen? It was a puzzle and September couldn't see an answer.

The old man escorted her to the heap of twisted iron that was the remains of the bridge. Some men were half-heartedly hammering at a girder, attempting to straighten it. The iron resisted their efforts. September guessed that to make the metal obey his commands the cludydd would have to assert his power, be aggressive even. She saw the red-faced angry Iorwerth fighting off the huge evil birds. Anger was the emotion of the warrior, but what about the peaceful ironsmith? No, September thought, though anger is the key it is not the wild anger of someone filled with hate or rage, such as the servants of the Malevolence, but a controlled aggression, a determination to make the iron fulfil its purpose. She could see the fierce, focussed anger of Iorwerth slashing with his sword or beating a red hot rod into shape. She was reminded of the fearful anger she had felt when Tudfwlch tore the Maengolauseren from around her neck and her iron blade had found its way into her hand and thrust almost of its own accord into his side. Wild, uncontrolled anger was bad, a tool of the Malevolence, but anger properly directed and tempered was a good emotion. She understood.

The stone responded and heated her hand. Stepping towards the ruined bridge she thrust her fist forwards, feeling her heart beating faster and her face glow with blood-red heat. She commanded the broken and bent bars of iron to remould themselves into their former shapes.

She was back amongst the ghostly red figures on the red planet. She panted.

"Did it work? Did the bridge rebuild itself?"

"Indeed it would have," chuckled Iddig, "You commanded that iron like a true cludydd o haearn."

"But it wasn't real," September said, "It was just a test to see if I could find anger."

"Which you did," Iorwerth acknowledged, "but you also realised that anger is a difficult emotion. Uncontrolled it is destructive. People who are angry are easy prey for the Malevolence if their anger is directed at their fellows out of disgust or envy."

Cynhaearn added, "Even some cludyddau have succumbed to the Malevolence because our emotion of power can be subverted to hate," September now knew why Tudfwlch had been converted by the Malevolence; when fighting the villagers of Glanyrafon his inexperience had allowed his anger to edge into hate and opened him up to infection by the evil.

Cynhaearn went on, "But kept under control and directed at the haearn itself the power of Mawrth is with you and you have the ability to bend haearn to your will."

"And I've had another lesson in understanding my feelings. Thank you." September felt herself moving away from the throng. "And now I think I've just got two more tests and two more planets to visit."

"Farewell, Cludydd," the men and women of Mars chorused.

September rose quickly from the surface. Her next destination was a distant bright spot in the star-filled sky. In fact it was some time before she was able to discern which of the stars was the planet until Jupiter took on the form of a silver-grey disc. Where are the coloured stripes and the great red spot? She wondered. All the pictures she had seen of the giant planet had pointed out the great storm cloud and she recalled how huge the planet was. But to her it was just a great dull silver sphere. Why did all the planets seem so featureless when telescopes and space probes showed that they were not? As she travelled through space unencumbered by a bulky space suit, September thought about the question. There were no telescopes in this world, she remembered, not even the astronomer of the Arsyllfa had one to look through. There certainly were no space rockets. She was seeing the planets as people had seen them and imagined them to be before telescopes changed astronomy. Before Galileo, she realised. This whole universe is a model of what people back home used to believe before Galileo and the others changed everything.

September felt triumphant that she had worked things out, but time for thinking was over. Her feet touched the dull silver surface of Jupiter. The anticipated ghostly figures quickly materialised around her. She looked for familiar faces and soon picked out the youthful features of Berddig, cludydd o alcam of Amaethaderyn and Betrys, the plump Prif-cludydd.

"Welcome Cludydd, it's lovely to greet you, my dear," Betrys said jovially.

"Thank you," September replied, "It's nice to see you too, but, Berddig, I'm so happy to see you again." September felt that she wanted to hug the young cludydd but she didn't think it was possible to grasp a spirit.

"And I too," Berddig said, "I am pleased that you completed your journey to the Arsyllfa and that you are now learning the powers that the Maengolauseren gives you."

September's happiness was dampened by the memories of her journey.

"I wish I could have come on this magic journey without all the travel. Then perhaps Tudfwlch and Cynddylig and the others might still be alive."

"Perhaps you needed those experiences to prepare you for your tasks and the trials that lie ahead," Betrys said, still smiling.

"We celebrate your survival and praise the memory of Tudfwlch and Cynddylig," Berddig said, "I hope the cloak of alcam and plwm carried out its purpose."

"I think so. We just kept running into things where I had to use the starstone to protect myself. I wasn't able to hide myself away under the cloak. But it is a marvellous thing."

"And now you have come to learn how the power of Iau passes into alcam," Berddig said.

"Alcam is a special metal," Betrys explained, "Alone it has little power, but when its qualities are combined with the other metals they are stronger and can withstand forces of decay. There is greater power in a union between metals."

Berddig nodded, "The same is true of people. Individually we can fall to the evil. Together we live in peace and prosperity and can oppose the manifestations of the Malevolence."

"You were the one who made that happen in Amaethaderyn," September said, recalling Berddig's role in welcoming her and organising the villagers to protect and support her.

The young man smiled.

"Your memories are important. We hope our task will delight you."

The crowd thronged around her. She hadn't seen so many people in one place since she had arrived in the Land. They were in some vast room. She had a sense of a ceiling overhead but the walls were so distant that they could not be seen. The room, however big it was, was filled with people and they all seemed to be addressing her.

September was standing on a low dais so that she could just see over the heads of the men and women pressed together facing her. They raised their voices, each struggling to be heard.

"Help us!"

"You must do…"

"Strike them…"

"You are the Cludydd…"

She saw from the implements in their hands and the adornments on their bodies and clothes, that some of the crowd were cludyddau. Here was a cludydd o haearn shaking a hammer; there a bearer of copper holding a small trumpet; beyond, a wielder of silver with an amulet of the shining metal. Each and every one was shouting at her. No-one was speaking to their neighbour or waiting for a moment to take their turn. The sound of the raised voices was deafening. September held her hands to her ears, the stone still gripped in her left palm.

Crowds had always frightened her. She never wanted to be the centre of attention, had never performed on stage. At home she would have crumpled into a sobbing heap if just a few people had appealed to her in the manner of this multitude. She wasn't at home though and September had learnt a lot about herself and about feelings. She didn't collapse. She breathed gently and smoothly, shutting out the noise and the sight of the people, thinking.

What did the spirits of Jupiter intend by this task? Here was a bickering mass of people acting as individuals ignoring each other. Would a cludydd o alcam be able to calm them, bring order and get them to cooperate? Was that the power that Jupiter gave to the bearers of tin? If so, how did she draw on it?

What was the emotion that was the key to untapping the planet's energy? She recalled Berddig's last words to her. Which memories were important? Berddig had been efficient in organising the people of Amaethaderyn. The people, including the other cludyddau, looked to him for guidance and leadership which he provided cheerfully. Was there anything there?

She turned her thoughts to Betrys. She hardly knew the portly, jovial tin bearer but for the glee with which she had greeted her at dinner at the Arsyllfa. What was it Betrys had said to her? That her name meant 'joy'. She seemed to be cheerful and jolly all the time. Indeed, although Berddig made serious decisions he too was always cheerful, always looking on the bright side, forever the optimist. What had he said? They would praise the lives of Tudfwlch and Cynddylig, not mourn them. Perhaps it was this feeling of optimism, of joy that drew people to them and gave them control over tin.

September was happy. She had the key to the power of Iau. She looked out again at the noisy, disparate crowd. She was not nervous of facing the mob. A feeling of elation filled her. She was jubilant. The stone warmed her hand. She raised her arms in the air and turned slowly in a circle radiating her smile.

"Friends. Listen to me," she said.

She was facing the silver wraiths of Jupiter, each of them grinning broadly and clapping their hands with glee.

"Well done, Cludydd," Betrys congratulated her, "You have indeed become a mistress of your emotions. You found the clues in our task most speedily."

"Now you understand joy, you will find it easier to wield all the metals and to guide the people who support you," Berddig said.

"Thank you," September said ecstatically. She was filled with euphoria and confidence that she had all the tools for the task ahead of her. Well, almost all; there was one planet left to visit. She was already rising from the surface of Jupiter. The spirits waved their farewells.

6

She looked up into the black starlit sky. One of the stars up there was Saturn, her final destination. Rapidly one point of light took on the appearance of a planet but there were no distinctive rings. Of course, September thought, they can't be seen without a telescope. What a shame, she thought, that the people of the Land do not know of the beauty of the rings of Saturn. The planet was a dull, pale grey, and as her feet dropped to the surface so a band of grey figures assembled around her. She recognised immediately the grey-haired, stooped figure of Padarn, the cludydd o plwm of Amaethaderyn. Alongside him was the shorter, stockier figure of Cynwal the Prif-cludydd from the mines of Mynydd Tywyll.

"We greet you, Cludydd, at the final stage of your long journey," Cynwal said gravely.

"We are relieved that you have arrived at Sadwrn," Padarn said, his face long and gloom-laden. "It shows that you have successfully completed the other six ordeals that equip you with the skills to face the Malevolence."

"I'm glad I've got this far," September replied cheerfully, "I'm looking forward to seeing what you've got for my last task." She knew that plwm, or lead, was a part of the cloak that had hidden her and the starstone from the Malevolence, but she wasn't sure what else the metal was good for."

"The task will certainly guide you to an understanding of the skills of a cludydd o plwm and show how the power of Sadwrn can assist in defending Daear from the incursions of evil," Cynwal continued sombrely.

"It will cause us great anguish if you are not successful, Cludydd," Padarn added.

Me too, September thought, having come this far I'm not going to fail at the final stage. She thought the cludyddau were being a bit negative. OK, so the Malevolence was a great threat but now that she had the Maengolauseren and the powers of the planets, surely she could succeed.

"Take care, Cludydd. Remember what plwm can do for you," Padarn said.

She stood on a battlefield. The ground was a dusty, desert plain that stretched to a featureless horizon in all directions. Overhead the Sun shone in a cloudless sky radiating a fierce heat that made the air difficult to breathe and burned her skin. Around her were the relics of battle; wrecked wagons, weapons of war and bodies. Everywhere she looked there were bodies. She was drawn to them, her horror of the sight surpassed by her need to find out how they had suffered and died. Some bore deep cuts from a sharp blade while others were gouged by claws and some had limbs ripped off or huge bites torn from them. There were burns on some and others were swollen with skin that had turned black. Still more were covered with pustules and sores, and over everything the dust drifted. A number had arrow shafts buried in them, apparently fired by their own comrades. Some amongst the dead appeared unharmed but were nevertheless lifeless. September recognised many of the injuries as due to the manifestations of the Malevolence or the weapons of the servants of evil.

September hurried to the nearest still form, a young man with a short sword still gripped in his right hand. There were no marks on his body but his eyes were open and staring. Surely I have the power to help, September thought. She held the dull, cool starstone against the young warrior's forehead and composed herself to feel compassion. The stone glowed with a silver light but the man remained unchanged. He was past the power of arian. September went to another lifeless form, a mature woman with a burn on her shoulder. She pressed the stone against the wound. Again it glowed without result. The energy of the Moon was of no use to her.

September leapt into the air becoming a great, blue-feathered eagle. She circled above the scene of the battle. It extended to the horizon in every direction. The same image repeated over and over again. The air was so hot that it was exhausting continuing to fly. Landing she changed into a panther with glossy blue-black fur and bounded over the ground, looking for something, anything, that was different but all that she saw was more death and destruction. In the heat she tired quickly and slowed to a loping walk, panting. She became a cobra with iridescent blue scales that slid over the hot sand examining each body for signs of what had befallen the great army but she found no clues other than the variety of injuries. She returned to her normal form and stood gazing at the endless field of bodies. The monotony of the scene drained the power of Mercury from her.

She raised her arm up and drew on her affection for all the people she had met in the Land. The stone glowed orange.

"Is anyone there?" she called. Her voice carried through the shimmering air. She was sure her question was transmitted around the whole globe. She waited, hoping for some answer, some reply that would tell her that someone still lived, but there was just silence. There was no-one left to whom the loving power of Venus could be extended.

She dropped her hand to her side. What else could she do? If there was no-one left what was the need for hope? If she expressed anger what was there to fight? If she could summon up just a smidgen of joy there was no-one to spread it to. Her powers were useless and without purpose.

The heat of the Sun was burning her up; sweat dripped from her, each breath of hot air scorched her lungs. She sat down feeling despair. What was she doing here? This was the seventh and last task. The other six planets, their metals and emotions were of no use. What was the essential feature of Saturn and lead? Lead was heavy and dull; the planet furthest from the warming, life-giving Sun. The cludyddau had appeared glum and woeful. Was that it? Was sadness the emotion she was expected to find? Was she supposed to feel sadness at all the death and destruction she was faced with here on this hot dusty plain?

Covering her face with her hands she looked up at the fierce sun. It was not the gently warming, benevolent Sun of the cludyddau o aur. It was a destructive ball of fire that was consuming the Earth and turning it into a hell. It was growing, the temperature rising ever higher. Was it the final onslaught of the Malevolence?

September felt as if she was in a furnace. It was becoming difficult to think. It was too much effort to even sit up in this heat. She lay in the dust as dejected and miserable as she could be. How could this agony draw power from Saturn and manipulate lead? It was such a negative emotion that no good could surely come of it. But, she thought, in feeling sorrow she recognised the consequences of actions and could contemplate pain and death. Lead was a barrier to radiation that killed; her cloak had defended her from the Malevolence's perception. Perhaps there was a link. Feeling sorrow made someone more aware of dangers that plwm and the power of Saturn could provide protection from. A shield of lead could block this burning heat from the Land.

She dropped her head onto her hands and felt an overwhelming sadness for all the people who had died at the whim of the Malevolence. The Maengolauseren went icy cold in her hand and as she took her final breath she commanded a shield to form over the Earth.

The cold revived her. She opened her eyes and raised herself up on her arms and felt the joy of cool air in her lungs. The hard, grey surface of Saturn was beneath her and the spirits of plwm were gazing down at her with concern in their eyes.

"You have recovered," Cynwal said, "we are relieved."

September pulled herself into a sitting position.

"I hope that wasn't real," she said.

"No, like all your tasks that was an imaginary situation," Padarn said, "but if, stars forbid, the Malevolence gained mastery over Daear then it is a possibility."

"But it achieved its purpose," Cynwal went on, "it forced you to consider the emotion that is the essence of Sadwrn."

"I couldn't see how being sad was useful."

"You thought that sorrow was a negative, destructive emotion that would disable rather than empower you," Cynwal said, nodding gravely.

"That's right,"

"Anguish and despair are indeed powerful emotions used by the Malevolence to render people incapable of resistance. Sorrow however is that feeling one experiences when faced by a loss of goodness or in the presence of evil and thus provides a defence against corruption and depravity. Sadwrn reinforces that protection and plwm gives us the ability to shield us from the wicked forces."

"I think I see. If I feel sad then that is warning that something evil may be happening."

"That is correct, Cludydd."

"But why, in your task, did all my other powers fail? None of the other feelings had any effect."

Padarn had been listening carefully but now answered September's question.

"That is because our purpose was two-fold. In addition to revealing the secrets of plwm, your visit to Sadwrn, being the last of the seven planets, had to show you how all the emotions, planets and metals are linked. In you they form a unique omnipotence that no normal inhabitant of Gwlad can possess. Only you, Cludydd, can wield all the powers of the planets and metals at once. This is the source of our hope that you can persevere against the Malevolence."

Once upon a time, September would have been overwhelmed by such expectation of her, but now she felt confident. She could feel all the emotions roiling inside her giving her the potential to wield the powers of all seven metals in addition to the Maengolauseren itself.

"I see."

"But you also should understand that the emotions complement each other – sorrow and joy, compassion and anger, the steadfastness of love with unexpected surprise, hope and fear, Sadwrn with Iau, Lleuad and Mawrth, Gwener and Mercher and lastly Haul with the stars. Each will support the other making you more powerful than any single cludydd, however talented."

"Thank you."

"No, we must thank you. You have proved yourself in each of the tasks. Now the power of the planets and stars is awakened in you. You truly are the Cludydd o Maengolauseren."

"You must leave us now," Cynwal said, "to follow your own will and choose your own path to confront the Malevolence. You are free but the powers of the stars and planets will always be with you. We wish you well and pray that you are successful in your endeavour."

The grey throng faded, merging with the greyness of the saturnine landscape. The sound of their farewells became like echoes diminishing to silence until September was left standing alone still contemplating what she had been told. Her training was complete. All the powers of this universe were hers. She could feel the energies of each of the planets flowing through her like electric currents. Her arms, legs, body and head tingled. She recalled that Padarn had referred to the seven emotions of the planets plus one more – fear. It was fear that she had used to ignite a response from the starstone when she was attacked. Now she understood that fear did not paralyse or turn her into a nervous wreck. Fear made her focus on the danger that threatened her, speeded up her thinking, gave her courage to respond. To fear evil was good.

What should she do now? Cynwal said she was free to do what she wanted. They seemed confident that she was equipped to fight off the Malevolence at the Conjunction. Except, she realised now, not one of the spirits of the cludyddau on any of the planets had mentioned Malice. Her twin didn't feature in their thoughts. Only she could figure out how her sister would affect the plans. More information was needed, but from where? Well, she had visited all the planets. That only left the stars, the source of the power of the Maengolauseren. Her mind was made up. She leapt into space reaching for the sphere of stars.

Which star should she head for? There were thousands forming the sphere that shielded the solar system from the evil beyond. The sphere of stars rotated at huge speed. She could match their motion effortlessly but there was one star that was special. Cynddylig had pointed it out as they crossed the lake; the star that didn't move, the Pole Star, the star about which the sky turned. She looked for Daear, a distant disc in the centre of the universe, and above the North Pole, a bright point amongst many. Instantly she was moving towards her destination at an inconceivable but unfelt speed. The sphere of stars span past her in a blur but the Pole Star was a fixed point ahead.

She had expected the stars to be like the Sun but, of course, the astronomers of old Earth and of Gwlad had no reason to suspect that each of the glowing points in the sky was a vast fiery ball of gas. They weren't. The sphere that was the Pole Star grew as she approached but was nothing like as huge as the Sun, nor was it hot. It was simply a light in the sky, one of the innumerable similar lamps that marked the boundary of the universe.

September's feet touched a surface that gave out a uniform blue-white light. It was cool and hard. No figures came to greet her. The Cludyddau o Maengolauseren that had come before her were inhabitants of her universe, not this one. She looked up. Displayed before her was the Solar System, the Daear at its centre and the seven planets including the Sun and Moon moving on their orbits around it, and beyond them the other hemisphere of stars fixed to the rotating sphere. It was like looking at a model of the universe, small and fragile and so unlike the concept of the universe she had grown up with.

There was no consciousness here amongst the stars but there was emotion. Fear. Fear of what was beyond, on the outside. That fear made the starstone glow in her hand, a miniature star. She had to test the fear. How far could she venture beyond the sphere of stars? She felt strong, full of the power of the universe that was above her head. Perhaps she could defeat the Malevolence on its own territory.

She leapt from the surface of the star and ventured into the space beyond. All the light and warmth and life of the universe was behind now; ahead was darkness. There was no feeling of crossing a boundary, no physical barrier at all, but she knew she had crossed a line.

At first it was just a faint murmuring like the buzzing of a distant swarm of bees, but as she ventured further into the darkness the sound in her head grew. Her birthmark began to itch. Then she began to sense it; the feeling, the emotion. Hate. There was no colour or gradation to it, just pure, black hatred. It was directed at the shining ball of myriad lights that was now behind her and it was all round her.

Her hip began to burn. The bitter screams of individual spirits could be identified now although their number was too great for her to count. The formless wraiths flew past her, heading for the light like moths towards a lamp. Some began to sense her and pause in their flight. They were drawn to her. Now she was the focus of their spite. The message spread amongst them. More and more crowded around her. She was pelted with their hate like cold hard hailstones falling from storm clouds. She summoned up a feeling of sorrow and drew on the power of Saturn to shield herself from the hateful sprites.

Would Malice appear to defend the realm of the Malevolence from her incursion? It appeared she wouldn't as more and more of the vengeful spirits hammered at her barrier. Her hip was really hurting now. She winced and panted trying to fight against the pain. Even with her shield of metaphorical plwm she felt the overwhelming hatred of the collective evil that was the Malevolence. What Aurddolen and the others had told was correct. There was no personality to it, no deliberate consciousness, just atoms of hatred. There was still no sign of Malice.

The pain was so bad now that she had to put a stop to it. Could she destroy all of the spirits of evil? She opened the palm of her hand and looked into the dazzling blue light of the starstone. The Malevolence certainly scared her and that was what she needed to invoke her command. She imbued it with all the energy she could summon.

"Ymadaelwch! Be gone!"

The sphere of blue grew from the stone in her hand and in an instant expanded. The spirits were blown away. The sphere grew and grew, sweeping out a space in the dark as large as the solar system, and stopped.

The blue light died and at once the spirits flocked into her again. Their hate redoubled.

Again she cried out and again the power of the Maengolauseren blew away the wisps of the Malevolence but she couldn't make it last. Her sphere of influence died and straight away the evil filled the space. She knew then that the cludyddau had been right. The Malevolence could not be destroyed. Its realm of darkness was infinite. Any power would drain away to nothingness in the dimensionless vastness. The hope was to evict it from within the sphere of stars and now she had to admit that was the limit of her power. She must return to the universe of good and perform her task there.

With her side hurting as if it was on fire despite her protective shield, she turned back to the distant light of the stars. The spirits hassled her like jackals after a wildebeest but she was still strong. The sphere of sparkling lights grew until they were around her and she was through the system of planets with Daear ahead of her. She was glad of the reassurance of the stars surrounding her and the familiar planets.

The pain in her hip subsided and she threw off her shield. Now she knew the extent of the Malevolence, the countless immortal souls that constituted the evil. She was aware of her limitations, but she still felt her power and knew that she could rid the Land of the evil, so long as she could defeat her twin – or turn her away from wickedness. She kicked towards Daear.

7

She was lying on a soft surface. September opened her eyes and saw the ceiling with the little glowing lights and the colourful wall hangings. She was back in her room at the Arsyllfa, back in the blue dress. Had she dreamt all that had happened to her out in space? The starstone was back in its silver locket resting between her breasts, the iron knife, Tudfwlch's sword, the copper horn and the vial of mercury lay on the table as before. How long had she been asleep? She didn't feel hungry, just a little thirsty perhaps.

She got up and went to the bathroom. She turned the tap on the bath but no water came out. That was unexpected but she wasn't troubled. Sieffre would get her some water; she was sure he would still be waiting patiently outside the door. The bolts were heavy and stiff but first the top then the bottom yielded to her. She pulled the heavy door open, took a step into the corridor and recoiled.

There was no roof overhead and rubble from the wall opposite was scattered across the floor of the corridor. Beyond, the outer wall of the Arsyllfa was breached. She could see daylight and clouds. A cold wind blew through the holes in the walls and made her shiver.

"So the Cludydd returns!"

September turned to see who had spoken. She recognised the voice. Standing at the end of the ruined corridor was Heulwen in her golden yellow dress and beside her stood Malice.

"What has happened?"

"Can't you see? The Arsyllfa has fallen, as I said it would," Malice sneered.

"How?"

"My powers plus a little help from my friend." Malice gave Heulwen a wink. Heulwen was impassive, standing still, eyes unblinking.

"No! Heulwen. What happened to you? What did you do?"

"She won't answer you. She only responds to me now. Not even her father could reach her."

"Aurddolen? Where is he?"

"Oh, he ran away. Couldn't face up to me. I'll catch him soon and then his soul will be just one amongst all the others that I command."

"He's alive?"

"I suppose you would call it that."

"Why was I left here alone?"

"You were locked in that damned room. It has resisted even my power. But now you have made my task easier. Instead of hiding away you have come out to play."

"I wasn't hiding. I wasn't there."

"No? Where were you then?"

"Among the stars."

Malice looked surprised.

"I'm not the same as when we met before," September said, unfastening the clasp that held the Maengolauseren. She let the stone drop into her hand. "I've been learning what I can do."

"Oh, really. Let's see what you can do about this." Malice flung a bolt of night-dark shadow that seemed like a rip in space. September felt sorrow and deflected it with a shield of plwm, then summoning up hope she answered with a beam of gold light. It hit Malice in the chest throwing her back. She landed amongst the rubble. Heulwen still stood unmoving. Malice picked herself up.

"So you have learnt to use the puny metals that these people wield. Well, let's see how good you are against my elemental forces." She raised her arms to the open roof. Three Adarllwchgwin soared down from the sky, the riders with their tridents raised to shoot their cosmic fire.

A surge of anger filled September and she flicked her fingers. Red-hot arrows of haearn raced to their targets. Each of the giant birds burst in a cloud of vapour. She raised the starstone and a violet cone of light formed, enveloping her twin. Malice twisted and clenched her fists as if in agony until she stretched her arms wide and the violet light disappeared. Malice stood, her chest heaving.

"Perhaps you have gained a little in power," she said.

"I've only just started," September said, feeling the power of all the planets and stars within her. She hadn't dreamed her tour of the universe, or, if it was a dream, then it was one that had given her control over her emotions and all the energies in the universe.

"And so have I," Malice cried. She waved her hands and from each end of the corridor a pack of baying dogs appeared. They flickered and were translucent as if they were made of flame. Each was bigger than a Rottweiler and when they opened their jaws to bark and pant, smoke and flame was emitted. They loped towards her, howling, but Heulwen stood in their path.

September jumped and took the form of the blue-feathered eagle. The tips of her wings brushed the stone that remained of the walls as she swooped along the corridor. She opened her talons and grabbed Heulwen's shoulders, lifting her from the path of the dogs. Her wings pushed down on the air and she soared up into the sky, out of the ruined Arsyllfa. With her eagle eyes she saw the flaming, ghostly hounds gazing up at her, whining. Malice looked up with fierce anger on her face.

September flapped her wings again and left the Arsyllfa behind and below her. Heulwen dangled uncomplaining from her claws but September worried that the sharp points must be piercing her skin. She must land to release her burden. Spiralling down around the peak that the observatory stood on, down into the valley, she looked and listened.

"Is anyone there?" she asked through the loving power of efyddyn. There was a faint response. She turned towards it. There in a cleft in the rock at the base of the cliff, a figure crouched. She slowed, catching air in her wings, hovering, laying Heulwen down gently on the ground, then landing on her feet.

September turned back into her normal self, the self that she had been on the planets; the self clothed in blue light. The figure emerged from the gap in the rock face. Sieffre looked exhausted, covered in dust and dried blood, his clothes in tatters.

"Cludydd?"

"It's me, Sieffre; September."

He saw Heulwen lying on the ground and stepped back.

"You brought her. Why?"

"It's Aurddolen's daughter, Heulwen. Don't you recognise her? Malice had her. She might have died." September went to Heulwen and felt her body. It was warm but her eyes, though open, were unseeing. Blood oozed from the gouges in her shoulders made by September's claws.

"She has died. She's a servant of the Malevolence."

"She's hurt." September knelt beside Heulwen and pressed the starstone against her wounds and let compassion well up inside her.

"She betrayed us, betrayed her father."

"Malice said Heulwen was a friend. I didn't believe her. She must have forced her somehow." The blood stopped flowing, the wounds filled up, new skin formed and the bruising faded. Heulwen looked healed but still lay silently staring.

Sieffre shrugged and sagged. He sat on the ground and looked up at September, noticing the radiant blue covering her body.

"You've changed. I can sense a new power in you."

"I have and there is."

"You were locked inside the room while we fought for the Arsyllfa."

"I wasn't there. At least part of me wasn't. As far as I was aware I was visiting the planets, tackling the tasks they gave me."

"They?"

"The spirits of the cludydds that live on each of the planets."

"Oh. You were shut up for so long; we thought you must have died. We couldn't open the door."

"How long?"

"Six, seven days."

"A week! It didn't feel anything like that time. I haven't eaten anything. I still don't feel hungry."

"That's good, because I have no food."

September span a web of silver around Heulwen and wished her to recover. Then she sat facing Sieffre. She looked at his thin, haggard face.

"Tell me what happened."

He took a deep breath and looked up anxiously at the peak and the ruins of the Arsyllfa.

"After I found you had locked the door I stayed in the corridor. Aurddolen said he had expected that you would shut yourself away and that we should not expect to see you for a few days. He continued to prepare for the journey. Other cludyddau came and went, and she," he pointed at Heulwen, "kept turning up asking for news. There wasn't any of course."

"What was happening outside? Did the attacks carry on?"

"Without ceasing. Every manifestation known was thrown against the doors and walls of the Arsyllfa without effect."

"So, how did Malice get in?"

"It was her I tell you."

"How?"

"After three days and you didn't reappear everyone started to get perturbed. Even Aurddolen was uncertain what to do. With little time to make the journey to Mynydd Tywyll he was eager to start, but not without you. Not even he could break the seals on your room. Heulyn used all his power and that of the other cludyddau to make it secure. Heulwen got more and more worked up. She started saying silly things, such as that you had left and gone to help the Malevolence; that your twin had taken you; that she, Heulwen, must take your place. She accused the other cludyddau of belittling her, not acknowledging her power. She declared that she was her father's successor and that she would be the greatest cludydd o aur."

"But she can't be. Only men can wield gold. They told me on the Sun."

Sieffre looked at her with something like awe.

"That's right. She'd always had this idea that she was more than the Mordeyrn's daughter, that she was his apprentice. I suppose people humoured her but when she started making these claims, the cludyddau told her that she was mistaken, she could not be a cludydd o aur."

"I suppose that didn't shut her up."

"No, she went berserk; accused everyone of being in the

service of the Malevolence and stormed off. We didn't know where she'd gone. The Mordeyrn was distraught. Then there was a shout that the doors were open and the Malevolence was inside the Arsyllfa."

"She'd opened the doors?"

"It seems so. We fought of course, but we were unprepared for fighting inside. A Cyhyraeth swept through and many were killed by its pestilence."

"But Aurddolen escaped?"

"Yes. When it was obvious that the Arsyllfa was lost, he and I and a few others fought our way out."

"Did you see Heulwen again?"

"No."

"What about my twin, Malice?"

"The woman in the gown as black as night?"

"Yes."

"Oh yes, she was there alright. I can hear her laughter now as she demolished walls with her beams of darkness. She saw us escaping. I saw her standing on the edge of the observatory. She threw the instruments over the edge. I think she let us go so that there would be someone to tell the tale of how Heulyn's Arsyllfa was brought down."

"Where is Aurddolen now?"

"Gone. Heading for the Mynydd Tywyll with Cynhaearn and Cynwal."

"But you stayed?"

"I've been waiting for you, Cludydd."

"Why?"

"I knew you would return and perhaps would need a guide again."

"I'm sure I do."

"I hadn't expected to see you in the form of a great bird, but I heard your call and knew it was you. You have changed."

"Yes, I've learnt how to do some things."

"I still don't know why you brought her." He gestured to the cocooned form of Heulwen.

"She was there. She's Aurddolen's daughter. It doesn't matter how it looks; I thought it was right to save her."

"Well, what are we going to do with her now? We can't

stay here. I've been lucky and managed to avoid the Malevolence. But you will attract the evil."

"That is true, although I have more ways of facing it now; but you're right we must catch up with the Mordeyrn."

"They're days away. I'm weak. I can't see how we can catch them."

"I'll carry you."

"What about her?"

"I'll carry you both."

"Even with your new powers I cannot see how your bird will be strong enough to bear two of us."

"Perhaps not as a bird."

Before Sieffre's surprised face September changed into the panther. He cowered back from the massive beast.

"Do not be afraid. You can both ride. Lift Heulwen onto my back."

"I'm not touching her."

September twitched her whiskered nose at the prone Heulwen. A grey coating of plwm spread over her.

"The lead will protect you. Now do it. Let's get away." She crouched down.

Sieffre lifted Heulwen onto September's broad back, then he climbed on. As September rose onto her four powerful legs he grabbed the blue-black fur on her neck. September could feel the weight of the two people on her back but she felt strong and full of energy.

"Which way?" she asked.

"Northwards, up the valley."

September started at an easy trot then, when she was sure that Sieffre and Heulwen were safe, she accelerated into a run. She travelled faster than a cheetah, faster than a car, faster even than an express train. The meadows of the valley passed in a flash beneath her paws, the air rushing past her face. Sieffre was bent low over Heulwen, his feet pressed against her side and his hands holding her fur in a grip so firm that she wondered if his fingers were frozen by the wind of their passage.

As she ran she called out to Aurddolen. A reply came to her.

"Cludydd, is that you?"

"Yes, it is me. I'm on my way to you and I'm bringing Sieffre and Heulwen."

"You have my daughter?"

"Yes, but there's something wrong with her."

"What?"

"She's alive and awake but doesn't speak or move."

"She has been touched by the Malevolence. Be careful."

"I have her wrapped in plwm to protect us. We will be with you soon."

The contact with the Mordeyrn showed her where she had to go. She turned to the north-east and bounded up a grassy incline to a ridge, barely pausing at the top before racing down into the next valley. She sensed it wasn't far now. Although the Mordeyrn and his party had been travelling for days their progress had been slow. As night fell they climbed another ridge and descended down into a valley filled with pine trees. She slowed a little as she entered the forest but soon came to a small clearing beside a stream. This was the meeting place.

Aurddolen and the rest of the party were sitting around a small fire. They leapt to their feet, Cynhaearn drawing his iron sword as September loped up to them.

"Stop," Aurddolen said, holding Cynhaearn back, "It is the Cludydd."

She knelt allowing Sieffre to slide stiffly off her back. Aurddolen rushed forward to lift Heulwen from her. Relieved of her burdens September transformed to her normal self. There was a gasp as Aurddolen's companions took in her luminous blue appearance.

"Hello," September said. There was a groan and she turned to see Sieffre lying on the ground. She rushed to him. "What's the matter?" He groaned again.

"I think every muscle I possess has cramped," he grunted out between moans, "I have never travelled so fast or been so scared in all my life. I couldn't move for fear of falling from your back." She knelt beside him and rubbed the starstone over his arms and legs while thinking compassionate thoughts. Sieffre recovered quickly and sat up.

"Thank you, Cludydd. Your skills with arian are most effective. I feel revitalised."

Hedydd, the astronomer's apprentice, approached with a bottle.

"I'm sorry we only have one flask between us but perhaps you need a drink." She offered it to September who took a sip and passed it to Sieffre. He drained it eagerly.

"You are changed," Cynhaearn commented to September, "I sense that you have achieved the powers of the Cludydd o Maengolauseren of legend. Come and join us by the fire and tell us your tale."

The stout Prif-cludydd o haearn led them to the campfire. Some pieces of cooked meat from an unidentifiable animal were set out on leaves along with fruit and nuts.

"Please eat," Cynwal said, "we have not had time to collect much but all we have is yours to share."

Sieffre tucked into the food, greedily making some recompense for his days of fasting. Aurddolen carried the limp body of Heulwen into the circle around the fire and laid her out. He continued to fuss over her while the others ate. September nibbled on a few nuts and was surprised that she did not feel as starved as Sieffre. Perhaps she was drawing energy from another source. She briefly described her journey among the planets and the stars, avoiding too many details but indicating that she had learnt the key to using the power of the planets and their associated metals. Modestly, she tried to show that she could not match the cludyddau in their many and subtle ways of using their skills but they congratulated her on achieving her new-found powers.

"We are in danger," Cynwal said, "The Malevolence is seeking all those adepts and the cludyddau in particular."

"Have you met any monsters since you escaped from the Arsyllfa?" September asked.

"We have been harried by Adarllwchgwin and Cwn annwn," Cynhaearn replied.

"Coon, what?" September enquired.

"Dogs of fire. Everything they touch is burned." Cynhaearn explained.

"Ah, yes. That's what Malice set on me. Heulwen was in their way so I pulled her out."

Aurddolen turned away from dealing with Heulwen.

"I thank you, Cludydd, for rescuing my daughter," he said.

The others looked away and September noticed various expressions of anger and irritation on their faces.

"We should think of ways of protecting ourselves for the night," Cynwal said.

"I think I can do that," September said, raising the hand holding the starstone. Sorrow welled up in her chest and she moved her arm in a semicircle. A dome formed over them, grey but practically transparent. Cynwal gasped in admiration.

"A shield of plwm. That is marvellous, Cludydd."

"I hope that will stop the monsters finding us or attacking," September said, then in a more jovial voice, "Now tell me what your plans are. Where are you headed? Did anyone else get out of the Arsyllfa?"

"We are returning to our homes in Mynydd Tywyll," Cynhaearn said, including Cynwal in his words, "The Mordeyrn is joining us to forge a new golden symbol of his power."

"But the journey is long and we have travelled slowly," Cynwal continued, "our home is our goal before we face the Malevolence at the Cysylltiad."

"I am homeless," Hedydd said sadly, "and all my work is destroyed along with the observatory."

"What happened to the astronomer, um, I can't remember his name?" September asked.

"Eryl. He died trying to protect his instruments. A Pwca swallowed him up."

"Now his spirit is amongst those that hate everything that he worked for," Cynhaearn said angrily.

The weight of their sadness and anger bore heavily on September.

"What about the others?" September asked.

"We became separated in the battle for the Arsyllfa," Cynwal said, "We do not know if anyone, cludyddau or others, escaped from being absorbed into the Malevolence."

"You think that the spirit of every person killed by the Malevolence has become its servant?" September said.

"That has always been the fate of those that fall to the Malevolence," Cynwal agreed, "a fate that everyone fears. To become the enemy that threatens us all is a constant horror."

"But that hasn't happened to Heulwen," September noted.

"What do you mean?" Sieffre asked, "She betrayed us, opened the doors of the Arsyllfa to the forces of the Malevolence. You said yourself that she was beside your twin. She must be a servant of evil."

"But she is not," September said, pointing to the still form of the young woman on the ground, "She is not a destroying zombie like the others, but in some kind of trance. I don't know what happened to her to make her open the doors of the Arsyllfa. I think Malice, my sister, found her and used her, but she didn't convert her spirit."

"The Cludydd is correct," Aurddolen agreed looking up from beside Heulwen, "I have not seen anything like this before. My daughter is alive and her spirit is within her still but imprisoned in some manner so that she is unable to respond to the world. Malice has some power that is preventing Heulwen from escaping from her."

"She is a danger to us," Cynhaearn said, "She may kill us or corrupt us or draw the Malevolence to us."

"No, I do not think so," Aurddolen disagreed, "I do not think Heulwen will act as a servant of evil. The covering of arian and plwm that the Cludydd gave her is both healing and shielding her, but I do not know if she will ever recover her senses."

"Hmm. Well, I am going to rest while we have the chance," Cynhaearn went on, "In the morning we can decide what must be done." He lay beside the dying embers of the fire and closed his eyes.

"Someone should keep watch," Cynwal said.

"I will," September offered, "I don't feel sleepy and you all look exhausted."

The travellers nodded in agreement and did not need any further persuasion to settle. Cynwal, Hedydd and Sieffre each lay down beside Cynhaearn and soon gave all the signs that they were fast asleep. Only Aurddolen remained awake at Heulwen's side. September sat beside him.

"I'm sorry about the Arysllfa," she said, thinking it sounded rather a pointless thing to say.

"It was my fault, and now I have the lives of many of its inhabitants on my conscience," the Mordeyrn said.

"Why was it your fault? Sieffre says it was Heulwen that let the Malevolence in."

"He may be right, but there is no proof that Heulwen opened the doors."

"Malice called Heulwen her friend."

"That's as may be but it doesn't make Heulwen responsible for her actions. It was my fault for failing to see the self-deception in my daughter. It was my mistakes as a father that allowed Heulwen to gain the impression that she could wield the power of aur."

"Your spirit on the Sun told me why Heulwen could not be your apprentice."

"You spoke to my spirit?"

"Yes, on all the planets I met the spirits of the cludydds, living and dead."

"You journeyed to the planets?"

"Yes. Well, I think I did. It felt real and the tasks they gave me were real enough although I was put in imaginary situations, like computer games I suppose."

"Computer games? I don't understand."

September described all that had happened to her once she had locked the door of her room on Sieffre. Aurddolen listened, nodding and gasping at various points in her story.

"If only we had held the Arsyllfa and could have met you when you emerged," the Mordeyrn said when she had finished, "we could have welcomed your transformation and discussed how to use your powers to confront the Malevolence."

"That's a talk we must still have."

"Yes, but without the security of the Arsyllfa around us and the knowledge that resided in the observatory, and while I and my companions travel to Mynydd Tywyll."

"But you had to travel anyway. You said that we have to meet the Malevolence at the Conjunction in the middle of winter."

"That is so, but the loss of the Arsyllfa means the loss of all our supplies for the journey to say nothing of the books of records. I cannot see how we can reach the mountains in time to prepare for the Conjunction."

September realised that Aurddolen had been shaken by the

defeat at the observatory and the change in his daughter. She had never seen him without hope before.

"You must use your power, Aurddolen. The hope that the Sun gives us. You will get to the mountains and help me face the Malevolence."

The Mordeyrn looked at her, perhaps recognising the growing power of the Maengolauseren in her.

"You are right. Hope. It is what gives us the strength to fight against the indefatigable power of the Malevolence. Hope that we can banish the evil from the universe until the next Conjunction." He took a deep breath, sat up straight and looked into September's eyes. "Hope and the power of all the planets and stars will help us to succeed."

September was delighted to see the golden glow reappear in the cludydd o aur and his aura of leadership restored. Having spurred him to his recovery she wondered whether now was the time to say what was on her mind.

"There is my sister," she said, deciding that it needed to be said.

"Malice?"

"Yes, or Mairwen. None of the spirits on the planets mentioned her. I don't think they realised that the Malevolence has changed because of her."

"She has given it focus."

"Yes. She can make the spirits do what she wants. She can call up manifestations whenever she wishes and has powers of her own. She and I are matched."

"Do you think you can defeat her?"

"I don't know. I think I surprised her when I used the powers of the metals but we haven't really tested each other yet. You say the power of the Malevolence will increase up to the Conjunction?"

"That's right. When all the planets are lined up, there are no barriers to the spirits of evil."

"So Malice's power will also be greatest then?"

"Yes."

"In that case I must get ready to face her. I need to practise the skills that the planets have given me and I will need all the support that you and the rest of your people can give."

"That we shall do, but first I must get to Cynhaearn's

stronghold in the mountains and there cast my new symbol of gold."

"It's a long way?"

"Many weeks of travel even when we are equipped for the journey and do not have to face attacks by the servants of evil."

"I can carry you there."

"Ah, yes. The panther or the eagle?"

"Either. As a bird I could fly you there very quickly."

"What about Heulwen? You said you could not carry her and Sieffre as the bird."

"No, two on my back were more than I could fly with but I could take you then come back for Heulwen."

"I cannot leave her again now you have restored her to me."

"The others would look after her."

"Are you sure? They see her as a betrayer, as a servant of evil. They fear her and would prefer her dead."

"We can persuade them and with my speed they would not be left with her for long."

Aurddolen thought quietly.

"We will put it to them in the morning, but now I fear I must sleep. It has been days since I could rest without agonising about the fate of you and my daughter and without fear of attack." He lay beside Heulwen and very soon was snoring gently.

8

The night passed slowly but September did not feel in need of sleep. It was dark beneath the trees with no glimpse of moon or stars. Silent too, with no sounds of creeping creatures or flying bats or owls. The transparently thin shield of lead that surrounded them was not threatened by manifestations of the Malevolence. All the travellers slept peacefully except for Heulwen who remained unmoving but with her eyes wide open. September wondered whether the girl was conscious and trapped within her body or whether her body was mindless.

September marvelled at her own wakefulness and lack of hunger. It seemed that the changes that had taken place in her during her journey to the planets had separated her physically from the Land. While she had learnt how to control her emotions and hence the powers of the metals and the starstone she no longer had need for the sustenance of life. Food and rest were not necessities anymore. She was clothed now in blue light and no longer had the objects that had accompanied her from Amaethaderyn to the Arsyllfa. Even the silver casing and chain which had held the starstone had been discarded. Now she held the stone in her hand and she never felt the need to release it. Even when she changed into one of the mercurial creatures the stone remained attached to her. While for a time it had seemed that she was an inhabitant of this strange world, now that she had gained unearthly powers she was apart from it although still bound to it. Nevertheless, she realised that she would not be permitted to return to her home until after the Conjunction when her task would, she hoped, be complete and the Malevolence banished beyond the stars.

What would become of her sister at that time? Would she be removed from the universe too or would she die for a second time? September wondered what it would have been like to have a twin sister. Perhaps they would have been inseparable friends, sharing pleasures and trials, be confidantes and partners. Did Malice or Mairwen have any such feelings or was she totally overwhelmed by the hate of the Malevolence?

As grey light filtered between the trees the others began to stir. Sieffre was surprised to find September awake and alert.

"Have you not slept, Cludydd?" he asked.

"No Sieffre. It seems I have no need of sleep just as I no longer have need of food."

The travellers ate the remaining nuts and berries left over from the evening's meal and prepared themselves to start the day's journey. Aurddolen looked after Heulwen but her condition had not changed.

When everyone was ready to break camp and had collected together the few possessions with which they had escaped the destruction of the Arsyllfa, the Mordeyrn called them together.

"There is a great distance between us and our destination. Many weeks of hard and difficult travel. But there is an alternative. With the Cludydd's ability to call up the power of arian byw she can carry us through the air to Mwyngloddiau Dwfn."

"All at once?" Cynhaearn asked.

"No. As a bird I can manage one passenger at a time," September said.

"It will surely tire you and take a long time to transport the five of us," Cynwal pointed out.

"Six. You are forgetting Heulwen," September said, "but I don't think it will tire me and you will be surprised how fast I can fly."

"If the flight of the eagle is faster than the pace of the panther then you will indeed cover the distance in a short time," Sieffre said.

"Oh, I think I can fly much faster than I run," September said cheerfully.

"So it is decided then," Aurddolen said, "we just need to choose the order in which the Cludydd carries us."

"Sieffre and I as warriors should remain till the rest have been taken," Cynhaearn said and Sieffre nodded in agreement.

"Cynwal. You should go first as Mwyngloddiau Dwfn is your home. You can tell your people what has happened and prepare for our arrival," Aurddolen spoke authoritatively and Cynwal nodded, "then Hedydd, you should go next. You are the astronomer now and must continue the observations."

"But I have no instruments or books of records."

"You have what you need in your head. Eryl trained you well. I know."

Hedydd blushed with embarrassment but nodded.

"Then it will be my turn," Aurddolen paused, "and I will leave my daughter in your care Cynhaearn." The stocky iron bearer momentarily looked as though the task was abhorrent and then he bowed his head.

"As you wish, Mordeyrn."

"Thank you. Then the Cludydd will carry her and return two more times for you my friends."

They all nodded and agreed.

"Despite the Cludydd's speed," Aurddolen continued, "it will take days to complete so you must prepare to make camp here for the duration. Perhaps the Cludydd will be kind enough to return with supplies to keep those that remain comfortable and satisfied."

"Yes, of course," September said, "Now let's make a start." She imagined a drop of mercury on a surface, running this way and that, its movement unpredictable. She leapt into the air becoming the blue eagle, flapped her great wings then settled back onto the ground on her taloned feet. The others gasped.

"You are beautiful, Cludydd," Hedydd said, "Your plumage is like the sky at dusk just before the Moon rises."

"You are indeed a magnificent creature," Cynwal said, "but how do I ride on you?"

September bent her legs and lowered her head.

"Sit on my back in front of my wings," she said, "and hold onto my neck." Cynwal cocked his leg over her and sat as she instructed. The others stood back out of the way of her outstretched wings. As she straightened her legs and raised her head, Cynwal flung his arms around her neck and held onto her tightly.

"Try not to strangle me please," September said.

"I'm sorry, Cludydd, but the thought of this flight scares me."

"I'll take care of you." She beat her wings and rose into the air. In a moment they were through the dome of plwm that covered the campsite, then they were over the stream and climbing through the gap in the tree cover. The canopy fell away below them. September circled over the small clearing fixing the position in her memory. Finding north-east she thrust herself higher into the sky. She found a thermal that lifted her to the clouds then she soared. Cynwal screamed with fear and delight.

The ground passed swiftly below them. Here and there amongst the trees were clearings where crops were grown but mostly the tree cover was unbroken. Soon they crossed a strip of white water that was the great southern river. Onwards they flew, swooping from one thermal to another, September's broad wings catching the air and pushing them on at great speed. It was not long before they crossed another band of water, the northern river. Before them now was the expanse of forest and in the distance the dark peaks of the Mynydd Tywyll. The sun passed overhead and still September continued on effortlessly while Cynwal clung on cold and nervous.

The trees were thinning now that they were passing over the foothills of the mountains. Below them September saw flocks of sheep on the cool, green hillsides. Cynwal shouted directions into her ear, as they swooped over ridge and valley. She rose higher to clear the first craggy ridges of the mountain chain, swooping down into the valleys beyond to increase her speed before catching the air in her wings to climb towards the next peak.

The sun was sinking behind the western peaks. Snow crept down from the mountaintops into the valleys until there was no longer the green of grass or black of rock to be seen but just the uniform whiteness of fresh snow. At last, ahead she saw a jumble of dark buildings and towers and chimneys with smoke belching into the cloud-filled sky.

"There," Cynwal cried, "Mwyngloddiau Dwfn."

The inhabitants might think I'm a manifestation of the

Malevolence, September thought, and summoned up the feeling of love to broadcast a message, "It is me, the Cludydd o Maengolauseren bearing your cludydd o plwm, Cynwal. Do not be afraid."

She soared down from the sky to the town built from black rock hewn from the cliffs. There was a track of compressed snow and ice leading up the valley to the town. September landed on it just short of the first dark, cold buildings. Already people were running from the streets and alleyways between the buildings, racing towards her. They were cheering and whooping with delight.

Cynwal slid stiffly from her back and struggled to straighten up. September shook herself and changed back into her normal form. The people skidded to a halt in front of them. Cynwal spread his arms.

"Friends, I am glad to be back amongst you and delighted to introduce the Cludydd o Maengolauseren to you but I bring you grave news. The Arsyllfa has fallen to the Malevolence."

A great groan passed amongst everyone and their heads drooped. One figure stepped forward, a woman dressed like the rest in a thick woollen coat that covered all but a small patch of her face.

"We welcome your return Cynwal, but are saddened by your news. What of Cynhaearn?" she said.

"He is safe," Cynwal replied. Turning to September, he introduced the speaker, "This is Ilar, the cludydd o alcam."

Ilar nodded her head, smiling at September.

"You are welcome, Cludydd," she said, "please accompany us to our home."

Cynwal went forward and was surrounded by his people. He realised that September hadn't followed.

"Come, Cludydd, let us get in out of the cold, the night is upon us."

"There is food and drink, and we would like to hear your news and the story of your arrival amongst us," Ilar said warmly.

September hadn't moved. She hadn't noticed the cold; either her cloak of blue light insulated her or she was impervious now to temperature changes.

"Thank you, but I must return to pick up the others."

"But it is dark," Cynwal said, "how will you find your way through the night?"

September tapped her head.

"I can feel the Mordeyrn and the others here. They will guide me to them." She changed suddenly into the giant bird, becoming almost invisible against the dark sky.

"I look forward to spending some time with you when I have brought all of them here."

Cynwal nodded gravely.

"I understand, Cludydd. May your journey be swift and safe."

September launched into the sky, and turned southwards following the faint call in her head. Soon the mining town had receded into the mountains and she was set for the long flight back. Why am I doing it this way? she thought, flapping her wings. I need to be in this form to carry passengers but when I travelled amongst the planets and the stars I moved many times faster. With that thought she reverted to her own body but soared like a rocket up into the sky. Her arm holding the starstone was stretched out ahead of her as if it followed some line of force. She arced out of the atmosphere and then fell back towards the Earth. The call of Aurddolen and Cynhaearn and the others grew in her head as she homed in on them.

And then she was standing on the ground under the dome of plwm beside the sleeping forms of the companions huddled together except for Sieffre who sat cross-legged by the fire. He leapt to his feet.

"Cludydd! We had not expected you so soon. Is there trouble? Where is Cynwal?"

"He is safe at his town in the mountains. I came back by a quicker method."

September smiled at the look of awe on Sieffre's face.

"You are truly a miracle," he said.

"There are things that I have found I can do," September said, "I don't know why but science must be different here to my world. I can't make anything happen there just by thinking of an emotion." It wasn't quite true; she could arouse her brother Gus to anger and frustration simply by reacting with glee when his favourite football team lost.

"You must be tired after such a journey."

"No, I think only fighting the Malevolence tires me now. Let us wake up Hedydd. The quicker I get you all to the mine the better I think."

The sound of their conversation had roused the others. They all looked in amazement at seeing September back amongst them and scarcely believed that she had made the return journey across Gwlad in little more than twelve hours. When he had recovered Cynhaearn spoke.

"Is all well at Mwyngloddiau Dwfn?"

"I think so. We were met by a crowd of people and I spoke to a cludydd called Ilar."

"Ah yes, Ilar has been guiding the people in my absence. She is an excellent cludydd o alcam and all the people work together for her."

"Well, I think it is time for me to take Hedydd. I hope to be back with you early in the morning and I will bring food for your breakfast."

In an instant September changed again into the blue eagle and lowered herself so that Hedydd could mount. With her passenger clinging on she rose into the night sky and beat her wings against the air. Now she had a picture of her destination in her mind she willed herself to fly as fast as she was able.

They saw nothing of the land beneath them as they travelled through the night until the northern dawn sent shafts of red sunlight across the snow-covered mountains. The sun had just risen above the eastern ridge when September dropped to the ground at the edge of the mining town. Hedydd dismounted stiffly, shivering with the cold. September became herself as Cynwal and Ilar emerged to greet them. Ilar gave Hedydd a woollen coat to wrap around herself and Cynwal handed two sacks to September.

"One contains food for a few days and the other warm clothing for the riders to wear when you carry them. I know how Hedydd is feeling."

September used the hand not carrying the starstone to lift the sacks onto her shoulder.

"Thank you. I will be back with Aurddolen before the end

of the day." She jumped into the brightening sky like a rocket launching.

She followed the same trajectory as before, chasing the dawn, but just as she was descending to the forest she felt a twinge in her hip. While still in the air she changed into the eagle with the unwieldy sacks dangling around her neck. She circled over the small clearing. There were fiery dogs prowling around the edge of the lead dome. It was deterring them for now but she wondered how long the shield would last particularly if Malice showed up. She thought of using the stone to blast the flaming hounds but paused. Using the power of the Maengolauseren itself might attract her twin. Perhaps if she just used the power of the metals the campsite might remain hidden for a while longer. She descended through the trees a short distance from the camp. She dropped the sacks and changed into the iridescent cobra, sliding silently through the thin undergrowth to approach the dome.

The dogs paced to and fro, pawing at the barrier. Every few moments one would howl with rage and throw its burning body at the shield. September could see that inside the grey hemisphere Cynhaearn and Sieffre stood with their swords raised. They were back to back circling slowly around the campfire. Aurddolen stood over Heulwen, holding a golden pendant.

How should she dispose of this pack of Cwn annwn? They had no physical form so iron blades or arrows would pass through them and lead would merely absorb their energy but something cold and wet would douse their fires. She knew what to do. As water flowed so did mercury. She slid closer to the dogs silently and secretly so that they were unaware of her presence. A suitable moment arrived.

She raised her head and changed into a wall of water like a tsunami wave which broke and cascaded down onto the fiery pack. Her water snuffed out their flames. Their howls became whimpers as their flames died and the Cwn annwn disappeared without a hint of smoke or smouldering ash.

September gathered her waters together and returned to her human self. She ran to retrieve the sacks then passed through the dome to be greeted by Cynhaearn and Sieffre.

"The deluge was you?" Sieffre asked. September nodded.

"You despatched those spirits of the Malevolence with ease, Cludydd," Cynhaearn said with admiration in his voice.

"You have learnt well," Aurddolen agreed. September felt a little embarrassed by their praise.

"Look, I've brought food from Cynwal and warm clothes for the journey. I think Hedydd was nearly frozen when we got to the mountains."

"You need to have been brought up there to feel comfortable in the cold," Cynhaearn said. Sieffre and Aurddolen agreed.

September turned to Aurddolen.

"Are you ready to go, Mordeyrn?"

"If you are sure you do not need rest, Cludydd."

"No, as I said, I've never felt like this before, so full of energy. I just don't get tired or hungry anymore."

"Well, if Cynhaearn and Sieffre will tend to Heulwen, I am ready to travel." Cynhaearn looked at the prone form of the Aurddolen's daughter. He seemed about to say something but finally just nodded.

Aurddolen donned a thick jacket from one of the sacks. Again September became the bird and dipped down for the Mordeyrn to climb onto her back. Then she was in the sky and once again flying through the daylight across rivers, forests and mountains.

They were greeted again by Cynwal, Ilar and the townsfolk and then September rocketed back to the campsite before nightfall. She was relieved to find Cynhaearn, Sieffre and Heulwen undisturbed.

Cynhaearn was glad to see her so that he could quickly get Heulwen off his hands, wrapped in a warm blanket and fastened with strips of sacking to September's back. September took off with her burden, the way now firmly lodged in her mind, and Aurddolen's powerful personality drawing her to the town in the mountains.

Aurddolen, alone, was waiting in the snow as she came into land at dawn. He hurried to release his daughter from the straps that held her. She sagged like a dead body in his arms but her eyes remained open, staring, perhaps seeing but not able to respond. He spoke.

"Thank you, September. Thank you for caring for my daughter. May your final two journeys be uneventful. I await your return so that we can rest and talk." He turned away to carry his burden into the town.

September leapt towards the stars and minutes later was back with Cynhaearn and Sieffre who were arguing about who should go next.

"I have the power of haearn to protect me," Cynhaearn insisted, "you go, Sieffre."

"No, I am unimportant. Your home needs you," Sieffre responded.

September stood by while the argument continued until Cynhaearn finally conceded. As he climbed onto September's back, she said, "I'll be back soon Sieffre. Please keep safe."

"I won't do anything to attract the Malevolence if I can help it, my lady," Sieffre replied.

As September flew she could feel Cynhaearn urging her on. The closer they got to his home the more concerned and eager he became. This time a large crowd of his people were waiting outside the town as the sun settled behind the western mountains. They cheered as September settled on the snow-covered ground and rushed forward to greet Cynhaearn as he dismounted.

Cynwal came to her.

"The people are pleased to see their mordeyrn and cludydd o haearn," he observed, "he has been away for months."

"What about Aurddolen? He hasn't come out."

"No. He has been ensuring that Heulwen is looked after, but the people are suspicious. They have heard what happened at the Arsyllfa and are afraid that she will bring the Malevolence to Mwyngloddiau Dwfn."

"With me and the Mordeyrn here I'm sure that will happen anyway."

"Yes, but Heulwen has become a scapegoat. You will be made most welcome when you finally enter the town."

"I'm looking forward to it. I must just get my last passenger. I hope Sieffre has been safe on his own."

"Take care, Cludydd. You have developed wonderful powers but the Malevolence and your sister are also strong.

She will be looking for an opportunity to strike you down." Cynwal spoke with the gravity she expected of a cludydd o plwm.

"I expect her at any moment. I'll be back soon – with Sieffre." She jumped and in seconds was far away from the mountain habitation.

The campsite was dark and quiet as September descended through the leaden dome. No fire burned. For a moment September feared that something had happened to Sieffre but as she landed he stirred from under a blanket covered in twigs and leaf litter. A thrill passed through her as she saw him rise to greet her. She opened her arms to hug him. He held back, perhaps a little afraid of her luminous blue clothing but she beckoned him and he stepped forward and embraced her. She felt his body pressing against hers.

"I'm so glad that you are safe," September said, "I was worried when I saw the campsite deserted."

"I thought it safer not to light a fire and to camouflage myself," Sieffre replied, "although some manifestations can sense one's spirit. After being alone at the Arsyllfa for days, I must confess to being somewhat afraid when left on my own again."

"So, let's get off to the mountains where we can be with lots of people." She became the eagle and ducked her head for Sieffre to clamber on.

"So the Cludydd o Maengolauseren bows to her servant, does she?"

Startled, September turned awkwardly to see the glowing, black-robed figure of Malice striding across the clearing.

"Sieffre is not my servant, he's a friend."

Malice looked puzzled.

"Friend? What is that?"

"Someone who helps you, who likes being with you, likes sharing what you do. Do you understand that, Mairwen?"

"Mairwen. Why do you call me that? Malice is my name."

"I told you before. Mairwen is the name Mother gave you, when you were born."

"I was never born. My spirit was cast out of your world. You had life, I did not."

"You may have been dead but Mother still gave you the

name."

"It is not my name. She named a spiritless corpse. I am Malice and this world will be mine."

"This is no more your world than it is mine. It belongs to the people who live here."

"Like your 'friend', Sieffre, I suppose."

"People like him, yes."

"They will all die and their spirits will join the Malevolence to do my will."

"Not if I can do anything about it."

"You are weak. You may have learnt some tricks from the planets but when the Conjunction comes, and I have the full power of the Malevolence to support me, you will not be able to stand against me."

Malice's confidence scared September. She wanted to get away from her. She spread her broad wings and scooped the air.

"Fly to your little refuge in the mountains."

"You know where I am going?"

"Of course. I can sense all your movements. We are joined you and I and I with Heulwen also. I will attack you and your 'friends' in the mountains like I did at your Arsyllfa and like that heap of rubble, your hideaway will fall."

Malice raised a hand to fire a bolt of cosmic darkness. September felt sorrow and surrounded herself with a globe of virtual lead. The ball of black light dissipated harmlessly. September flapped her wings and rose above the trees. A dozen Adarllwchgwin descended from the night sky from all sides; only the glowing red eyes of the birds and their riders making them visible. Sieffre's legs dug into her sides and his arms gripped her neck as September turned and twisted striving for height. As her attackers dived towards her she became angry. Fiery iron arrows flared from her talons. Each sped towards a target and one by one each of the evil birds detonated and disappeared in a blast of hot air.

From below, September heard a cackling laugh, fading as she sped way to the north-east.

9

It was another dawn when September swooped into land at Mwyngloddiau Dwfn. Sieffre slid off her back and shivered.

"I don't know how people can live and work in these temperatures," he said.

September changed into herself and shrugged.

"They're used to it. I used to be like you; I hated the cold, but now it doesn't seem to bother me."

A crowd of the mining community had come out to meet them. For the first time September looked closely at them. They were generally darker and shorter than the people she had met further south along the warm reaches of the southern river. In their thick woollen clothes the miners looked stockier too. Cynhaearn came forward and clapped Sieffre on the back.

"Welcome my friend. I'm glad to see you again," he said then turned to September, "and thank you Cludydd for saving all of us a journey of many weeks."

"I'm just sorry that more of the people from the Arsyllfa were not with you. We must find out if more escaped."

"Yes, we have that and much more to discuss. Come inside. The Mordeyrn is eager to start work."

Cynhaearn guided Sieffre and September towards the town, the crowd around them. They had to thin out to a crocodile to pass down the narrow, icy alleyway between the dark buildings built from rock hewn from the mountains. Windows were few and the buildings seemed forbidding. They clustered close together as if for warmth. People could flit from one building to another, hardly stepping out into the bitterly cold mountain air. Towards the centre of the town, the pathways were slushy rather than covered by ice and dark because the closeness of the two and three storey buildings blocked out the light.

They came into a small, open square which had one

building where a wide door was flung open. They entered. Inside the feeling was different. There was warmth from fires burning in hearths and light from specks of starstone that were arrayed like the stars themselves across the ceilings. There were low tables, like the walls, carved out of rock and polished. The floors were covered in brightly patterned carpets strewn with equally colourful cushions of various sizes.

Cynhaearn flung off the coat he had been wearing as did the townspeople who had followed them in, but Sieffre refused to remove his woollen coat.

"It is warmer inside than out but still cold for my liking," he explained.

"Hah," laughed Cynhaearn, "The air has been too hot for me to breathe while I have been down in the south. At least the Arsyllfa is on top of a mountain and comfortably cool. I'm glad to be back in my own climate, with my own people."

September was again surprised that though she could detect the change in temperatures she was untroubled by being too hot or too cold – very different to being at home when at the first sign of the sun she felt hot and bothered and the first hint of frost made her shiver.

"Come, sit, make yourselves comfortable. I'm sure you are ready to eat a proper meal, Sieffre, and perhaps you too, Cludydd." Cynhaearn gestured to the cushions on the floor and the steaming dishes of food that were being brought to the tables.

September agreed to try the food out of politeness but didn't feel hungry. As Sieffre tucked into multiple bowls of broth, and she nibbled on a piece of delicious, sweet bread, Aurddolen appeared among them.

"Ah, Cludydd. You have arrived. I am relieved."

"How is Heulwen?"

"Slightly improved. She can sit and even stand unaided but still does not respond."

"You realise that she is still a danger to us and all these people."

Aurddolen's face darkened.

"How can that be, Cludydd?"

"Malice has a link to her. Perhaps she can even command Heulwen to do something. I don't know."

"How do you know this?"

"Malice told me. She was at the camp just as Sieffre and I were about to leave. She told me that she can sense my movements and Heulwen's."

"She knows you are here now."

"Yes."

"Then we must defend this place."

"We must, and I will help you, but I think it better if I do not stay. You have things to do to prepare for the Conjunction. If I am elsewhere then perhaps I can draw Malice's attention away from you and leave you safe."

"You speak wisely, Cludydd. You have certainly developed since your sojourn amongst the planets and the stars."

"I know I have changed but I am still not sure what is going to happen when this Conjunction comes or whether I can stop Malice's plans for world domination."

"You must destroy her. She gives purpose to the Malevolence's hate."

"I'm not sure I can. When I see her I see myself. I see what I might have been. She's my sister."

Aurddolen sagged as if the weight of his responsibilities had become too much.

"I understand. I feel the same about my daughter even though I know she has been touched by evil and maybe will never again be the woman she once was." He took a deep breath, re-fortifying his resolve. "Nevertheless, we must make a plan to face the trials ahead. Your idea to travel around Gwlad is good, but we must put the defences of this town in order before you go. I will get Cynhaearn to call the other cludyddau together urgently."

He bustled off to talk to the mordeyrn of the mining area and soon returned.

"Come with me to a meeting room where we can discuss matters away from these crowds. The others will join us as soon as they are able." He led the way from the large communal hall through a door into a smaller room. It had a single, circular slab of rock as a low table surrounded by soft cushions. Aurddolen sat and September joined him, crossing her legs, something else that she could not do comfortably at home.

"I am glad we can have a few moments of private conversation, Cludydd. There is so much I would discuss with you but I do not know how much time we have."

"We can talk wherever we are. I can always link to you."

"Ah yes, the power of efyddyn as granted to you by Gwener. Your skills amaze me, Cludydd. You have gained strength in diverse ways. You spoke briefly of tasks set you by the spirits of the planets. You say you even met my spirit."

"Yes. It was just like talking to you as we are now, except you were surrounded by other gold bearers including Heulyn and you appeared ghostly."

"I knew that as cludyddau our spirits travel to our planet, but I had no idea that they have a separate existence there, whether we are alive or dead. It does however explain a little how we draw our powers from the planets. But to return to the skills of efyddyn. Do you think you can communicate with other cludyddau?"

"I think so, especially those I have met. I can control my emotions much better now and that helps me to form a link even without the copper horn I had before."

"That is good. I would like to try to make contact with everyone who was in the Arsyllfa – if they have survived; many didn't. They will not have a cludydd o efyddyn with them so they will not be able to communicate. Anarawd was a victim of the Cyhyraeth that swept through the Arsyllfa when the doors were opened."

"I will try to make a link when we have had our meeting."

"Perhaps you can also locate Malice, so we can predict when and where she may strike next, since she can sense your whereabouts."

"I haven't tried, but I will when I am far from here. Just in case making the contact brings her to me."

"That is wise. You have been filled with wisdom as well as power, September."

"I amaze myself, Aurddolen. I don't feel at all like the fat teenager who had no confidence at all. I feel full of energy and strength and sure that I can use the powers of the planets and metals to do good things. The only worry I have, and it is a big one, is how to overcome Malice and the Malevolence at this Conjunction."

"We have just a few weeks to solve that conundrum, longer than I expected as I thought most of our time would be taken in travelling here. Nevertheless, I am sure the time will pass quickly and we will be kept busy by the manifestations of evil and by your twin. My first target is to prepare the aur to forge my new symbol of power so that I can stand beside you once again and support you with all the energy of Haul."

The door opened and Cynhaearn and Cynwal entered followed by a young dark-haired woman, a white-haired woman of a similar age, and a golden-haired youth. Ilar, the cludydd o alcam, was last to enter the room. They spread out around the table, the three who had not yet met September staring at her with wonder in their eyes.

"Please sit and join us, friends," Aurddolen said, "September, may I introduce you to Cari, the cludydd o efyddyn." The dark woman gave September a loving, welcoming smile. "Ariannell, the cludydd o arian." September nodded a greeting to the white-haired woman who she had guessed correctly was the silver bearer. "And Heulfryn, formerly my pupil and now cludydd o aur of the Mynydd Tywyll." The young man grinned at September.

"We are missing a cludydd," September noted.

"Isfoel, our cludydd o arian byw," Ilar said, "he is under the mountains."

"He spends much of his time in the form of a bat, searching the mines," Cynwal explained.

"Searching for what?" September asked.

"In good times he looks for traces of new veins of metals in the rocks. Now he seeks out manifestations and warns us before they get close to the miners," Cynwal said.

"You find manifestations in the mines?" September had thought of attacks from above and over the mountains but hadn't considered that here they might be attacked from beneath their feet.

"Oh yes," Cynhaearn said, "particularly the earth manifestations, Gwyllian, Coblynau, Tylwyth teg."

"I've met the first – old witches that turn people to dust – but not the other two," September said.

"Let us hope that you do not have to, Cludydd," Cynwal said, grimly, "although I fear that you will at some point."

September wondered if Tylwyth teg or Coblynau could be worse than Gwyllian or Pwca or any of the other manifestations.

"Has Isfoel seen many?" she asked.

"Certainly," Cynhaearn said, "and their numbers have been increasing. Not surprising as the Cysylltiad approaches. Their presence scares away the miners and so our production of metals has dropped. It will be difficult to get into the deep lodes to collect all the aur that Aurddolen needs for his symbol of power."

"Just another problem to overcome," Aurddolen said in a tone which made it difficult for September to decide whether he was depressed or upbeat.

"The more manifestations there are, the longer Isfoel spends down there," Ilar said.

"So, we won't be seeing much of him," Cynhaearn said, "We must get on. What is your plan, Aurddolen?"

"A plan! Would that I had one. Originally it was to build up our strength and then travel with the Cludydd o Maengolauseren onto the ice cap to the meeting with the Malevolence at the Conjunction. I suppose that is still the plan except it has been complicated with my need to regain my power and the appearance of Malice, the Cludydd's twin. Malice has given direction to the evil and now the appearances of manifestations are less random and hence much more dangerous."

"The fall of the Arsyllfa showed that," Cynwal said gravely, "The presence of the Cyhyraeth and other manifestations as the doors were opened was not a coincidence. It was planned and prepared for by Malice."

"That is correct, Cynwal," Aurddolen said, "and for that reason we are in great danger here. The presence of the Cludydd, myself and my daughter, to say nothing of your collected powers will draw Malice and her forces to us."

"What can we do?" Ariannell asked.

Aurddolen replied, "The Cludydd has an idea – to travel

the length and breadth of the Land, facing whatever she finds and perhaps drawing Malice's attention from us." There were murmurs and nods of approval around the table.

"But we will still be a target," Cynhaearn said.

"Of course," Aurddolen agreed, "so we must do all that we can to improve the defences of the town. We must consider ourselves under siege."

"I wonder if something like the dome I made at the campsite would help," September said.

"A dome?" Ilar enquired.

"Yes, a dome of plwm," Cynwal said excitedly, "the Cludydd summoned the principle of plwm to surround us and keep out all evil manifestations. Do you think you could do the same here, Cludydd?"

"You mean to encircle the whole town?" Heulfryn said. The young blonde man's voice carried a note of awe.

"Yes. I'm sure that with Ilar and Cynwal we can produce a shield that will stop your enemies from getting in, so long as no-one lets them." September was conscious that the Arsyllfa's defences had been proof against anything that the Malevolence could do until the doors were opened from the inside.

"That will be a great reassurance for the people of Mwyngloddiau Dwfn," Ariannell said.

"We will still have to clear the mines of manifestations in order to get at the aur for the Mordeyrn, but that is within our powers." Cynhaearn looked satisfied. He stood up, "Right let's get to work."

"One moment," Aurddolen said, raising a hand, "Cari, are you in touch with other settlements?"

"Yes, Mordeyrn," the young woman replied, "Each day I receive messages from across Gwlad through my speaking horn."

"Good. The Cludydd wishes to establish contact via the power of efyddyn with those that are under attack. You can help her to establish the links."

"Yes, Mordeyrn," Cari agreed then looked at September, "I will help you in any way I can, Cludydd."

"Thank you," September said. She realised that Aurddolen had given her a number of tasks and that she wouldn't be leaving the mining town immediately.

Now the meeting did break up. Cynwal guided September to his own home in a small stone house, with Ilar accompanying them. He poured cups of steaming drink and offered them to September and Ilar. September took a sip. It tasted like a mulled wine.

"How do you suggest we construct the shield?" Cynwal asked.

"Well, all I did at the campsite was imagine what I wanted while summoning the emotion that links us to Saturn and makes the lead metal work."

"But you didn't have any plwm," Cynwal said.

"No, I don't need it. Since I visited the planets I seem to be able to use the powers of the metals even without having the metals in my hand. The starstone itself is sufficient."

Ilar shook her head in wonder. "That is miraculous, Cludydd. You are using the essence of the metals direct from the planets. We, the humble cludyddau, must have the real materials in our hands to draw on our planet's power."

"I suppose it is a gift of the spirits on each planet," September said, not wanting to show off in front of the cludyddau.

"It is a marvellous skill," Cynwal said, "and it is most fortuitous that you are with us at our time of greatest need. Now the questions are, can you make a dome big enough to protect the whole town and how can we help you?"

"I don't know how it happens but if we work together, I'll do my thing and you do whatever you do."

"We can only give it a try," Ilar said, "the power of alcam will reinforce your plans."

"Let us get to the centre of town and put our powers to the test," Cynwal said. He led September and Ilar from the house and they followed the narrow, dark alleyways until they reached a small open space. There was nothing to distinguish it from any other space in the town. It was surrounded by the tall, brooding, windowless buildings with just a small patch of clear blue sky directly overhead. A cold wind blew down the alleyways forming eddies of chill.

"This is just about the central point in the town," Cynwal said. He drew a short but thick metal bar from the leather pouch he wore attached to his belt. It was dull grey and much scored and gouged. September recognised it as lead. Ilar also produced her symbol of power, a roll of wrinkled, silver-grey tin which she unrolled into a sheet.

"So we need to invoke a dome surrounding the whole town," Ilar said.

"A sphere not just a dome," Cynwal said.

"A sphere?" September asked.

"Yes, to protect us from attacks from the rocks beneath us," Cynwal said.

"Oh, of course," September said, wondering how she could have forgotten the threat from the earth manifestations.

They stood in a triangle. September raised her hand holding the starstone and the two cludyddau lifted up their samples of lead and tin. Cynwal and Ilar began to chant in the old language that September did not understand. She closed her eyes and tried to summon simultaneously the sorrow of Saturn and the joy of Jupiter. Joy and sorrow together, how do I do that? She wondered. For a moment she was lost for ideas then she recalled the memorial service for her grandfather, her father's father. Like everyone else she was sad at his death and missed the love he gave her whenever she visited him, but there in the church, relatives and friends told amusing stories about things he had done in his life; they played the music he had enjoyed and sang uplifting hymns. She remembered the feeling – joy and sorrow. She imagined a globe covering the whole town like the glass around a snow scene. Cynwal and Ilar sang loudly.

A silver-grey dome formed above their heads. For a moment the curved shield hung there and then it expanded faster than they could follow. Now they were looking at the sky through a veil of pale silver-grey.

September lowered her arm. Slowly Cynwal and Ilar did the same.

"I feel it," Ilar said slowly, "it is as if the energy is still flowing through me."

"Yes. I am the same," Cynwal said, "the song continues. The metals are ringing, sustaining the shield."

"You will have to keep it going when I am gone," September said, realising that her power was different to that of the cludyddau. Her job was done but they remained as the source of the dome's energy. "Can you manage?"

"Yes," Cynwal said, standing as if he was unsure of his balance, "It is like having a continuous sound in my head, a wordless song that goes on and on, repeating. It is a strange experience but I'll get used to it."

"Me too," Ilar agreed.

"Let us return to the Meeting Hall," Cynwal said. Once again he led the way through the narrow passageways.

They found a small crowd outside the building, all staring up at the grey sky. Cynhaearn saw them approach.

"You have done it?"

Ilar and Cynwal nodded distractedly.

"Yes," September said, "You and your people should be able to pass through it freely but evil will be stopped. I hope it will last."

"So do we, Cludydd, but you have our thanks."

"Now, I must see Cari."

"I'll guide you to her home."

Cynhaearn led September into another part of the town through yet more, dark, narrow passageways. At last they climbed stone steps to a doorway. The door opened and the dark young woman welcomed September in.

"I sensed your arrival," Cari said. Cynhaearn said his farewells and departed into the alleyways. Cari led September into a small workshop with a furnace and bench on which were articles made of copper, both small and large. September recognised the small speaking horns like that which Catrin had given her and she had left in the Arsyllfa. There was a copper rod with a ball at the end such as she had seen Catrin wield against the Gwyllian all those weeks ago at Amaethaderyn, and there were artefacts of other shapes for which she could not guess the purpose.

"Please sit," Cari said, sitting down on a stool by the workbench and indicating another stool near the furnace. "The Mordeyrn said I could help you to contact other settlements, but I do not understand quite what he means."

"The spirits of Gwener have given me the power of efyddyn to use through the Maengolauseren," September said.

"Ah, you have spoken to the spirits."

"Yes. I visited Venus, uh, Gwener. They gave me a task which I must have done well enough for them. Now by calling up the emotion of love I can use the power of copper, although I am sure I do not have the skill that you have."

"But you do not carry any efyddyn with you Cludydd. Do you need a horn?" Cari indicated the speaking tubes on the bench.

"I don't need one. The starstone is enough on its own," she explained, showing the clear stone in her hand, "but I need to have some way of recognising who I am speaking to. I can speak to Aurddolen, but I don't know many people across the Land."

"I see. Well, I'll speak to other cludyddau o efyddyn." She picked up a horn and sang a brief song into its mouthpiece. Soon there was a reply. September heard the voice of another woman in her head and had an image of waves crashing on a beach. Cari changed her tune and another voice answered with a picture of tall, dark trees. Then there was another voice and scene and another and another. To September the voices and pictures appeared in her head like a slide display, one after another flickering into her vision and hearing. She had no idea whether her brain was taking in what she was experiencing or whether the stone itself was recording the voices and images. She did however begin to appreciate the number of places of habitation spread across the continent of Gwlad and the variety of people who lived in them.

A long time passed before Cari finally sighed and laid down her horn. She yawned and got stiffly to her feet.

"I think that is all the cludydd o efyddyn that remain. Many have been lost to the Malevolence," she said. September felt Cari's sadness made stronger by the love that linked all the copper bearers.

"Thank you. I hope that will be all I need to tune in to each of them. It's like a mobile phone with lots of contacts."

"Mobile phone?"

September noticed Cari's mystified look, "It's how we communicate on my world."

"Oh."

"I don't think I can explain it, but we have instruments like your horn which allow us to speak to each other."

"You have cludyddau?"

"No, everyone can use a phone."

"Everyone. Surely there is not enough efyddyn for everyone to own a speaking horn?"

September felt the conversation was taking her into areas she didn't know about.

"Perhaps you're right. Look, thanks, I'd better get back to Aurddolen before I leave you."

"I'll guide you back to the meeting hall."

Cari led September back through the alleyways although September could not tell whether they used the same route as when she had come or whether it was a different path through the maze of buildings. Soon, however, they arrived back at the large hall which was now deserted. Cari took her inside and upstairs to a door that stood ajar.

"These are the Mordeyrn's rooms," Cari said, "I will leave you here, Cludydd. May you have success in your tasks." The cludydd hurried off and September felt that she did not want to see Aurddolen, or perhaps it was his daughter she was keeping away from.

September tapped on the door and stepped inside. Aurddolen was emerging from another room.

"Ah, Cludydd, you are back. You have completed your tasks?"

"Yes. Hopefully the shield will defend the town and I can keep in touch with people across the Land."

"So, now you intend to leave?"

"Yes, I think I should. My hip hasn't itched at all since I've been here but who knows when Malice might seek me out."

"Ah, yes, your birthmark. It gives an indication of when the Malevolence is approaching?"

"Yes, but the warning time is short. I hope I can do better by linking to Malice."

"Well, take care. That one has powers that are outside my knowledge. Her influence over my daughter is an aspect of evil that I have not experienced before."

"Is Heulwen here?"

"Yes, in there." Aurddolen indicated the room he had just emerged from.

"May I see her?"

"Of course. I have you to thank for rescuing her from Malice. Who knows what her fate would be if she had remained in Malice's hands."

Aurddolen led her into the room. It was a small bedroom furnished with a fur covered mattress, carpet and wall hangings that gave it a warm feel. Heulwen sat cross-legged on the bed, back straight, head up, eyes open, looking ahead but totally devoid of consciousness.

"Hello Heulwen," September said. There was no reply or movement from the young woman. "She doesn't respond?"

"She will swallow food and drink placed in her mouth. She balances, sitting and standing. Her body works, but she has no will of her own."

"Do you think Malice can make her move?"

"I don't know. I have seen no sign that Malice can control her since you returned her to me, but that does not prove that Heulwen cannot be manipulated like a puppet. You say that Malice has a link to her. That worries me."

"What will you do?"

"I will look after her, talk to her, try to get through to her using my powers and those of the other cludyddau but I must ensure that she is kept secure at all times and not able to endanger the people here."

"The others will help."

"Reluctantly. I think Cynhaearn would prefer it if she was cast out onto the ice, but he and the others will do my bidding – for now at least."

"If you think of anything more that I can do, call me."

"I will Cludydd. We will talk wherever you may be. Now, I have held you up long enough. The rest of Gwlad has need of your powers."

"Yes, but don't forget I can return here in minutes."

"I know."

They embraced. It felt like more of a farewell than it needed to be. September had decided to stay away from Mwyngloddiau Dwfn unless the town was under threat. She would do her best to draw the Malevolence away while Aurddolen prepared for the Conjunction.

They parted and September returned to the main hall.

Hedydd and Sieffre were there, standing close together. Both were now dressed in thick furs. September was certain that they had been holding hands. Sieffre took a step towards her when he saw her.

"Cludydd. We are glad to meet you. We have been told that you are leaving this frozen town."

"Yes. It's for the best. Do you want me to take you somewhere warmer?"

"No, well, yes, I want to return to the warmth of the southern lands, but it appears that I have a task to perform here."

"The Mordeyrn wants me to continue making observations of the heavens," Hedydd said.

"But your shield will obscure the stars and the mountains press too close, limiting the view of the sky," Sieffre said, "so Hedydd will have to travel to a peak to make her measurements and I will be her protector."

"I see." September noticed that Sieffre was less relaxed with her than he used to be and had transferred his duty of care to Hedydd. "That is good. Your work is very important, Hedydd, and Sieffre is the best bodyguard you could have."

Hedydd gave Sieffre a look of admiration.

"He says that he thinks your powers mean you have no more need of his services, Cludydd," Hedydd said.

"I wouldn't say that," September said, remembering the gratitude she had felt for Sieffre's willingness to remain at her side and his heroic vigilance in awaiting her return from the planets, "I will always want you as a companion Sieffre, but Hedydd is right, she has more need of your skills now."

Hedydd and Sieffre looked at each other with satisfaction and relief.

"And now I really must go," September went on, now sure that she wanted to be somewhere else. She left the building and stood in the square. The Sun was dropping towards the western mountain tops just visible above the roofs and while it was still autumn there was an icy chill in the air. Some people going about their business stopped when they saw her iridescent figure. They cried out when she changed into the giant blue eagle.

September spread her wings, cupped the air and rose.

10

September circled over the rooftops beneath the silver-grey dome, just looking at the buildings beneath her. At the northern end of the town there were towers and gantries and chimneys – the mines and foundries that were the purpose of the settlement. There were few people visible – the miners must be underground, September realised. She strove for height in the thin, cold air. The shield was close; then she was through and the blue sky shone above her. Now the town below was hidden beneath the grey curved surface. She hoped that she, Ilar and Cynwal had done enough to protect the community.

She flew up to the western ridge and followed it southwards until it fell away to the wooded plains below. Swooping down she landed on the final promontory and perched there, folding her great wings to her side. With her eagle eyes she peered northwards at the distant dark speck that was Mwyngloddiau Dwfn at the head of the snow-covered valley, turning to look southwards at the seemingly unending forest. There were people down there, beneath the tree cover and beyond, beside the northern and southern rivers, in the far east on the coast of the ocean, to the west in the Bryn am Seren and further south still on the dry plains that became desert. They were all hers to guard and protect, at least until the Conjunction signalled the final battle. There was just seven weeks until the fateful alignment of the planets but time enough for the Malevolence and Malice to work their evil as their powers grew. September had no doubt that her time would be filled but she was confident that she could face the threats of the manifestations and of people turned to evil. It was Malice that still troubled her. She had no idea at all how she could confront her and halt her plans to destroy the Land. If she could only follow her movements then she would at least have a chance to prepare.

How could she find Malice? She opened her mind with love and was assaulted by the chatter of countless conversing people. She didn't try to identify individuals but there was no beacon of burning hate so she knew that Malice wasn't among them.

Instead she summoned the closest feeling she could to Malice's hate and spite – anger. The power of haearn filled her – clashing blades and pounding hammers, clanking chains and thudding machines – but there was no contact with Malice's raw emotion. There didn't seem to be a way to form a link with her twin using her metal skills. The source of her power was the planets and the stars; Malice's came from the lost souls above the stars. Their only contact had been in their mother's womb. September remembered her birthmark. She changed into her human form and pressed her right hand to her hip where she had the crescent shaped birthmark. It always began to itch and burn when the manifestations appeared. Was it a link to Malice or just the Malevolence in general? She rubbed the mark gently and tried to concentrate on the sensations that it gave her. She felt a warmth in her side but nothing else happened. She had to accept that she could not reach Malice, but Malice had said that she could locate September. How did she do it? Was it the disturbance in the universe caused by the starstone, the same disturbance that drew manifestations to her? If that was the case then the link was indeed one-sided because Malice was just one amongst the innumerable lost souls, made most powerful by having September as her twin.

September realised that she was not doing much good perched on a mountaintop. Perhaps she should search for Malice. Maybe she had adopted the Arsyllfa, the scene of her greatest victory, as her base on Earth. September launched herself into the sky on a trajectory that brought her, in minutes, to the ruins of the observatory.

She landed on what remained of the observing platform. The marble floor was cracked and the instruments gone. Even the girders of iron, gold, lead and tin that had protected it were twisted and broken. The stairway was destroyed so September changed into her cobra-shape and slid over and around the smashed stone. She surveyed one floor after another. All was quiet but nothing remained undamaged or unviolated. The books in the Mordeyrn's study were torn and burned; each cludydd's room was ripped apart; even the room that had kept her safe while the Arsyllfa was being invaded had been destroyed after her departure. She found tiny scraps of paper – all that remained of Heulyn's journal -, bits of soiled cloth among the splintered wood of the wardrobe and a fused puddle of metal that she guessed was the fate of Tudfwlch's sword and the gifts she had received from the cludyddau of Amaethaderyn. This destruction was a sign of Malice's spite – it had done her twin no good but was just an outlet for her anger when September had escaped with Heulwen.

September slithered to the lower floors finding the decaying bodies of victims of the Cyhyraeth, and others burned by Cwn annwn or turned to dwindling heaps of dust by Gwyllian.

She listened carefully, broadcasting her love, reaching out tentatively, tuning out the continent-wide chatter of cludyddau o efyddyn. The Arsyllfa was silent and dead, but there was a distant whisper. People she knew were somewhere – not near but not that far away either. She slid to a gap in the walls, changed into the form of the eagle and launched herself into the air.

The voices were still there. She circled until she was sure of their direction then soared away from the observatory heading southeast. High she flew, over hills and valleys and the voices in her head grew stronger. Then in the dying rays of the day's sun she saw four figures, trudging through meadowland beside a stream. She swooped down to them.

The leader, a man, looked up and saw her. He shouted with alarm and the small group scattered. September landed and turned into her normal self.

"Don't worry. It's me," she called. Each of the figures paused in their effort to escape and turned to look at her. The two closest to her she recognised as Heini and Arianrhod, the elderly bearers of mercury and silver. The two who had run the furthest were a young man and woman who September vaguely recalled working at the Arsyllfa. Each of the four retraced their steps to approach her.

"Cludydd? Is it really you?" Arianrhod said.

"You were transformed into a bird." Heini marvelled. The two young people were silent and awestruck.

"I have gained new powers," September explained.

"Tell us, please," Arianrhod said, "but night falls and we must make camp."

"Not that we possess the means to entertain you or indeed to satisfy all our needs," Heini said.

"We escaped the downfall of the Arsyllfa with nothing," Arianrhod explained. Nevertheless they quickly chose a spot beneath a group of trees, found wood for a fire and a few handfuls of nuts to eat. Soon all five were seated in a circle and September explained quickly what had happened to her among the planets, her rescue of Heulwen and meeting with Aurddolen and the others.

Heini's and Arianrhod's faces darkened at the mention of Heulwen but their relief that there were at least some other survivors of the disaster at the Arsyllfa was clear.

"We thought we were all that were left alive," Arianrhod said, "we saw so many die and I could do nothing to heal the fallen."

"You must have gone in a different direction to Aurddolen and his group," September said.

"We headed south at first," Heini explained, "and we are hoping to return to Dwytrefrhaedr, but Arianrhod and I are old and slow. We are holding these young folk back."

"Are you sure there is no one else from the Arsyllfa alive?" Arianrhod asked.

"No. I have just come from there and I saw lots of bodies. I listened hard but you were the only people I could locate close to the observatory. I don't think there is anyone else. Aurddolen said he knew that Eryl the astronomer and Anarawd had died."

"And Betrys was overwhelmed by Cwn annwn as she tried to get people out of the Arsyllfa." September felt sad to hear of the death of the jolly tin bearer.

"The question is, what do you want to do next?" she asked and explained what was happening in the dark mountains and what her intentions were.

"I don't think we will be much use when it comes time to

trek onto the icecap," Arianrhod said, "We will just slow everyone down."

"Arianrhod is right. I think it would be best if we returned to our homes and helped their defence against the Malevolence," Heini agreed.

"I can carry you if you wish."

"From what you have told us it seems you have already performed that service a number of times," Heini said, "but you do not have to worry about me. If you can look after Arianrhod and these two youngsters I can transform and fly to the coast myself."

The young man and woman were still overawed by being in the presence of the radiant Cludydd o Maengolauseren and said that it was no more than a couple of days walk to their parents' homes so only Arianrhod was left for September to carry. They agreed to stay where they were for the night and travel at first light. They talked for a while of their regrets at the loss of many friends at the Arsyllfa, of what lay ahead in the fight against the Malevolence and the prospects for a successful resolution at the Conjunction. September appreciated Heini's and Arianrhod's confidence in her new powers but they knew little of the threat that Malice posed. The two aged cludyddau were obviously exhausted from their days of walking and soon dozed off while the youngsters were too shy to talk. September alone remained wakeful and alert. The peace and calm of the setting was pleasant but September felt that she would soon be thrust into battles to protect the people she had come to love and respect.

The sky was just taking on the colours of dawn as the four sleepers stirred. There was little to be done to break camp and soon farewells were being said. Heini transformed into a seagull that squawked as it took to the air and headed east. September changed into her eagle and Arianrhod clambered stiffly onto her back. The young people waved as they dwindled to specks below them while September climbed into the lightening sky.

She beat her wings and headed northeast, soon swooping across hills and valleys. The southern river flashed past below them and then they were over forest. They remained high in the sky when they passed over small clearings containing settlements.

Soon Arianrhod pointed down at a ribbon of water.

"Afon Gogleddol, the northern river," she shouted beside September's feathered head, "follow it to the east." September swooped along the course of the mighty river.

After a short while September saw something ahead and at the same time an itch began in her right hip. Although the sky was clear and the sun shining brightly there appeared to be a dark smudge over part of the river.

"There," Arianrhod shouted, pointing a finger at the part of the river shrouded by the cloud, "My home is being attacked by the Malevolence."

As they approached, the burning in September's side increased and she could see that the cloud was a sulphurous fog such as had been wrapped around the Arsyllfa on her arrival there. Within it were the shadowy figures of a swarm of Adarllwchgwin. Flashes of yellow light signified a barrage of fire from the red riders aimed towards the ground.

September kept her height until she was over the cloud of attackers.

"Hold on," she commanded Arianrhod, then she stooped to the attack. As she streaked towards the ground she composed herself to unleash the power of the starstone. Then they were in the cloud and amongst the Adarllwchgwin but still descending at great speed.

"Be gone!" September screeched from her beak. A sphere of violet radiated out from her. It touched one of the evil birds, which disappeared in an explosion of hot air. Then another and another puffed out of existence. It was a chain reaction that increased in ferocity as the sphere expanded until all the manifestations were consumed. September's screaming dive generated a vortex like a tornado that blew away the noxious smog. The air cleared and below them, rapidly approaching, was the surface of the river. September spread her wings, scooping the air and pulling up. Her talons scythed through the water and then they were flying gently towards the southern bank, the sky clear of attackers.

Smoke rose from various points along the riverside and

there were boats in the water but September could see no sign of a settlement until Arianrhod tapped on her neck and pointed up at the tall trees that lined the bank. There September saw platforms and houses amongst the branches. She rose until she was amongst the sparse foliage at the top of the trees and settled onto a floor of wooden planks. Arianrhod slid off her back as faces appeared at the tops of ladders and people climbed up to greet them. September transformed and soon she and Arianrhod were surrounded by adults and children.

With everyone chattering together September found it difficult to follow a conversation until Arianrhod lifted her hands to quieten everyone and turned to September.

"My people and I want to thank you for driving away the Malevolence. It's not the first time that Trefyncoed has been attacked and it will not be the last but on this occasion you have prevented much death and destruction." September accepted her words modestly and decided that hanging around to hear the inhabitants' gratitude for her efforts was an embarrassment she could avoid.

"Thank you too for the journey," Arianrhod continued with a smile, "it was breathtaking."

"I enjoyed seeing a part of the Land that I have not seen before," September said, "but now I think I am needed elsewhere." It wasn't a made up excuse as there was a distant murmur of fear and desperation in her head.

"Good bye. I'll call here again," September said, transforming again into the eagle and launching herself off the platform.

September began her task of responding to the calls for help from the people of Gwlad. Across the seven regions of the Land she destroyed manifestations that appeared and fought off the bands of humans turned to evil. Not only was the power of the Maengolauseren used for her purpose but as in the tasks she faced among the planets she also used the powers of the metals. With the Moon she healed injuries and sickness like a silver bearer. The skills of Mars enabled her to restore iron bridges and machines. She reinvigorated the gold nuggets that energised machines and invoked the Sun to bring hope amongst the inhabitants. The joy of Jupiter helped to unite communities and reinforce their defence and Saturn provided shields to repulse the attackers. Through it all the love of Venus linked her to the appeals of people across the Land and the transformations of Mercury saw her appear as the eagle in the skies, the panther among the trees, the cobra in the plains and the desert and a blue-grey seal in the water of the eastern ocean.

Sleep was not necessary and September never tired but she grew weary of the constant burning in her side and disillusioned with the repetitive task. While the people hailed her as a saviour every time she destroyed manifestations or ended conflicts, she was aware that she always arrived after the attacks had begun. The calls that came to her were always from people besieged; there were no early warnings. Despite the supersonic speed of her trajectory that took her missile-like from one site to another, it still took her minutes to arrive. That was time enough for a herd of Ceffyl Dwr to drown a village in a watery stampede, for a pack of Cwn Annwn to torch a settlement, a Cyhyraeth to blow its pestilence over a community, or a coven of Gwyllian to turn all in their path to dust.

The people celebrated her arrival amongst them. They always invited her to stay and share what they had but September sensed that their joy was tempered by sadness at the death and damage caused by the Malevolence. The people wanted to reinforce their defences and rebuild, so were reluctant to waste time and resources on frolicking. The loss of the Arsyllfa, the observatory built to prepare for the next rise of the evil above the stars, was a constant reminder of the power of the Malevolence.

The attacks of the manifestations went on; more people fell into the thrall of the evil and broke up their communities with riots and murder, but there was no sign of Malice. September wondered if her twin was directing the attacks, keeping her busy criss-crossing the continent, but she never appeared when September arrived to fight her minions. September thought she knew why. Malice was avoiding direct confrontation while her powers grew and the days to the Conjunction ticked off one by one. September was aware that the Malevolence was growing stronger. The number and ferocity of the attacks was steadily increasing. Now as autumn turned to winter there were often two attacks simultaneously. Being in two places at once was a gift that September did not have and so people were left to defend themselves on more and more occasions.

September discussed her worries with Aurddolen in their frequent conversations. The Mordeyrn was sympathetic but the situation was as he expected and his principal concern was to restore his power by casting a new symbol of gold. The miners had found a new vein of gold-bearing ore in the rocks deep beneath the Mwyngloddiau Dwfn and were digging a new tunnel to extract it.

Then one day, as she snuffed out the last of a pack of Cwn annwn, while around her the tents of the desert nomads burned, Aurddolen's cry filled September's head.

"Cludydd! We need your assistance."

"Where are you? What's happening?"

"We are trapped by manifestations in the deep mine. Tylwyth teg fill the tunnels and Coblynau are tearing the roof down on our heads. We cannot defeat them alone."

September trembled with fear. She was at the extreme end of the continent from the mines of Mynydd Tywyll. It would take her many minutes to make the journey even at the speed of a space rocket. How could she reach the people deep underground? She could not see how she could help the Mordeyrn and the miners but there must be some way that the starstone could assist her, some power she had not yet discovered how to control. She needed a way to instantly transport from one point to another.

She recalled her arrival in the Land, many weeks ago. The starstone had brought her here from her own world, apparently in a moment. Could she activate the same mechanism to carry her to the Mordeyrn's rescue?

September held up the stone in her hand. It was clear and she could see the cobalt blue of the sky through it. She manoeuvred it until the Sun swam into view. Its golden light fell on her face. Perhaps the planet that gave Aurddolen his power could connect them. She closed her eyes to avoid the blinding brilliance.

"Take me to the cludydd o aur," she muttered.

Even through her closed eyelids she saw the shaft of sunlight increase in intensity. She felt her whole body heated by the rays and sensed the moment when her feet left the hot sand.

11

There was darkness beyond her eyelids. Cries and screams, clashes of iron and the rumbling of falling rock assaulted her ears. The heat was at least as intense as it had been in the southern desert. September opened her eyes. Compared to the bright desert it was dark but there was just enough light to see bodies crowded into a small cavern. Her back was against a rough-hewn rock wall, the floor strewn with rubble and beside her was the Mordeyrn holding a lamp containing a tiny fleck of starstone that illuminated his face. She saw an expression of wonder.

"Cludydd! You have learnt the art of symudiad."

"Sim what?" September was confused.

"Symudiad, migration, removing yourself from a place. I had not dared hope that you could respond to my appeals."

September tried to make sense of the melee around her. Bodies moved in a strange uncoordinated dance in the flickering light of other starstone lamps.

"What's happening? I can't make it out."

"Tylwyth teg are attacking from the tunnel we dug, and Coblynau have broken into the chamber by their own means and are tearing at the rock. Cynhaearn, Isfoel and the miners fight but are outnumbered."

One of the jerking bodies suddenly fell back and rolled at September's feet, screaming in agony. There was a hissing, fizzing noise that September recalled from school chemistry experiments when acids were added to powders. She knelt down beside the miner and saw vapour rising from his face and clothes. A liquid was dissolving his skin, exposing bloody flesh and bone beneath.

"It is the spit of the Tylwyth teg!" Aurddolen shouted over the noise of the battle, "It burns like fire and consumes flesh and anything else it touches."

September held the Maengolauseren over the man's

wounds and summoned compassion. The hissing ceased and his screams turned to moans.

"You must help the others," Aurddolen insisted.

September stood up and pushed forward through the struggling bodies to get a better view of the skirmish. She saw that the cavern was roughly rectangular, about five metres in width. The miners forming a line across the chamber waved short swords and poked spears at the manifestations pressing forward towards them. Most of the attackers were pale, thin creatures, the size of children but with lined, ugly faces and long, straight, white hair. They resembled the figures of elves and fairies that September recalled from picture books but these were not kind, benevolent creatures. They shrank from the scything cuts of the iron blades of the miners, but at every opportunity advanced on their spindly legs and spat at their opponents. Wherever their saliva landed it hissed and burned and gave off wispy fumes. The Tylwyth teg crammed the cavern and the tunnel beyond but amongst them and particularly at the edges were other creatures. The Coblynau were stockier and dark but barely taller, with round, whiskered faces. It was their hands that drew September's attention. They were broad with long fingers that ended in claws. Some ripped at the rock of the walls of the chamber and flung the rough pebbles at the defenders. Others groped forward clawing at the bodies of the miners. September glanced up and saw Coblynau clinging to the ceiling and gouging out great shards of rock to drop on the people below.

September took in the scene, lit by lamps of starstone, in a moment. The miners were hard-pressed, forced back shoulder-to-shoulder with little space to swing their weapons. Some, she saw, lay fallen, writhing or still. At the centre was Cynhaearn, roaring defiance and thrusting his sword. Beside him was a giant black rat that tore at the Tylwyth teg and Coblynau with its own claws and long teeth. In places the rat's fur was burned by drops of the acidic spit and was bleeding from scratches made by the Coblynau.

September had seen enough. Despite the heroic efforts of the defenders, she feared that their time was running out. She had no idea what effect the explosive power of the starstone would have in the confined space of the mine; nevertheless she raised her hand.

"Be gone!" she commanded. The familiar blue beam shot from the stone, widening to fill the width and height of the cavern. The light dazzled her, and she saw the miners raising their arms to cover their own eyes. In a moment the blue light filled the mine and the tunnels into it and the Tylwyth Teg and Coblynau were transformed into clouds of fine powder. Dust devils curled in the air, settling to the rock-strewn floor. The noise was replaced for a moment by silence then the cheering began.

The miners turned to face her, clustering around her, shouting out their thanks and admiration. September pushed through them to find the fallen. As many as half of the miners lay on the ground. Some were silent and motionless but others writhed and moaned. September held the starstone over their acid burns and gouged flesh and emptied her mind of everything but compassion. One by one the injured men were calmed.

"We can look after them now, Cludydd," Cynhaearn said, kneeling beside her, "Thank you. I don't think the powers of Aurddolen or Isfoel or my own could have prevailed against such a force of Tylwyth teg and Coblynau."

"Your arrival was timely, Cludydd." The speaker was a small, wiry old man. He was naked but covered in hair and rock dust. His face was hidden behind long grey whiskers which were flecked with blood.

"You must be Isfoel," September said, deducing the identity of the mercury bearer from his appearance.

"I am pleased to make your acquaintance, Cludydd," he responded with a slight nod of his head.

"You were a rat but I was told you often take the form of a bat."

"That is true, lady. A bat can flit through the tunnels easily but the form of a rat is better for fighting."

"I can see that, but you are injured." Blood dripped from burns and cuts all over his body.

"Just a few scratches and acid drops," Isfoel said.

"Let me heal them." September passed the starstone across Isfoel's face and body. The burns and cuts disappeared.

"Thank you, Cludydd. You display a great deal of skill."

Aurddolen appeared at September's side.

"We should return to the surface and leave the miners to their tasks," he said. Isfoel agreed and led them along the tunnels, dark except for faint pools of light around the widely spaced splinters of starstone. Neither heat nor cold affected September anymore but she was amazed at the high temperature in the mine. The miners worked stripped to the waist, hammering spikes into the rock face to shatter the stone. September commented on the contrast with the cold at the surface.

"This is the deepest mine," Aurddolen explained, "two thousand arm-reaches below the surface. The temperature rises the deeper you dig. Some say there is a fire at the centre of Daear that will burn for eternity. The metals are born as liquids which run through the cracks in the rocks."

They reached a vertical shaft with a basket hanging from a rope. It reminded September of the lift that had carried her up the cliff between the two towns beside the waterfall. Isfoel held the side of the basket and helped Aurddolen and September into it.

"Aren't you coming with us?" September asked.

"No, Cludydd. I will resume my patrol of the tunnels but I hope your assistance will not be needed again." He transformed into a bat and fluttered off down the tunnel. The basket jerked and began to rise.

"It will take some time to reach the surface," Aurddolen said, "A chance to talk perhaps."

"Yes."

"Your symudiad astounded me. I did not think it was possible to control that aspect of the Maengolauseren."

"I'm not sure how much control I have. I just pointed the stone at the Sun and hoped."

"It is just another indicator of how well you and the starstone respond to each other."

"Perhaps. I hope I can do it again. Anything that can enable me to reach people faster will help."

"You have seemed rather despondent when we have talked, Cludydd."

"Yes. Every day I see the results of the attacks by the

Malevolence – more dead, more destruction – and that's at the places where I arrive in time to help. There are other places being attacked which I can't get to until the people have suffered a lot worse."

"I know how it seems, September. The Malevolence grows stronger and will do so right up to the Cysylltiad. The people know what is happening and are doing their best. Everything that you do helps them and gives them hope."

"But why does the Malevolence get stronger? I have destroyed thousands of manifestations." There were tears in September's eyes and a lump of misery in her chest.

"That is true but the spirits that inhabit the manifestations cannot be destroyed, they are merely flung back to their realm above the stars joined by the spirits of those they have killed and those who have turned to evil. The Conjunction is not far off and already the planets are beginning to line up. Iau and Sadwrn have already disappeared in the radiance of Haul and the other planets approach it. The shielding influence of the planets is weakened and more of the spirits can descend from the dark reaches of space."

"So there is nothing we can do."

"We are doing all we can for now. The people must hold out – and they will."

"And at the Conjunction – what happens then?"

"That is the moment when Daear is most exposed and the spirits of the Malevolence have their opportunity to descend in their greatest numbers, but you will be at the focus of their influx and you, with the power of the Maengolauseren and all the planets combined, will repulse them."

"Except there is the matter of my twin."

"Ah yes. You have not seen her?"

"No, but I'm sure she is in charge and sending me here and there to deal with incidents she has planned. She won't face me until she has the full power of the Malevolence to back her up."

"You will prevail, Cludydd. I know you will and soon we will have enough aur to cast my new symbol of power. Then I will stand beside you."

"Why don't the Cemegwr help?"

September felt the Mordeyrn's body stiffen.

"Why do you speak again of them?"

"Well, if they are the creators of this universe perhaps they have an interest in what goes on in it."

"No, that is nonsense. There are no such creatures. Whoever the creators of the world were, there has been no evidence for their existence since time began other than the silly stories people tell to make sense of what they see."

"You're sure?"

"I am. Do not anticipate help from these imaginary beings. You are our salvation, Cludydd. You alone have the power to overcome the Malevolence – and your sister."

A draught of cold air signalled that they were approaching the surface. A spot of grey sunlight appeared above them, which grew until it was the size of the shaft. The basket slowed and stopped when it was level with the ground and hands grabbed it. September saw that the rope bearing the basket had wound around a great iron wheel connected to a huge heavy beam that rocked on a pivot. Clouds of steam emerged from below the contraption.

"Is it a steam engine?" September asked.

"A machine, driven by steam that is heated by the power of aur." Aurddolen seemed to confirm her suggestion. He stepped out of the basket and held out his hand to help September. "I am sure other communities await you, Cludydd, but please come and see my daughter." He guided her into the crowd of miners that parted to let them through. The dark skinned men gazed at her dazzling blue appearance in wonder.

Aurddolen clutched his arms around himself. It was late autumn and high in the mountains it was already cold enough for a thick layer of snow to be lying on the ground. The grey shield overhead also reduced the amount of sunlight warming the town. Aurddolen took long swift strides down the street from the mining sector of the town to the living quarters. September kept pace with him.

"How is Heulwen?"

"Little changed."

A few minutes' walk brought them to Aurddolen's residence. Heulwen was in the same room as she had been on September's previous visit. She sat upright on a chair, her eyes open but unseeing.

"Hello, Heulwen," September said. There was no response. Heulwen's eyes continued to stare vacantly ahead. September bent to look closely into Heulwen's face, but she did not flinch or avert her gaze.

"She eats and drinks, sleeps and walks but still shows no consciousness," Aurddolen said.

"Do you think Malice is still linked to her?"

"There has been no evidence of that but I fear that if called upon then she would do your sister's bidding. Hence the door to this room is kept locked when my daughter is alone."

"I'm sorry, Aurddolen. I can't think of anything we can do for her."

"Neither can I." He fell silent.

"Is there anything else?"

The Mordeyrn looked thoughtful. "There is. As we expected, the shield over the town has acted as a beacon to the Malevolence. Manifestations are drawn to it."

"They can't get in."

"No. Everyone inside is safe, but as you have seen, in the deep mines, beyond the safety of the sphere, we are beset by manifestations of the earth. More seriously the manifestations that besiege the town are interfering with supplies. Mwyngloddiau Dwfn and other mining settlements are unusual in the Land in that they cannot produce their own food. They rely on other communities to supply them in return for metals."

"I see. What is happening?"

"We are running out of food. People are starting to go hungry. No supply caravan has been able to get past the manifestations this month. They are attacked when they approach the town."

"I haven't been aware of these attacks."

"No, Cludydd. You have been answering much more important calls for help, but the townspeople are becoming worried and do not know how they will be fed."

"What do you suggest?"

"Cari is in communication with the cludydd o efyddyn of the nearest settlement in the forest, from which most of the supplies come. We are planning a large caravan which will bring enough food to last us until the Conjunction is past. It will be escorted by warriors and a number of cludyddau, but your help will also be very useful."

"I'll be ready," September agreed, "just call me when you need me."

"Thank you, Cludydd. I knew you would help us despite all the demands on you. But now I have detained you long enough. Thank you again for saving us today."

"It seems to be all I can do at the moment," she replied putting a hand to her head, "I am feeling a call for help. I will try to – what did you call it?"

"Symudiad."

Aurddolen led her to the narrow space between the buildings. The Sun was not visible in the small patch of sky between the tall walls but nevertheless September raised the starstone and looked through it. She held in her mind the picture she was getting from the people who were appealing for her help.

"Take me – there," she muttered.

Golden light poured from the starstone, spinning around her like a whirlwind, dazzling her eyes and obscuring Aurddolen and the dark rock. Her feet no longer rested on the hard cobbles of the town's streets.

September returned to her unending chore of defending the people of Gwlad. Now at least, her transport by symudiad was instantaneous on receiving an appeal for help. Each migration was unsettling – the dazzling light, the change of footing, the sudden immersion in a battle against various forms of manifestation or hordes of maddened people driven to evil. She quickly learnt to close her eyes at the moment of displacement and to be ready for action as soon as the light cleared. At first the people were astounded by her sudden appearance but they appreciated her immediate response to whatever was attacking them. The number of casualties and the damage caused by each incident was reduced but as the days went by there were more of them and the size of the force of manifestations increased.

Each hour passed with September relocating from one part of Gwlad to another. She no longer knew where she was as she responded to the appeals in her head and barely had time to notice whether the community was in the hills or by the coast, under trees or on open plains. The different locations flickered past her eyes almost unseen.

She found herself in a familiar setting. Around her there were low, round, thatched buildings surrounded by trees. She recognised some of the faces that clustered around her thanking her for destroying a swarm of Adarllwchgwin.

"Berddig, Iorwerth!" she cried, "It's you."

"Welcome back to Amaethaderyn," the young, jovial bearer of tin said.

"We are delighted to see you again, Cludydd," the warrior agreed.

September looked at them closely. They looked tired and worn. Iorwerth in particular displayed scars and fresh wounds on his arms and face. The other people around them were thin and their clothes were battered and torn. She looked at the buildings. While there were some that were new, many were damaged.

"This was not the first time you have been attacked since I left," September said.

"No, it was not but it was the largest group of manifestations we have faced. We have managed to deal with the others ourselves," Berddig said, "but on this occasion we needed your help."

"I can see you have had a difficult time."

"Life is hard under the threat of the Malevolence. Growing crops, looking after the animals, fishing, all have been disrupted by the attacks. Our food stocks are low and sometimes we are hungry, but we survive."

"Come with us. There are others that will wish to meet you again," Iorwerth said.

For the moment there were no cries for help in September's head. She followed Iorwerth and Berddig between the round mud huts until they came to the village meeting area. The space now had a canopy of reeds and was laid out as a treatment centre. A dozen or more men, women and children lay on bed mats and walking between them was the silver-haired figure of Arianwen. She looked up as September and her attendants arrived and smiled warmly.

"Cludydd, you have returned to us."

"And driven off the Malevolence, for now," Iorwerth said.

"Hello, Arianwen." September drew the older woman into an embrace. Arianwen held back at first, confused by September's gleaming but insubstantial dress, but then hugged her.

"We have heard so much about you," Arianwen said as they parted, "the great deeds you have performed, the powers and skills that you possess. It is wonderful to see you again after all these weeks."

September lowered her head modestly.

"It's true that I've learnt how to do some things, but I don't know about great deeds. The Malevolence still grows stronger and people are still dying just as they've done ever since I arrived here." A picture of Tudfwlch appeared in her mind and a tear rolled down her cheek. Another image came to her; the prone figure of Eluned. "What about Eluned? Is she alright?"

"Oh yes," Arianwen nodded just as the white tiger bounded into the clearing and transformed into the naked bearer of mercury.

"September!" she cried, "You're here." They too embraced.

"You look OK," September said, stepping back to look at the young woman.

"I'm fine. Arianwen healed me."

"I'm glad."

"But you! You're magnificent. I knew you would come into your powers."

"Thanks, but there is still the Conjunction to face."

"You will defeat the Malevolence," Eluned said forcefully and the others nodded and agreed.

"What about Catrin and Padarn?" September asked, "Where are they?"

"They are here," Berddig said, "Catrin is communicating with our neighbours. She keeps in touch as much as she can."

"Padarn is resting," Arianwen said and September detected a sad note in her voice, "he is tired. He uses so much power to shield us from the Malevolence that he is weakened. We hope he will make it to the Cysylltiad."

"Perhaps I can help and throw a shield over the village like I have over Mwyngloddiau."

"We have heard of that great application of the power of Iau and Sadwrn," Berddig said, "but does it not require the energy of the cludyddau to maintain it?"

"Hmm, yes. Ilar and Cynwal are holding it in place, but couldn't you and Padarn do the same here?"

Berddig looked miserable, "I fear that Padarn is no longer strong enough to sustain the effort such a structure would demand. I can support him, but I am not sure it would be enough."

"We could try."

"Yes, Cludydd, but there is another matter. The shield will attract the Malevolence."

"That's happened at the mine, yes."

"But here we need to get out into the fields to grow our crops, sail on the river and lake to fish and move among the trees of the forest to collect wood and nuts. The shield would have to be huge to protect all our people while they carry out their tasks."

September could see Berddig's point. Was her power sufficient to protect all the people? She didn't feel confident that it was.

"We can defend ourselves," Iorwerth said defiantly, "and call on you only when it is necessary." The others nodded and called out their agreement.

"I am sorry," September said.

"What for?" Arianwen asked.

"For not being able to do more."

"You are doing what you can and you will be victorious at the Conjunction," Eluned said, drawing another chorus of agreement.

Once again September did not feel as confident in her abilities as the people of Gwlad felt. Their faith in her embarrassed her.

"I must go," she said.

"May the Cemegwr be at your side," Iorwerth said. September turned to him.

"You believe in the Cemegwr?"

Iorwerth shrugged, "It's just a saying."

"Aurddolen says they don't exist, they're just tales."

"The Mordeyrn is correct," Arianwen said.

"We don't know," Berddig said, "We have seen nothing that suggests they are part of this world but the stories persist and some people look to them for support as much as they look to you to defeat the Malevolence."

"Put the Cemegwr out of your mind," Arianwen insisted, "Now you must leave us and go to help others in need."

"Please come and visit us again, when there are no manifestations about," Eluned said.

September was already holding the Maengolauseren to the sky, "I will," she called as the golden light surrounded her.

12

She was back amongst the dark buildings of Mwyngloddiau Dwfn. Winter had come to the mountains. It was late morning but the Sun was below the rooftops and the alleyways were in dark shadows. The Mordeyrn was standing alone.

"Welcome, Cludydd," Aurddolen said warmly, "Thank you for responding. I hope we haven't interrupted you."

"I was at Amaethaderyn. They'd been attacked by Adarllwchgwin."

"Ah, how I wish I had been with you. How are they there?"

"OK. Well, they're coping. They all look tired and Padarn is exhausted. They have managed to defend the village so far but like everywhere it's getting more and more difficult."

"I know, but let us hope that normal life can resume in a short while."

September was not quite sure what normal was for her. What would it be like to go home after all her experiences in the Land?

"Yes, but there's the Conjunction to face first. What have you called me for? You are not under attack. The shield hasn't been broken?"

"No, but the people are starving. The time has come to try to get supplies through. We need your help to guard the convoy on its journey from the forest."

"How long will it take?"

"It is three days travel from the village."

"Three days. That is a long time for me to leave the rest of the Land on its own."

"I know, Cludydd, but without these supplies, Mwyngloddiau Dwfn will not survive and we will not be prepared for the Conjunction."

"I understand. What do you want me to do?"

"Thank you, Cludydd. Cynhaearn and a body of his best

warriors are already there and about to set off but they will need your assistance I am sure. When the caravan arrives I will also be ready to cast my symbol of aur."

"I'd like to see that."

"You will. Now I will show you where you have to go."

September probed the Mordeyrn's mind. She saw the location he had visualised – a village in the forest on the foothills of the mountains. She raised the starstone.

"Three days," she said, "I'll be back with your supplies."

When the dazzling light cleared she was under the canopy of tall trees. All around her between the trunks were laden horses and their handlers. Striding towards her was Cynhaearn, sword at his side and carrying a circular iron shield on his back.

"Cludydd! Welcome. We are just about ready to set off at last. You can't know how difficult it has been to prepare all the people as well as all the horses. I wish Ilar was here to do the organising; she's a lot better at it than me. I suppose that's what being a cludydd o alcam is all about."

September smiled at Cynhaearn's rambling; he was as worked up as it was possible to be.

"What do you want me to do?"

"Just being with us will encourage everyone."

"You know my presence will probably attract the Malevolence."

"We are going to face manifestations in any case. With your protection we might actually get most, if not all, of these supplies to Mwyngloddiau."

"Right, well let's make a start."

Cynhaearn strode off shouting instructions and slowly, one by one, the horses began to move in the same direction between the trees. September transformed into her panther and ran amongst them. The horses were not frightened by her but seemed to recognise her as a guardian. The handlers and guards were initially shocked by her appearance among them but when they realised that the Cludydd o Maengolauseren was travelling with them, their spirits were lifted and they cheered whenever they saw her.

Gradually the convoy converged into a single file following

a trail through the forest. Each handler led up to five horses heavily laden with sacks and packages. At the head of the convoy was a group of warriors. September recognised some as being miners from their dark skin and short stocky build. Others were taller, fair fighters from the forest settlements. A young cludydd o haearn led them, his bright sword drawn and pointing the way. More of the guards walked beside the caravan on the lookout for attacks from manifestations and another cludydd commanded a group that brought up the rear. Cynhaearn seemed to want to be everywhere at once, running to catch up the lead group, hurrying back to check on the rearguard. September, too, loped up and down the long line of packhorses expecting to feel the imminent arrival of the Malevolence in her birthmark at any time. She did not have to wait long.

The caravan was still plodding through the forest, climbing slowly, when her hip began to itch. What were the manifestations? Where would they make their attack? September was at the head of the procession when her keen hearing picked up a cry of alarm from behind. She raced to where the call had come from, the pain in her side growing stronger as she went. Then she saw them – a pack of flaming Cwn annwn amongst the trees howling and baying as they bounded towards the party.

She skidded to a halt and without transforming raised her front left paw. Violet light engulfed the pack dousing their fire, but as one group were defeated another cry went up further along the line. September leapt to meet them again dissipating the fiery dogs before they could harm the horses or their guardians. And so it went on throughout the afternoon, September leaping from one point to another to face one pack of burning hounds after another. Those few that escaped her violet beam were cut down by the warriors with their iron swords forged in the furnaces of Mwyngloddiau Dwfn. The horses plodded on, calmed by their handlers, but September was sure that their progress must have been slowed.

At nightfall Cynhaearn called the convoy to form into a cluster to make camp. They were still under the cover of the trees but September cast a shield over them all to give them peace overnight. She joined the guards to watch throughout the night and saw the flickering flames of dogs prowling around the edge of the dome.

In the morning, September cleared the vicinity of the camp of manifestations before dissolving the shield. The caravan slowly got under way and September stood guard counting the horses that passed her. There were over two hundred heavily laden beasts. From what she had seen of the way of life of people across the Land this must have been one of the biggest and most complex expeditions they had ever organised. No wonder that Cynhaearn was in a constant state of tension. September worried that he would exhaust himself long before they reached the mining town.

They continued to be harried by Cwn annwn and when they emerged above the tree line onto the grass covered slopes of the Mynydd Tywyll, squadrons of Adarllwchgwin descended from the sky. September dealt with them with little inconvenience to the plodding train of horses.

They crossed a ridge and joined the valley which the town stood at the head of. Llamhigwyn y dwr, the flying frog-like creatures, rose from the fast-flowing river; later a Draig tân roared across the sky. September dealt with all the manifestations, returning them to their inanimate elements and dispatching the spirits. Cynhaearn's warriors were grateful that they only had the occasional creature to deal with and their weapons, imbued with the power of Mars, were a match for them all. Patches of ice and snow appeared on the rocks and grass and icy rain fell on them.

After a cold night in the valley, the journey went on, climbing now into the rugged mountains. Now they walked through snow and ice; when the clouds covered the sky, heavy snow fell on the heads of man and beast. Ceffyl dwr rearing up from a mountain lake, and a Pwca in the form of a mountain bear, joined the hordes of Adarllwchgwin and Cwn annwn that attempted to break up the convoy, with no success against September's all-powerful beams of light.

Higher in the mountains where the track zig-zagged up the steep valley side, Coblynau emerged from newly gouged tunnels, Tylwyth teg skittered amongst the rocks spitting acid and Gwyllian staggered towards them reaching out with their knobbly claw-like hands. September gave Cynhaearn's men the chance to demonstrate their skill. They scythed through their enemies but September made sure that none of the manifestations caused any harm to the horses or their baggage.

On the final stage of the journey they tramped through thick snow, a blizzard in their faces. They were almost caught out by a Cyhyraeth, its moans lost in the howling wind, but the itch in September's side gave warning of the attack and she blew the wraith away before it could bring its pestilence to the trudging band.

During a brief respite in the storm, September transformed into the eagle and circled high above the convoy. She could see the dome covering the mining town just a couple of hours march away together with its ring of besieging manifestations. She flew down to the caravan and joined Cynhaearn.

"It's not far now," she said.

"Yes, I know, but it will be dark before we reach the town."

"And I will have to drive off the Malevolence before we pass through the shield."

"Are there many servants of evil there?"

"Yes, and more will probably come as we get closer."

"I'll tell the handlers to get the horses to bunch together. There is no need to be strung out in a line."

"You'll have to watch the back of the caravan while I deal with the manifestations ahead of us."

"I'll put my warriors in a circle around the horses. That should safeguard them."

The plans were carried out, all the while with harrying by packs of Cwn annwn and swarms of Adarllwchgwin attacking from all sides and above. September, in the form of the eagle, swooped around the caravan radiating violet light while Cynhaearn's guards fought tirelessly.

Once the horses were circled by a defensive ring, September diverted her attention to the hordes of manifestations besieging the town. She changed back to her normal form and stood on the snow-covered slope a little way from the dome. The blizzard had stopped and the clouds cleared away revealing the star-filled sky. The snow-covered ground seemed aglow with its own radiance, illuminating the domed town and its besiegers.

September raised her hand holding the starstone, closed her eyes and imagined every one of the evil spirits blown away. A great cone of light erupted from the starstone expanding to engulf every entity that was outside the shield. The manifestations were destroyed at once with explosions, fireballs, dust devils and deluges. The way was clear.

She waved the convoy on and ponderously it began the final trek to the safety of the town. September became an eagle again and circled overhead supporting the guards in defeating the remaining attackers.

The horses were led through the grey curtain and into the narrow alleyways of the town lined with cheering townspeople. Cynhaearn and his warriors stood guard until the very last packhorse was safe and then they too passed through the shield. September saw yet more manifestations amassing to renew their siege, but they were too late. The convoy was safe. She entered the town to find Aurddolen striding towards her.

"Well done. You did it with no losses," Aurddolen congratulated her.

"Not here, no, but my head has been full of appeals for help elsewhere in the Land all the time. I have no idea how many have died while we were travelling here."

"You can't be everywhere, Cludydd, and you can't take responsibility for every attack by the Malevolence."

"Perhaps not, but the calls are in my head and it feels as if it's my fault if I don't try to help."

"I understand and I know you'll want to go and do what you can, but please come with me now as I cast my new symbol of power."

The pull of the appeals was strong in September's head but she heeded the Mordeyrn's request and followed him through the town towards the mines and workshops. She felt a question burning in her.

"I didn't read all of Heulyn's account of the last Conjunction, but was it as bad as this one?"

"Ah, that is a difficult question to answer. Heulyn recorded reports from across Gwlad and there were many attacks by manifestations, a great deal of destruction and many good spirits were turned to evil and lost above the stars. I do think however that the attacks this time have reached a higher level of intensity sooner."

"Is that because of Malice?"

"I don't think so. She may be directing them but my feeling is that the Malevolence is stronger."

"Why?"

"I do not know what gives the Malevolence its power but the records of earlier conjunctions, patchy though they are, suggest that the evil is growing stronger at each event."

"You told me once that there have been five or six conjunctions before. Is that right?"

"It is a guess. There are few records of earlier conjunctions. The populations were so reduced that contact was lost between settlements. Surviving was the priority. It took many years to re-establish contact and trade across the Land. It was Heulyn's great gift of foresight that preserved so much knowledge into this cycle."

"So is this the sixth or seventh conjunction?"

"Legends tell that Daear was formed during a Cysylltiad, when the good of the universe coalesced to form the land, the seas, the air and the fire at the heart of Daear. The Malevolence attempted to destroy the good but was driven off by the first Cludydd o Maengolauseren. If that is true and there have been five further conjunctions since then this is indeed the seventh."

Aurddolen had confirmed September's suspicions.

"Doesn't that tell you something?" she said.

"What do you mean?"

"The number seven. Is it a coincidence that there are seven planets, seven metals, seven this and seven that. Seven is a magic number here. Doesn't that make the seventh conjunction something special?"

The Mordeyrn was thoughtful as they tramped up the dark, cold lane. Finally he spoke.

"I have been extraordinarily blind," he said, "I am not worthy to be a successor to Heulyn. Of course. Seven is the number of power. Not only is the seventh conjunction a special event but you, as the seventh Cludydd, must surely be endowed with extraordinary powers. Thank you, September, you have restored my hope." He increased the length of his stride, his back straightened a little and he held his head up a little more.

"I shall create my new symbol with renewed faith in the strength of Haul."

September, however, was worried. Did being the seventh bearer of the starstone automatically make her the greatest? There was a nagging doubt in her mind that the existence of her twin was still important.

They had reached the tall stone workshops of the miners. Aurddolen pulled open a huge wooden door and such a blast of heat came out that the ice and snow lying on the ground outside the building immediately melted.

The workshop was a place of fire and noise. While the outside was dark, inside flames roared underneath huge furnaces illuminating the machines of iron and copper that clanked and rattled. The fires and the machines were tended by the dark squat people of the mountains. There were many of them throughout the building. Heulfryn, the young cludydd o aur, ran towards them.

"The aur is prepared, Mordeyrn. It awaits your command," he said.

"I am ready," Aurddolen said. He strode to a waist high hearth covered in glowing coals and threw off his long, heavy gown. He stood naked except for a cloth wound around his waist and groin. "Bring me the aur."

Heulfryn ran to one of the furnaces and began pulling on a chain made of links two centimetres thick. September watched as a large crucible lifted off the furnace and travelled through the air to halt above the hearth where Aurddolen stood. The crucible itself glowed red hot and vapours rose from it.

"Now!" Aurddolen commanded.

The crucible began to tip. The interior was revealed – a liquid mass of glowing gold. The gold started to pour. September was suddenly afraid. The molten metal would fall on Aurddolen and burn him. The Mordeyrn did not flinch but held out his hands. The liquid gold fell but did not reach his hands; he was not scorched. The glowing mass of metal was suspended in the air a few centimetres above Aurddolen's hands, a few more centimetres above the hearth. September heard Aurddolen chanting. The words were the old tongue, which she could not understand although she made out some words such as 'aur' and 'haul'. The amorphous mass of liquid gold roiled and flowed. It became a perfect sphere about thirty centimetres across with spikes growing out of it. September counted eight of them arranged in a cube. One spike grew longer and thicker turning into a two metre long rod. Aurddolen grabbed hold of the rod and turned away from the hearth. He held the rod with its glowing, spiked orb, aloft.

"Behold! I am restored as the Prif-cludydd o aur. The power of Haul is with us. Let every one of us have hope." There was loud cheering thoughout the vast workshop.

September looked around and saw that all the workers had stopped to watch what the Mordeyrn did. He lowered the staff so that it rested on the floor. The metal stopped glowing and became simply golden. Aurddolen looked at September.

"It is done. Now I can draw on all the energy of Haul and help you defeat the evil of the Malevolence."

"Isn't it heavy?" September asked, wondering what a head-sized ball of gold would weigh.

"For someone who was not a cludydd o aur it would indeed be too heavy to lift, but for me it is weightless. It is carried by its own energy. Ignoring his gown which lay discarded on the ground he strode towards the door and stepped out into the cold mountain air. September followed.

There were more cheers. It seemed that the whole town was waiting outside in the freshly fallen snow. Every single person seemed delighted that the Mordeyrn had his new symbol of power. He marched between the people, heading down hill towards his lodging, his bare skin apparently unaffected by the cold. In fact, September thought, he seemed to be glowing like his golden staff.

They reached the building where Aurddolen lived. The people stopped outside as he went in with September close behind. In his main room he placed the staff on the floor and let go. September expected it to fall but it remained balanced on the single rod. Aurddolen looked exhilarated.

"Now we shall be ready. We set off to meet the Malevolence in one week."

"Who is 'we'?" September asked.

"All those who have vowed to join us. I sent out the call some time ago. Those cludyddau that could be spared from their communities, warriors, healers, anyone with skills that we will need on our trek into the whitelands I invited to join us. Some have arrived, more will come. All are dedicated to support you, Cludydd."

September had a flash of her and Aurddolen leading a motley band through blizzards and ice like Captain Scott crossing the Antarctic. She wondered what they could do.

"A week? But it is still four weeks to the Conjunction."

"It will take that time to reach the focus of the evil. It will be a long and arduous trek for us, if not for you."

"Hmm, I'd better see if I can help some of the people who are left to fight the Malevolence in their own homes."

"Yes, September, you do that. We will continue to prepare."

September focussed on one of the images in her head with a desperate appeal from a copper bearer. She prepared herself for symudiad.

13

The week passed in a rapid succession of days and nights. Without pause September flashed from one confrontation with the Malevolence to another. The manifestations were no match for her power but she knew that she was only tackling a fraction of the incursions. The clamour for assistance was a continuous roar in her head. She was glad that she didn;t have to sleep as it would have been impossible to settle with the voices screaming and crying for help. As she travelled across the Land she saw more of the effects the Malevolence was causing. People were starving because their food stocks had been destroyed or they had been unable to bring in harvests. Many of their homes had been ruined and the tools they needed lost. People were falling ill with sicknesses of deprivation. Some people lost faith in the power of the cludyddau to protect and succour them and turned on their neighbours. They became servants of the Malevolence and added to the destruction. September realised how the past conjunctions had kept the population of Gwlad small and isolated. The Land was forever struggling to recover from one episode of the Malevolence after another, despite the efforts of her predecessors.

It was early in the morning that Aurddolen announced that they were ready to set off from Mwyngloddiau Dwfn. September transported to the space where the motley army was assembling near to the mine entrances at the top end of the town. The company was not as large as she had expected. There were about a dozen miners led by Cynhaearn and a similar number of other men and women from other parts of the Land. In addition, Heulfryn, Cari and Ariannell from Mwyngloddiau stood with a handful of their fellow cludyddau. Hedydd and Sieffre were also there. Each of them were dressed in thick woollen clothes with rucksacks on their backs. Even wrapped up they looked cold in the pale winter light with snow falling gently on them.

September approached Hedydd and Sieffre.

"You are going too?" she asked.

"Yes, I am needed to guide you to the spot where the Malevolence will be concentrated. I am the Seryddwr now," the young woman replied.

"Of course, the last astronomer. You must return to make sure that you pass on your knowledge."

"I will make sure of that," Sieffre said, placing an arm protectively around the young woman. Hedydd looked at him with love rather than mere gratitude. September thought she knew what that feeling was. There had been a time when she thought she might have fallen for Sieffre's charm and dedication.

"Good luck," she wished them. She looked up, beyond the town to the white, jagged peaks that rose one on top of the other to the north. "Do you have to climb over that to reach the ice cap? It looks impossible."

"We go through them," Cynhaearn said, joining the trio, "Through the years mines have been driven right through the mountains and onto the ice covered plains beyond. It would take days of travel if we had to walk but we have some assistance. Come to the adit and see."

He led them through the various pithead buildings until they approached the near-vertical cliff that was the head of the valley. There was a dark hole in the rock and, emerging from it, a pair of rails. Standing on the rails was a row of wheeled trucks.

"A railway," September said.

"Yes," Cynhaearn agreed, "We have already taken supplies and equipment to the end of the line. Now it is ready to carry us, and you too if you will join us for the start of our journey."

Other members of the group were already scrambling into the trucks, two or three to each one.

"I can't see what makes it move?" September said. There were no horses to tow the wagons and no engine.

"The Mordeyrn provides the power of Haul," Sieffre said.

"Of course," September nodded, although she still could not understand how gold could be a source of energy.

Aurddolen appeared now from the lower town, striding towards them with his golden staff and orb. He climbed into the lead truck and beckoned to the others to join him.

"Join me here, Cludydd," he called to September, "perhaps you will accompany us on the first part of the journey."

September was torn by the appeals in her head, but something told her that the party would need her help. She climbed into the lead wagon with the Mordeyrn.

"What about Heulwen? Is she coming with us?" September asked.

"No. Ilar will look after her while I am gone. I have told her to keep Heulwen locked in her room until we return. I do not want there to be any chance that she might escape under Malice's control."

By now more of the townspeople had emerged into the freezing cold to bid them farewell. Aurddolen planted his staff firmly against the floor of the wagon and muttered something that September did not understand. The orb began to glow and the train of wagons started to roll, the iron wheels scraping against the rails. The people cheered.

The black maw of the mine was in front of them and then they were swallowed up. The wagons increased in speed, the noise ricocheting off the walls. In moments the dim light of the entrance had diminished to a distant spot and only Aurddolen's orb lit up the tunnel. The track was initially straight but began to twist and turn, the wagons rattling and rocking from side to side. To September they seemed to be travelling incredibly fast, the walls and low roof flashing past.

Minutes had gone by and September guessed that they must already be one or two kilometres into the mountain when her hip began to itch.

"Aurddolen," she shouted over the noise of the trucks, "the Malevolence is near. We may be attacked."

"I expected it," the Mordeyrn replied. Their speed decreased. He leant forward to try to see further. September too peered into the gloom. Only a patch of tunnel twenty or thirty metres in front of them was illuminated by the golden glow. Suddenly September saw a sparkle ahead then light was reflected back instead of being lost in the gloom of the tunnel.

"Stop!" she shouted, "There's something there." The grinding of the braking wheels against the tracks made her ears ring but the trucks slowed.

"The tunnel's blocked," September cried out. The tunnel was filled from the rails to the roof with fallen rock. The train halted with the lead wagon pressed against the boulders. For a moment there was silence, then more noise, this time of rock crumbling and falling. Dust and bits of stone dropped on them.

Coblynau appeared from fresh holes in the walls, roof and ground and hobbled towards the party on their short legs, groping with the rock-grinding claws on their hands. September heard shouts from behind as the miners swung their short swords. The tunnel was filled with dust and cries. She knew what she had to do.

September raised her hand and shouted her command. Violet light beamed up and down the tunnel turning every one of the Coblynau to clouds of fine dust that settled in heaps where they had fought.

Now silence did fall. Aurddolen climbed from the wagon and inspected the blockage. Cynhaearn came from the rear truck.

"It looks pretty extensive," Cynhaearn said, "Could take hours to clear. I suppose we'd better get started." He shouted to his fellow miners to take out their picks and shovels and get to work.

"Perhaps there is a quicker way," September said, joining them.

"What do you mean?" Cynhaearn asked, looking mystified, "No one can work faster than my miners equipped with iron tools assisted by the power of Mawrth."

"That's right," September said, "but your iron tools are small. I can use the power of Mars without the iron. I think I know what to do. Tell everybody to get into the wagons and keep down."

"Do as the Cludydd says," Aurddolen said. The message was passed along and the party hurried to hide themselves in the trucks.

September look around to check that everyone was safe

and then faced the rockfall. She raised her hand holding the starstone and summoned up anger. She was angry with the Coblynau for slowing them down, angry with the stone itself for blocking their path and angry with the Malevolence for all its destructiveness. The starstone began to glow a deep red colour and there was a sound like a whirling fan. Wind blew her hair. September thrust her hand forward. The invisible blade bit into the stone. There was the roar of fractured rock. Across the full diameter of the tunnel the fallen boulders were ground to dust illuminated by crimson light. The dust was blown back, far down the tunnel. It blew a fierce tornado of rock fragments over and around the line of wagons.

Slowly September advanced forward. The obstruction was eaten away like a drill through butter. Metre after metre she edged forward, every piece of fallen rock ground to fine dust which was carried on the gale and passed beyond the train.

At last she broke through the rockfall. There was no more rock on the line ahead; the tunnel was clear. September lowered her hand and the red light faded. The last of the dust settled to the floor of the tunnel and the members of the company raised their heads above the wagons, every one of them covered in the fine powder. They cheered and called out September's title.

She climbed back into the lead truck and Aurddolen powered them onwards. Their speed increased until once again the walls of the tunnel flashed past. Every so often the track divided and a tunnel went off to the right or left, but they continued onwards, the track level but now with thousands of metres of rock above them.

For hours they travelled through the clattering darkness. September had been free of pain in her side but now it began to itch again. She warned Aurddolen.

"We're nearly at the end of the track," he shouted over the noise of the wheels on the rails. He reduced speed and again they peered ahead for some blockage.

The wagon slowed to a stop against a buffer. They'd reached the end of the track and the tunnel had opened up into a chamber. Her hip was burning.

"There should be guards here," Aurddolen said, commanding his orb to brighten. Golden light filled the cavern. September saw bodies lying motionless and a mess of scattered and torn packages. They all climbed out of the wagons and went to investigate. September and Auddolen examined one of the fallen warriors. She looked away, not wanting to look at the burned flesh.

"Tylwyth teg," Aurddolen muttered bitterly. There were cries from all parts of the chamber. September looked up and saw the white, sparkling manifestations attacking from all sides. The members of the party retreated away from the acid-spitting figures and clustered together. Dark and fair warriors drew their swords but they flinched from the showers of acid.

September raised her arm and commanded the starstone to respond. The chamber and the adjoining tunnels filled with violet light, turning the fairies of the Malevolence, like the Coblynau, to dust.

Silence fell and the party spread out again looking at the bodies of the fallen. Aurddolen went to examine the stores that were spread round the chamber. Packets of food were ripped apart and scattered, thick furs were torn into shreds and sleighs were smashed to pieces.

Aurddolen slumped in despair.

"All the guards have been killed and the supplies we put together for the journey into the whitelands have been destroyed. Without them we will not survive the cold and lack of food."

"Let's look carefully. Perhaps it isn't all gone," September said.

Aurddolen commanded each member of the party to collect together what was left that was useable. They searched every square metre of the cavern using lamps containing splinters of starstone. When the search was complete they had collected together a pitifully small pile of uncontaminated rations, a few items of cold weather clothing and one intact sleigh.

"There's nothing like enough for everybody," Cynhaearn said.

"Is everybody necessary?" September asked.

"What do you mean?" Cynhaearn said.

"I know everyone has volunteered because they want to

help but from what I've been told the big thing at the Conjunction is between me and the Malevolence, and Malice. I don't think a lot of people need to get into danger. In fact, perhaps they're needed more protecting their homes."

Aurddolen had been listening to her.

"But Heulyn gathered together a large army at the last conjunction."

"Yes, and you told me that they all stayed and watched and waited while my mother went to face the Malevolence."

"Hmm, you are right. Perhaps a small party to accompany you is all that is necessary."

"You need me to guide you to where the Malevolence will strike," Hedydd said.

"And I must escort her," Sieffre added.

"And I will contribute my power," Aurddolen insisted. Cynhaearn, Heulfryn and others insisted they were essential.

"No," September said, "I think only Hedydd and Sieffre are needed to show me to the spot. Aurddolen your power may be needed to help keep the people of Gwlad together. Cynhaearn, your people need you to protect Mwyngloddiau."

Aurddolen was thoughtful.

"Perhaps you are right, Cludydd, and I was mistaken. You must face the Malevolence, an astronomer is needed to fix the position and, apart from Sieffre to protect Hedydd, that is all. We will return once we have seen you safely out on to the ice."

Some of the other cludyddau and warriors were disappointed not to be part of the expedition but most accepted the wisdom of returning to their communities as the Malevolence reached its peak. September noted that everyone was confident that she would overcome the evil, a confidence that she did not share. She did not reveal her doubts.

September had intended to leave the party while they made their slow progress across the icecap. She had expected to continue to respond to appeals for help from across the Land but she realised that her priority had to change. Now, she must guard Hedydd until they got to the site that Eryl had identified. The persistent clamour for her assistance must be ignored. She knew it meant more pain and death but facing the Malevolence at the Conjunction was her most important, and perhaps her only, task.

All the supplies were piled onto the remaining sledge. Sieffre and Hedydd put on the thick furs that would prepare them for the ultra-cold that they would face when they emerged from the mine. A group of miners dragged the sledge through the final few hundred metres of tunnel with the rest of the party following.

Pale light showed from the tunnel opening. The days on the icecap would be short and they would be travelling as much through night as through daytime. Icy air blew into the tunnel, making the unprotected party retreat. Hedydd and Sieffre put their heads through the halters of the sledge, as did September.

"Farewell," Aurddolen called, "I had hoped to be beside you when you faced the Malevolence for the last time but I accept that your plan is for the best. Our best wishes go with you." There were loud calls of agreement.

The three travellers pushed forward and dragged the sledge over the remaining few metres of rough rock. They reached the ice and as the runners began to slide more smoothly, they emerged from the tunnel and were surrounded by the white wilderness. Their breath froze in the air and fell as fine snow.

They headed north. At first all three of them pulled on the sledge but it soon proved easier for Sieffre and Hedydd to walk while September, in the form of the panther, towed the load. They travelled for hours under the star-filled night sky until Sieffre decided that Hedydd needed to rest. They set up camp with September calling up a protective dome of plwm and using the power of aur to warm them. After eating, Sieffre and Hedydd slept together in the single tent while September watched.

In the morning they set off before it was light, setting the pattern for the following days. It wasn't long before the first attack by a manifestation; a Pwca in the form of a giant polar bear. September vapourised it, and destroyed all the other forms of the Malevolence that harried them.

Day after day they pushed northwards through blizzards and fair weather, meeting manifestations time after time. The Sun spent less and less time above the horizon until one day they did not see it at all. All the while, Hedydd directed them. She carried an instrument which she referred to frequently. It was a metal-framed box, with sides of a clear material.

"What is that instrument you use?" September asked Hedydd.

"Eryl gave it to me just before the Arsyllfa fell. He said that we should both have one just in case something happened to his."

"I can see from the red colour that the frame is made of copper, but what is the clear material?" The only glass September had seen on Gwlad was cloudy and occurred naturally.

"Eryl told me it was cut from a material found in the rocks of Daear."

September was little the wiser. Inside the box a needle hung from a thread so thin as to be almost invisible. The needle was able to swing horizontally and vertically. When Hedydd held it really still it stopped swinging and pointed in one direction, somewhere northwards and at a steep angle to the vertical.

"The needle is made of haearn," Hedydd explained, "but carries a tiny piece of another kind of rock that exerts an influence on the haearn."

"It's a compass!" September exclaimed.

"I do not know that word," Hedydd said, "But Eryl said that when the Cysylltiad approaches we should follow the direction pointed to by the needle. We will be at the focus of the Malevolence's arrival on Daear when it hangs vertically."

September didn't understand fully how the instrument worked but she knew that it was vital if they were to arrive at the correct place.

Whenever the sky was clear Hedydd also observed the stars and checked her observations with figures in a book she carried. She told them precisely how many days it was till the winter solstice and the day of the Conjunction.

The days went by and they travelled constantly but September saw the effect that the cold and the constant attacks by manifestations were having on her companions, especially Hedydd. They got slower and slower and covered fewer and fewer kilometres towards their destination. With a few days to go to the Conjunction it was apparent that they would not reach the point that Eryl had calculated. As they rested in their grey cocoon, September made a suggestion.

"We are not going to be in position if we go on as we are so I suggest that I carry you."

"You cannot carry us and our sledge, Cludydd," Sieffre said.

"I know. You must leave it hidden here with the tent and most of the supplies. Just bring enough food with you to give you energy to walk back here. I can carry you to the place of the Conjunction quickly but it will take you days to make your own way back."

"Can you not bring us back after your confrontation?" Sieffre asked.

"No, I probably won't be here. You know the stories about the last Conjunction better than I do. You know that Breuddwyd never reappeared once the Malevolence was defeated."

"That is true," Hedydd nodded.

"You are exhausted," September went on, "I think you should rest for a couple of days, get your energy back so that you can walk once you have led me to the place I need to be."

"Your suggestion is sensible," Sieffre said, "We should bury most of our equipment in the snow but make a beacon that will guide us back here."

They built a snug igloo from the ice in which they stored the equipment and food and rested in comparative warmth for two days. Sieffre devised a flag and pole that he hoped would survive the fierce winds that blew across the ice.

On the morning of the day before the solstice according to Hedydd's calculations, September changed again into the panther. Hedydd and Sieffre mounted her, wrapped in their thickest, warmest clothes and carrying packages containing food rations. Hedydd grasped her instrument. September set off, racing across the flat plain of ice and snow. She leapt across crevasses, bounded up hills of ice, galloping as far as possible in a straight line in the direction given by Hedydd. They moved so fast that attacking manifestations were left behind. They travelled through the dark day and into the night. Hedydd leant forward to shout in September's ear.

"Stop please, I must check the instrument."

September skidded to a halt in a flurry of ice fragments. Hedydd sat perfectly still.

"We are nearly there, just a few hundred more paces in that direction." She pointed across the white wilderness. September trotted on for a few minutes more until Hedydd called a halt again and dismounted. September returned to her normal self and the three of them looked into the instrument. The needle glinted in the starlight hanging vertically from its thread.

"We're here," Hedydd announced, "and the solstice will not be long."

"Right, that's it," September said, "Go now. Get as far from here as possible. I don't know what's going to happen but I don't want you harmed."

Sieffre and Hedydd knew she was right.

"Goodbye, Cludydd. May all the planets be with you," Sieffre said.

"They will," September agreed, "Make sure Hedydd gets to safety. The Land needs her knowledge."

The man and woman trudged off occasionally looking back over their shoulders.

September watched them go feeling a great sadness. Was this the last time she would see them or any other inhabitants of the Land? Was her time in this universe really nearly over? She looked up into the sky. There was no cloud and it was full of the sparkling points of stars. She knew that there were no planets to be seen. They were all lined up with the Sun on the other side of the Earth. At this very moment the Moon was sliding across the face of the Sun causing an eclipse. All seven heavenly bodies were hidden from view. The time of the Conjunction had arrived.

14

The air was still and September felt calm too. This was the moment all her time on Gwlad had been aiming towards; her destiny, if anyone believed in that idea. She wasn't sure if she was afraid because she did not know what she had to fear. She just stared up at the hemisphere of stars, almost as bright as when she travelled amongst them.

Directly overhead there was a spot of dark amongst the stars that seemed wider than others. She looked at it, intrigued. The patch of black grew, but unlike a cloud obscuring the stars it seemed to push the stars around it apart. Space itself was being distorted. The circle of dark grew and the bunched up stars formed a bright ring around it. She watched, uncertain what she was seeing. The air around her started to move. Air was blowing down on her from the sky and then she understood. Her birthmark was hurting. The Malevolence was coming.

The circle of darkness covered a quarter of the sky above her and the wind had grown into a hurricane that swirled about her. The darkness from above the stars was coming down to Daear and blowing away everything before it. Descending to her was a funnel so black it didn't just absorb light, it destroyed light.

Then she heard the spirits. They didn't make any noise but they were in her head. There were no words, just a single raw emotion – hate. They were coming down to her, descending from their realm above the stars to claim the world. This wasn't just the few hundred or thousand spirits that gave a semblance of life to the manifestations, but millions, billions of them, all with one aim – to destroy.

She knew what her task must be. She had to stop them, send them back to their place above the stars. They must not be free to roam across the Land. Now was the time to use all the power of the Maengolauseren, all the power of the stars, to throw back the tide of Evil.

The wind whipped her hair but her glowing raiment was unaffected. September stood firm and raised her hand bearing the starstone high above her head. Now she was scared. The Malevolence filled her with fear for the people of Gwlad, for the communities, for the rivers and forests, the mountains and plains, the desert and the ice. If she was unable to stop the evil coming then all would be destroyed. Oh yes, she was afraid. But fear gave her power. There were other emotions that filled her- anger at the Malevolence, compassion and love for the people of Gwlad, sadness for those that had died, joy that she had the power to oppose the evil, surprise that she, September, was here as the saviour of the universe and lastly hope that the final battle would be won. The energy of all the stars in the sky and all the planets was channelled through her.

"YMADAELWCH!" she shouted, "BE GONE!"

A cone of violet sprang from the stone and rose up into the sky spreading swiftly. It climbed higher and higher, opposing the dark, throwing back the screeching spirits.

"You won't do it you know."

September flinched, dropping her hand and turning around. The light died. Malice stood on the ice, clothed in darkness, with her arms folded nonchalantly.

"You!" September cried and was left speechless. She had expected Malice to appear but her casual stance took her by surprise. The wind roared around her but her twin appeared unconcerned. She looked at September with a sly grin. September felt her anger grow stronger, wilder.

"What do you mean? I have the power of the stone and all the stars and planets to call on. I will push the Malevolence away from the Earth."

"No you won't. Your tiny universe is nothing compared to the infinity of the dark. You cannot plug the hole caused by the Conjunction because you do not hold all the power of the stars."

"But I do. I am the Cludydd o Maengolauseren."

"No, I told you once before. It should have been me but regardless of which of us lived and which of us died we grew in the same womb. There is a bond between us. I realise that now and it is what gives me strength. The power in the universe is shared between us, but whereas you have just a few thousand stars to help you, I have the billions of spirits that have been driven into the dark."

September didn't want to believe what Malice said but what confidence she felt was ebbing away.

"You haven't seen me for months. You don't know what power I've got."

"I have and I do."

"What do you mean?"

"I have followed you for every moment of your crusade across this pitiful land. I have been your shadow, hidden from sight, but there behind you or by your side. I have watched you show off your minuscule powers to oppose the forces I sent to test you."

"You were there?"

"Every moment. I saw you proudly come to the rescue of those feeble creatures you called friends. They hailed you as their saviour but they didn't know how mistaken they were. And now you think you can oppose the Malevolence. You have no chance and I will dispose of you myself."

Her grin was replaced by a grimace of concentration and she thrust her arm towards September. A bolt of pure blackness hit September in the chest. She sprawled on the ice, the gale roaring around her filled with the screams of the descending spirits. She raised herself up onto her knees and threw her own violet light at Malice. Malice staggered but didn't fall. She took a few paces towards September and fired another black hole of darkness at her. September fended it off, but the force pushed her down again. Another followed, and another. She sank lower and lower, stretched out on the frozen plain. Above her, the dark spread across half the sky.

Malice stood over her.

"I could have just blown you away, but I wanted you to know that you had failed."

September tried to lift her hand holding the starstone. It felt so heavy. She opened her hand and willed the violet beam to ignite. A pale wisp of light appeared that Malice just dismissed. September sank back exhausted for the first time since she had returned from the planets.

"Seventh born you may be, but this is the seventh coming of the Malevolence and now, with me, it is has grown to such power that no Cludydd can oppose it."

This wasn't how it was supposed to be, September thought, I am not strong enough.

"And now I will destroy you, take your power for myself," Malice went on, extending her hand down to September, "and claim your spirit for the Dark."

A dark shadow sprang from Malice's hand, enveloping her. September felt bitter cold touch her skin, the cold of the Dark. Her body was becoming numb, her mind filled with the chants of hate. Her limbs stiffened, her heart-beat slowed. She must get away from Malice's power. Symudiad was the only way out. She forced her hand holding the starstone to open.

A trickle of blue light sprang from the stone, it ran down her arm, flowed across her chest. Where it met the darkness it crackled and spat. The trickle became a stream washing across her body, fizzing and spitting where it met the cold shadow. The two forces fought for supremacy. September could no longer see Malice or the darkness of the Malevolence. She could not feel the wind or the ice on her back. She was engulfed in blue light.

Part 4

~

Partnership

15

She kept her eyes firmly shut, her fists clenched and did not move. The ultimate cold of Malice's black light no longer burned her skin. The symudiad had worked; she had moved out of Malice's reach. The surface beneath her was not hard, cold ice. The softness and warmth was familiar and yet she did not recall experiencing it recently. There was something between her and the surface, something that covered her body but was not the incorporeal light which had clothed her for weeks. Memory came.

Home! She was in her bedroom, lying on the floor, the carpet beneath her, wearing her sleep shirt. Relief washed over her. She was safe; no longer the subject of the Malevolence's hate; away from Malice's spite. Relief was soon replaced by another emotion – regret. No more was she the Cludydd o Maengolauseren with miraculous powers. She was back to being simple September Weekes, fat and weak and stupid. She cried and sobbed for the fit, firm body she had lost and the respect that people gave her.

Another memory and emotion washed over her – guilt. She had failed. She had left the Land under the Malevolence's dominion. Malice was free to wreak her vengeance. She had failed the task that had been set her and now Aurddolen, Hedydd, Sieffre all the other cludyddau and the people of Gwlad were left to their own defence. It was too much to bear. She screamed and thrashed, hammering her hands and feet against the carpeted floor.

Distantly through her tears and misery she heard movement. Running, shouting, more hurrying feet. Fingers gripping her flailing arms, her body held against another, her closed hands pressed against her chest, a face close to hers. A familiar smell and feel - Mother.

"What's the matter, Ember? A bad dream?"

She struggled to speak. Words spilled out incoherently

"Starstone. Malevolence. Land. Malice."

Breuddwyd gasped and held her tighter.

"Go, Julie. Get a glass of water or something, but leave us. Ember needs quiet."

Feet retreating. Peace.

"What did you say, Ember? Slowly now. Tell me what is troubling you."

She drew a deep breath, "I failed. I couldn't send the Malevolence back above the stars. I failed the Maengolauseren. I let everyone down and now they will all die."

"No. It can't be true. That is my dream."

September opened her eyes and saw the horror in her mother's face.

"A dream? No. I've been away for months."

"No, Ember. You have been nowhere. It is still the night of your birthday. You've had a bad dream."

She couldn't believe it. Her experiences were so real, particularly the most recent ones - the ice and cold and the disappearing stars, the descending spirits, and Malice's assault.

"No, I was there. I travelled across the Land. I was the Cludydd o Maengolauseren. I had powers. I disposed of all sorts of manifestations that were killing people and destroying their homes. I was supposed to send the Malevolence back. I didn't."

"But that was my dream. I had it more than thirty years ago, before I had April, before I met your father. Dream or vision, it was God testing me. He sent me to a place that was a kind of hell. A hell filled with kind people who respected me but knew nothing of Jesus or our Father in heaven or the goodness of the Holy Spirit. They did not believe in the love of God. They just believed in evil, the Malevolence as you and they called it. I did what they wanted and learnt their ways hoping they would turn to Christ, but the vision ended."

"It wasn't a vision, Mother. It's real. I don't know where or how but I was there and you were too."

"I don't know how you could have the same dream. Or perhaps God is testing you too but it was not real for me and it is not real for you. Like you I thought I was there for months but no time had passed when I awoke, so it could not be real. It has stayed in my memory, but it was a dream, it must have been."

"Look, Mother. It has nothing to do with God or what you believe in. The People needed me to clear the Malevolence from the Land as they needed you before me. I don't understand why time passes differently there, but it does. You were there a thousand years before me. It is real, I know it is. Look."

September opened her hand. In her palm was the starstone, the Maengolauseren, clear as glass, cracked into two pieces.

"My stone!" Breuddwyd gasped.

"It's broken!" September cried.

"I found it before I went to the Land," Breuddwyd went on, reminiscing. "It was cloudy at first and then became as clear as it is now. I looked through it at the stars and suddenly I was surrounded by light and then I was there. But when I woke up at home after I performed my task it was gone. I haven't seen it since."

"It was the same for me. I found it, or perhaps it found me. It took me to the Land one night. I only stayed a few hours then, but a couple of weeks later, tonight I suppose it must be although it doesn't feel like it, it took me again. What does it mean that I still have it? Why is it broken?"

Breuddwyd was thoughtful.

"You knew that I had dreamed the same dream?"

"It was not a dream. I was told that the last Cludydd was called Breuddwyd and that we looked similar and that the Cludydd is always the seventh child. Our family has had some kind of link with the Land thoughout their history and the stone appears when the Cludydd is needed at the Conjunction."

"Seventh child. I am the seventh child of my mother, but you're not, you're my sixth child."

"You're forgetting my dead twin, Mother."

"What do you mean?"

"She was born before me, wasn't she?"

"So that was why you asked me if I had given birth to any other children. I wondered how you could have guessed. She was dead in my womb. They had to get her out first so that they could save you."

"She may have been dead but she counts and she exists in the other world, in the Land."

"She does?" Breuddwyd looked excited and happy, "Mairwen lives?"

"She's a servant of the Malevolence. She doesn't know the name you gave her."

"A servant of evil? No!" Breuddwyd's expression had changed to one of horror.

"She calls herself Malice because that's what she feels. She wants to destroy everything because she couldn't live a normal life. She is what stopped me from finishing the task as you had done. She attacked me as I was trying to stop the Malevolence coming down to Earth. I had to get away from her. The starstone brought me back here."

"My child, part of the evil?" Breuddwyd cried, "I was right all along. It is a test from God to prove my faith in his love." She paused to sob; great breast-shaking sobs. Then she stopped and looked straight at September. "It is not finished yet, is it? I have to go back and turn my daughter away from sin so that she can rest in peace."

"What are you talking about Mother? God's got nothing to do with it. I've been sent back; Malice and the Malevolence have won."

"No, it's not over. You still have the stone. It can take you or me back there. Perhaps I can go and rescue Mairwen."

"Is it possible?" It was September's turn to ponder. She looked at the stone in her hand, "Could I really have another chance to save the People?" She was September, the flabby dumb teenager of whom nobody expected anything, but now she had a memory of being fit and mature, of being powerful and someone that people respected and looked to for survival. Whether she had been away for months or no time at all she was changed. She was the Cludydd and perhaps she still had a chance to defeat the Malevolence.

"Yes," Breuddwyd replied, "Once I had used the power of the starstone to drive the Malevolence away from the Earth I found myself back in my bedroom and my hand was empty. That is why I thought it must have been a dream or vision after all. There was nothing to show I'd really been away.

The fact that you still have it must mean that the vision is not over."

September looked at the two pieces of the Maengolauseren. The stone had been cut precisely in half but both parts were clear as they had been when she had used the stone to travel to the Land.

"But why is it broken in two?"

"Perhaps it isn't broken," Breuddwyd said, thought creasing her brow, "Perhaps it has divided itself into two starstones, each able to act like the one did."

"Two starstones?" September picked out one piece from her palm and held it between her thumb and forefinger and manoeuvred the other piece to hold between the finger and thumb of her other hand. She held them up and looked through each in turn. The image seemed to swirl in both of them but there was no whirlpool of light.

"Two starstones for two Cludydds," Breuddwyd said, "You and me."

"You mean we could both go back to the Land?"

"Why not? Together we could deal with Mairwen and get rid of the Malevolence."

"We could save the People."

September gave one piece of starstone to her Mother. Breuddwyd closed her hand around it and a blissful look came over her face.

"Save them from sin and bring them to God."

"I don't think there is a god, Mother, either there or here."

"We shall see my dear. Now shall we try?"

"Yes. No. Wait."

"What is it? You know time passes more quickly there than here. Who knows how much time has passed since you came back."

September leapt to her feet and went to her desk, turning her computer on. A thought was burning through her brain.

"I know, but I need to find something out before we go." The screen lit up and the processor began its laborious boot up sequence.

"What do you want to know?"

"You know how different the universe of the Land is to here. The Sun, Moon and five planets orbiting around the

Earth, or Daear as they call it. The stars which are not stars like the Sun. Nothing else – no galaxies, no other planets. And just the seven metals with amazing powers tied to the planets. Manifestations that are formed from the four elements."

"Yes, I remember Heulyn telling me all that."

"But don't you get it? It's what people thought our universe was like, oh, four or five hundred years ago. Here and now we know that our universe is not like that, but there it really is."

"I don't understand. I never learnt much about space or science. What do you want to find out?" Breuddwyd was mystified.

"I need to understand how the metals and the elements are linked and I want to know what the starstone is made of. I thought it was diamond but the stars aren't diamonds so I wonder what people used to think the stars were made of."

Her computer had woken up and September quickly logged into the internet and started googling frantically. Pages flickered across the screen. Breuddwyd watched from behind her shoulder bemused by what she was seeing. Finally September exclaimed "Yes!" and shut off the computer.

"Have you found out what you wanted, Em?" Breuddwyd asked.

"I think so."

"What is it?"

"I'll tell you when we're there. Let's go."

Breuddwyd looked at the stone in her hand.

"Will it really happen? Will we go to the Land?"

"I don't know, but if there is a chance that I can save the people I met then I've got to give it a try."

"You've changed, September. You're not the silly girl I despaired of anymore. You're intelligent and decisive."

"I've had months to change, Mother. I learnt a lot while I was there. I learnt to use the powers of the starstone. I helped people and they respected me. I had a body I was proud of. Now I'm back here and I look like this," she picked up a roll of fat from her waist. "I'm sick of being this fat, blobby thing. If we get through this I'm going to make sure I'm fitter; and I want to show I'm not a thicko."

Breuddwyd hugged her.

"You're not. You are my darling, brave daughter. We will defeat evil and open people's eyes to Christ."

September didn't reply but pushed herself away from her mother. She reached across her desk and pulled the curtains apart. The sky was dark but for the full Moon now well past its zenith. Only a few stars were visible.

"Let's get going, Mother. You know what to do."

Mother and daughter stood side-by-side holding their pieces of the stone up to the window. September looked through her piece. There were more stars, and yet more appearing, filling all of space, replacing the dark. They coalesced into a bright spot that grew and grew.

The avalanche of violet light burst through and overwhelmed her. She had a glimpse of her mother by her side submerged in light and then she closed her eyes, staggered, reached out to steady herself on her desk. There was nothing within her reach. She fell.

16

She hit the ground, rolled, and continued rolling down a slope. She twisted, dug her heels in, came to a stop, lay on her back and opened her eyes. It was dark; night time without stars or Moon. She was sitting on a hillside. Her hip was sore. There was a smell of burning and decay.

"Em, are you alright?" Breuddwyd ran to her side, hand outstretched to pull her to her feet. September stared at her mother. She was clad in violet light with her white waves of hair framing a young pale face.

"Yes, I'm fine. Mother, you look like, uh, me."

"And you, my daughter, look like I remember myself appearing when I was your age."

"It must be the Maengolauseren – it gives us the body we wish we had." She rubbed her hip; it was itching terribly.

"What's the matter? Why are you rubbing your side?" Breuddwyd asked.

"It's my birthmark. It always itches and gets sore when the Malevolence is near."

They both looked around apprehensively.

"I don't see any manifestations," Breuddwyd said.

"No, but I feel spirits all around me."

"I feel them too. Their hate burns like fire."

"It felt like that when I passed through the sphere of stars into the Dark."

"I didn't do that. I visited each of the planets but didn't wish to go beyond the stars."

"I thought I could defeat the Malevolence before it came to Earth but I was scared stiff. I was surrounded by all their hate. It was the same at the Conjunction when the Malevolence came down and Malice stopped me from doing anything about it."

Breuddwyd gave her a look of sympathetic love.

"Em, my darling. You experienced things here which I

never had to face. At my Conjunction I just raised the starstone. It exploded and that was the end of it; I found myself home in my bed."

September shivered and wrapped her arms around herself.

"They are here now. Their hate is everywhere."

"You're right. It's like a persistent chant in my head."

"The Malevolence must have spread across all the Land after the Conjunction." September felt the consequences of her failure but she saw her mother was thinking.

"They will be aware of us. The Maengolauseren is like a torch that attracts insects. They will take on the form of manifestations and attack us."

"We must cloak ourselves, to hide us from the Malevolence, and Malice."

"A cloak? How?"

"Like this." September waved her hand holding her starstone in a circle over her head. Silvery grey threads appeared winding themselves about her until she appeared to be enclosed in an almost invisible cocoon.

"What did you do?"

"It's alcam and plwm. Do you remember? Tin and lead. They make a shield against the Malevolence. I made it using the emotions, joy and sadness."

"Ah, yes, joy for Iau and sadness for Sadwrn. It's coming back to me now." Breuddwyd copied September's movement and soon she was similarly cocooned in a faint grey shield.

"It seems I have the skills still," Breuddwyd said then looked around. "Now Em, where are we? I don't recognise this place."

September examined their surroundings. There was very little light but she saw that she had rolled a short distance down from a ridge. She took the few steps back to the top. The grass under her feet crumbled to dust. Down below she could just make out a river, a black shiny snake amongst dull black trees.

"I think we're at Amaethaderyn, or to be exact the ridge of the Refuge above the village."

"Amaethaderyn? I don't know it."

"It's where I arrived both times after the Mordeyrn summoned me."

"Ah, Heulyn."

"No, Mother, Aurddolen. Heulyn was your Mordeyrn, a thousand years ago."

"I keep forgetting the time. Where is this Refuge?"

"At the top of the hill, this way." September set off eastwards. After a few paces she spoke.

"Something's not right."

"What isn't?"

"Well, both times I arrived before there was cool damp fresh grass under my feet. This feels dead."

"It feels burned."

"And the air was clean and fresh."

"It smells of death now."

As they approached the summit of the ridge, a dull red glow spread up from the eastern horizon revealing the sky to be covered by an overcast of brownish cloud. The light revealed their destination. September gasped.

"The first time I came there were rings of trees around a stone altar," she explained, "The second time I arrived they had been blown down by a Draig tân."

"It looks as if more than one Draig tân has been here," Breuddwyd said. The fallen trees had been reduced to grey ashes. In the centre was a heap of white dust.

"I think Malice has been here and destroyed every trace of the Refuge out of spite."

"I can't imagine a daughter of mine being so vindictive."

"She may have been your child but she guides the Malevolence now."

Breuddwyd looked sadly at the destruction.

"I wonder if there is any of God's love left in her."

"I didn't see any love of any sort, just hate."

Breuddwyd turned away hiding her face from September.

"Well, there's obviously no-one here. Where is the village?"

"Down by the river. Shall we go?" She pointed down the hillside across what had once been a gently sloping meadow of grass and wild flowers and now looked to be a barren wasteland. "We don't have to walk. Shall we fly?"

Breuddwyd turned back to her, wiping a tear from her cheek.

"Fly, ah, yes. Now how do we do it?"

"Remember the seven emotions, one for each planet?"

"It's coming back."

One moment Breuddwyd was standing in front of her and then there was a giant raven with iridescent blue-black feathers. It flapped its wings and took off. September transformed into her eagle form and joined her mother in the sky. They circled around each other.

"You are beautiful, my love," Breuddwyd cawed.

"And so are you, Mother," September squawked back, "follow me."

She climbed with the raven close behind her. The light was spreading across the ground below, but the Sun was hidden behind the sulphurous clouds. September was dismayed by what she saw. All the grass on the hillside was scorched and the trees beside the river were blackened stumps. The river moved sluggishly as if a thick, oily emulsion. Across the river the clearing where the village stood was an indistinct chaos.

September swooped down and landed beside the lake in what she thought was the centre of the village. She returned to her normal self. The raven landed beside her and became Breuddwyd. September looked around. Nothing was as she recalled. Every wooden hut was flattened, the posts and thatch reduced to splinters and dust. The lake was no more, just a dry shallow depression of cracked mud, the reeds burned to ash.

"This was Amaethaderyn?" Breuddwyd said.

"Yes. It was where Berddig and Arianwen greeted me and Eluned, Catrin, Iorwerth and Padarn gave me gifts. I sailed away from here with Cynddylig and Tudfwlch." Saying the names filled her with a great sadness which fought against the hate she felt from the spirits that occupied the world.

Breuddwyd walked around, kicking at the dust and ashes.

"There's no one here now."

"They must all be dead," September cried, "It's all my fault. I let the Malevolence through. Perhaps everyone in the world is dead."

"You don't know what happened to the people who lived here. Maybe they escaped. Look there are still trees standing." Breuddwyd pointed to the edge of the clearing.

There were burnt stumps of trees at the margins of the village but beyond there seemed to be trunks with branches and leaves.

"Let's explore," Breuddwyd said, transforming into a blue-grey wolf. She ran off. September changed into the panther and followed. They ran across the scorched soil of the allotments where the villagers had grown crops and on into the forest. At first the trees were mere dead poles of charcoal but further on they found signs of life: brown bark, moist green leaves. The trees were packed close together so that Breuddwyd and September had to slow down. They paced warily between the trunks. It was dark as little light filtered down through the canopy from the overcast sky. September noticed a flash of something pale, some distance away between the trees. She set off towards it with Breuddwyd close behind. There it was again, a glimpse of white before it was hidden from view. September hurried, weaving between the trees. This way, that way; there a tail, a leg, a head.

September planted her paws in the leaf-mould and skidded to a halt. In front of her a white tiger stood poised ready to leap at her.

"Eluned?"

The tiger took a step towards her warily, sniffing the air.

"Cludydd?"

The wolf closed up behind her. The tiger retreated. September transformed.

"It's me, Eluned. Don't be afraid."

The tiger changed into a white-skinned, naked young woman. She ran and embraced September.

"You are here!" Eluned cried, and then stepped back in shock as she saw the other glowing blue woman beside September, "Who is this?"

"This is my mother, Eluned. Breuddwyd, the Cludydd before me."

Eluned's eyes were wide with surprise.

"Two Cludyddau o Maengolauseren. It is not known."

"I know. But a Cludydd has not let the Malevolence through before. I failed Eluned. I'm sorry."

Eluned looked grave. "We knew that you had not succeeded on the night of the Cysylltiad. The stars disappeared from the sky. In the morning dark clouds spread down from the north, covering the Sun. There was a stinking wind and dirty rain. Then the evil spirits arrived." Eluned paused, "But it is not safe for us to talk. Manifestations will soon come to hunt us. Follow me quickly."

She transformed back into the tiger and ran away. September and Breuddwyd followed as panther and wolf. Zig-zagging between the trees, they ran as if being chased. Soon September realised that they were. Materialising from the air and springing up from the ground were numerous manifestations of various forms – Cwn annwn, Adarllwchgwin, Tylwyth teg. They were drawn to Eluned as she sped through the forest. They were followed by fire, shafts of flame and gouts of acid. At first Eluned outpaced the manifestations but more appeared through the trees in the direction they were fleeing. Eluned stopped.

September skidded to a halt transforming into her human appearance at the same moment. She raised her starstone and commanded the manifestations to be gone. Violet light exploded out in all directions, disintegrating the manifestations. In a moment the dim light of the forest was restored and they were alone.

"There will be more. Come quickly. It's not far now." Eluned set off again at an even greater pace. She ran so fast that September worried that they might collide with the trees.

They came to a place where the trees were more widely set apart. A thin curtain of silver grey threads hung from the branches. Eluned stopped and became herself. She brushed the threads to the side and stepped through as screeching Coblynau crawled out of the ground and hobbled towards them. September and Breuddwyd followed Eluned through the grey net. September looked back and saw the manifestations halt as though perplexed by the disappearance of their victims. Then she turned to look ahead and her heart leapt with joy. There were people here.

They lay or sat or knelt between the trees, a couple of dozen of them. Eluned stood facing September and Breuddwyd.

"Welcome to the new Amaethaderyn."

September's joy turned to sorrow as she realised that the

few people she could see were the survivors of the destruction of the village.

"Is this everyone?" she asked to confirm her fears. Eluned looked sad.

"It is. The day after the Cysylltiad we were attacked by a huge force of manifestations. We did what we could but few of us escaped."

"You have a shield. Padarn and Berddig are here?"

"Yes, here's Berddig now."

The young cludydd o alcam was approaching them but September was shocked by his appearance. He looked as if he had aged two or more decades and his face showed extreme exhaustion."

"Am I seeing double? What other explanation is there for the appearance of two Cludyddau so alike," he said in a voice lacking the joviality September recalled of him.

"Hello Berddig. I'm September and this is Breuddwyd, my mother, the Cludydd before me," she explained.

"So, you have returned to us. It is unheard of to have two Cludyddau o Maengolauseren" Berddig said wearily, "I am sorry that we have no means of celebrating your appearance among us. Indeed you are lucky to have found us at all."

"You are well hidden," September agreed.

"I didn't mean that. I meant that we will all be overcome by the Malevolence in a short while."

September was horrified by his expression of doom.

"You seem to have no hope," Breuddwyd said.

"Unfortunately that is correct," Berddig admitted, "We lost hope when the Malevolence descended on us at the Conjunction. Now it is just a matter of time before we are all corrupted. Already many have died or turned to evil."

"But you have a defence of alcam and plwm."

"Soon our shield will fail. Padarn is weak to the point of death and I too am tired."

September felt the hopelessness and the sense of defeat that Berddig expressed.

"We can support your powers," she said, raising her stone and summoning a dome of grey to reinforce the metal threads festooned from the trees.

"Thank you Cludydd, but without your energy it will soon

fail and in any case we have no food or water. Only Eluned can venture outside and then only for a short time before she attracts manifestations."

"We saw that," Breuddwyd said, "the wickedness is everywhere."

"The same is happening all over the Land?" September asked as if the thought had just occurred to her.

"Presumably," Berddig shrugged, "The spirits of the Malevolence cover all of Daear. I cannot believe that Amaethaderyn was so special as to be the sole target for the evil wrath."

"Have you not heard from other places?"

"No messages can be sent or received. The atmosphere of hate hinders the power of efyddyn to communicate."

"You mean Catrin can't get through to the other cludyddau?"

"That is what I meant."

September remembered with a shock that since arriving all she had felt was the hate of the spirits and not the chatter of the people that had filled her head before.

"So Catrin is cut off, Padarn weak, you are exhausted, Eluned is hounded by manifestations. What about Arianwen and Iorwerth?"

Berddig's face took on an expression of grief.

"They are gone; to their planets or the Malevolence we do not know, but they are no longer with us."

September felt the loss in her heart.

"What happened?"

"Iorwerth led the defence of Amaethaderyn, of course. He stood firm while all fell around him. With his great sword, Aldyth, he despatched many of the manifestations that attacked us, but their number at last overwhelmed him. I did not see his passing so do not know whether it was the fire of Cwn annwn, the spears of Adarllwchgwin, the spit of Tylwyth teg or the stone hand of Gwyllian, but he was overcome."

There were a few moments of silence and contemplation.

"What about Arianwen?" September asked, trembling with anticipation of the bad news.

"While we ran away to safety, she stayed to bring peace to

the dying and succour to the injured, but she too was a target of the Malevolence. Great numbers of manifestations attacked her and she succumbed to them."

"Iorwerth and Arianwen gone," September sobbed, "All because I couldn't do the job I was given." Tears rolled down her cheeks and she cried. Breuddwyd gathered her to her breast.

"Now, now, my love. It's not your fault."

"Yes, it is. The starstone gave me the power to stop the Malevolence but I didn't use it."

"You said Mairwen stopped you."

"Yes, but I should have dealt with her."

"But from what you said, she has great power too. It is going to take the two of us to tackle her and the evil."

Berddig and Eluned were staring at the two Cludyddau.

"Your sister stopped you sending the Malevolence back above the stars? That is why our People are on the brink of annihilation?" Berddig said.

"Yes." September explained what had happened on the icecap at the time of the Conjunction.

"She was here," Eluned said, "looking like you but clothed in black. She stood at the centre of the village directing the assault, but impervious to any force we used against her. It was she who ensured that the whole village was turned to dust and ash."

"She does indeed wield great power," Berddig agreed, "I do not know what you can do."

September took a deep breath.

"We must do something, but first, tell us how long it has been since the Conjunction. For me it is just a couple of hours."

"This is the dawn of the third day since that night," Berddig said, "On the first day the evil spread across the Land. Late in the day we were attacked. Those of us who escaped made camp here. Yesterday and through the night our shield has been tested by manifestations."

"I ventured out a few times to try to find food and water," Eluned continued, "but as you saw, I am soon beset by the evil."

"You have no supplies?" Breuddwyd asked.

"None," Berddig replied, "We cannot hold out for long. We will weaken quickly and then our defences, even strengthened by your power, will fail and the manifestations will overrun us."

"It must be the same everywhere in Gwlad," Eluned said.

"We have very little time, then," September replied, feeling her resolve returning. "Mother, we must find a way of finishing the task today."

"Yes, Ember, but how?"

"I'm not sure, but first we must find Aurddolen."

"Your Mordeyrn?"

"Yes."

"Where is he?"

"I left him in the mountains, at Mwyngloddiau Dwfn."

"Let us pray that he still lives."

"I hope the Mordeyrn can help you," Berddig said.

"Gold is part of the answer, I'm sure of it," September said, "but you're all important."

"We all want to help while we still live," Eluned insisted.

"Just hold on," September urged, "You must save as many people as possible."

"If Padarn lives today then our defence will hold, but the strain of holding the shield is using up the little energy that he has left." Berddig was still solemn but he had regained some of his customary joy. "We still have faith in you, Cludydd, um, both of you."

"Well, there is no time to lose, we must be away to the mountains," September said.

"How?" Breuddwyd said, "It's a long flight."

"We can go by symudiad."

"What's that?"

"The way we got here. Instant teleportation, like on those Star Trek shows that Father and Gus watch."

"I never learnt how to do that."

"Perhaps you didn't need to. I'll show you. Hold my hand and just think of being with me."

They gripped hands, and September visualised the mining town with its tall grey buildings surrounded by the snow-covered peaks.

Golden light engulfed them.

17

She staggered on the uneven rock of the sloping ground and Mother's weight pressed on her. The golden spots slowly cleared from her eyes but her vision was still obscured by a swirling blizzard. Dark grey walls were dimly visible through the flurry of snow.

"Do people really live here?" Breuddwyd asked. "The temperature must be well below freezing."

"You don't feel cold, do you?"

"I don't feel cold but I feel *the* cold."

"Good. For a moment I wondered if it was just me that the starstone prevented from sensing heat, cold, hunger or thirst."

"No, it was, is, the same for me. It was that lack of need for food or drink or shelter that convinced me that I was living through a dream or vision, despite everything appearing so real."

"I think it is just the Maengolauseren looking after us."

"I prefer to believe that it is God that does that."

September did not want to reply so took a few steps towards the buildings. Breuddwyd hurried after her.

"Where are we? Is this the place you mentioned?"

"Yes, this is Mwyngloddiau. We're on the edge of the town, just inside the shield I put up. That's if it is still here, I can't tell in this blizzard." The sky was dark grey. The Sun had not yet risen over the ridge.

"Well if the buildings survive and there are no manifestations then presumably your defence has held."

"But I can feel the hate of the evil spirits and my hip still hurts."

"Yes, the Malevolence is all around. Where is everyone?"

"Sheltering inside I expect. Come on, we must find Aurddolen."

September marched up an alleyway between the towering walls, with Breuddwyd following after her. They soon reached the small deserted square that September recognised. As they approached the building where Aurddolen lived the door opened and a figure in a golden dress stepped out; a female figure.

"Heulwen!" September exclaimed, astonished at her appearance.

"You have returned," Heulwen said in a strange, resonant but halting, voice, "Who is it that accompanies you?"

September turned to take her mother's hand and draw her forward.

"This is my mother, Breuddwyd, the Cludydd who came before me. You seem to have recovered Heulwen."

The young woman took a moment to take in what September had said.

"Mother? Your mother?"

"Yes, Heulwen. Where is everyone? Is Aurddolen inside? Can we come in?"

Heulwen came out of her contemplation. She stood up straight and tall and seemed to become radiant.

"They have fled to the mines."

"Why? Surely it is safer here inside the dome."

"They ran away, scared and frightened."

"Scared of what? The Malevolence can't get through the shield we put in place."

"They were in awe of my power."

Heulwen glowed with a golden light. She raised her pendant above her head. Red lightning sparked from the golden sun.

"Heulwen!" September screamed.

"What is she?" Breuddwyd shouted.

"You should not have returned here," Heulwen's voice boomed. She directed shafts of orangey-golden light at September and Breuddwyd. They fended off the flashes of energy but stone crashed to the ground beside them, torn from the buildings.

"This is my province now. I hold it for my mistress." She thrust both her hands in their direction and fired bolt after bolt of crimson light at them.

September and Breuddwyd raised their hands holding the starstones. A violet wall appeared between them which the red light broke against and dissipated. The air churned, stirring up vortices of dry snow and rock.

"Who is she?" Breuddwyd shouted, parrying the waves of light.

"The daughter of the Mordeyrn. She fell under Malice's influence. It appears that she has gained some of Malice's power."

"Unless it is Mairwen working through her."

"We must overpower her and drive the Malevolence out of her."

"Together, we have the power, September. Summon all the energy of the Maengolauseren."

Mother and daughter stepped forward, projecting their violet shield before them. Gradually they pushed back the golden torrent that streamed from Heulwen's hands. The girl shouted defiance and redoubled her efforts, but step-by-step September and Breuddwyd approached her. Heulwen continued to fight but her look of shock showed that she realised that she had met a power greater than hers. She edged back towards the doorway.

September and Breuddwyd parted, moving to each side of the golden girl, closing in on her. The violet planes of light encircled and pressed against the desperate golden beams that Heulwen cast at them. The golden light diminished, guttered and was extinguished. The violet shield enclosed her. Heulwen fell to the ground.

The light died from the two starstones and September knelt to examine the young woman.

"She's like she was before, when Malice took her. She's alive but not responding."

"We can't leave her in case the evil power returns to her and she becomes a danger again," Breuddwyd said.

"We had better carry her inside and see if we can find Aurddolen."

They stooped to lift her up and carried Heulwen through the doors into the communal area of the building. There was no sign of a cludydd or the townspeople. They lay Heulwen on one of the stone tables.

"Stay with her, Mother, while I look for Aurddolen. His rooms were upstairs."

"I'll pray for her and keep her under control if she wakes. Take care, my love, there is evil all around."

September nodded and went through the door to the stairs. There was silence as she climbed and no sign of anyone in the first room she came to but a glow emerging from Aurddolen's bedroom attracted her. She stepped through the doorway and stopped in shock.

The room was almost filled with a sphere of reddish-gold light. It was so bright that she shielded her eyes. Its surface flickered but in the moments when the fire almost died she had a glimpse of what was inside the sphere. It was Aurddolen. He was standing with his golden staff and orb raised. It too was radiating light, the almost white, golden light of the Sun. He was unmoving, apparently fixed in his position.

September struggled to find a solution to the puzzle. Aurddolen seemed to be a prisoner trapped inside the sphere of energy. From the colour of the light the sphere had been generated by his daughter. What must she do to overcome it and release him? Why had it not collapsed when Heulwen was defeated by their power?

There was a cry from down the stairs. September turned and ran. Mother was in danger. She leapt down the stairs and ran into the ground floor room. Breuddwyd was retreating from the figure of Heulwen who was now erect on the stone table. Erect but not standing.

Some force was holding her up but her head still lolled to one side and her limbs were limp. She was held in a shaft of red light.

September reached for her mother and drew her back to her. Breuddwyd turned in surprise but relaxed when she saw who was gripping her.

"What happened?" September asked.

"She was as when you left then suddenly this red glow came over her and she was lifted up. I think she is still unconscious."

Heulwen's lips began to move and a voice emerged, but not her own.

"Who opposes my servant?"

"It's Malice. She's controlling Heulwen and speaking

though her," September said.

"No one on Daear can equal my power," the voice of Heulwen went on, "My vengeance will be terrible on those who think they can strike at my servants."

"That is Mairwen speaking?" Breuddwyd asked.

"Mairwen. Malice, whatever. She thinks she has all the power."

"My daughter," Breuddwyd cried and pulling her hand from September's, stepped forward, "Mairwen, listen to me if you can hear me."

"Who speaks?"

"I'm your mother."

The column of red light was convulsed. Heulwen's body was tossed from side to side and shaken. The light seemed to fade for a moment and then was restored.

"Mother? I have no mother. I was born in the dark. Dark was all I knew for an eternity."

"No Mairwen. I carried you, with September, but you died."

"I was denied life. You cast me away. You, like everything in the universe, living or material, will feel my vengeance."

"There is no need for revenge. I held you after you were born. Your body was cold. Nothing could have been done to save you. I loved you. I named you. You are called Mairwen."

"Malice is my name and malice is my nature. You will feel my wrath as my sister did."

"You didn't defeat September. She is here now and together we will make you understand that there is no need for hate when God loves you."

"God? What is god? You shall not stand against me. The Malevolence will complete its destruction of this world and I will direct its power."

"No, Mairwen. That is not the way." Breuddwyd appealed to the figure of Heulwen hanging in the air, "Leave this poor girl. Let us meet so I can show you what I mean by God's love and salvation."

"She has served her purpose, this daughter of the Mordeyrn. Her powers are weak. I will meet you myself with all the powers of the Malevolence to torment you."

The red light died and Heulwen fell to the stone table. She lay in a heap of contorted limbs. Somewhere above them there was a crash of thunder.

"See if she is still alive," September shouted as she ran from the room and bounded up the stairs. She ran into Aurddolen's quarters. The bedroom was in ruins, furniture destroyed and stone ripped from the walls but the golden sphere was gone. Aurddolen was kneeling, his right hand still gripping his golden staff. September ran to him.

"Aurddolen, are you alright?" She righted a stool and helped him on to it. His face was drawn with fatigue and his shoulders shook uncontrollably. He sagged in her arms and looked up at her, at first not seeing her. Recognition came.

"Cludydd! You are still here," he murmured, his voice weak and faint.

"I've come back. I'll explain later, but are you OK? I saw the golden light surrounding you."

"For an unfathomable time I have had to oppose that constricting light. It was the work of my daughter, or rather Malice working through her."

"What happened?"

Aurddolen took several deep breaths, licked his dry lips and spoke.

"It was the time appointed, the moment of the Conjunction. We were in the square – the cludyddau and the people. We expected a feeling of release and hope as you defeated the Malevolence and drove it back above the stars. We thought there might be a visible sign in the north, a burst of your violet light. Instead there was darkness. The northern sky became black and the stars disappeared. The darkness spread. Then the spirits came."

"They couldn't get through the dome?"

"No, but they were all around. We could feel their hate. Cari collapsed, her head filled with the cries of the spirits which deafened her to the calls of other cludyddau o efyddyn. Hordes of manifestations appeared all around and above the barrier. Ilar and Cynwal felt their energy drained by the forces trying to gain entry but thanks to you it held."

"I thought you would be safe inside the dome."

"So did we. Of course we knew something had gone

wrong. We realised that somehow you had been unable to drive the Malevolence from the world and that its full power was being unleashed on the Land."

"What did you do?"

"We didn't know what to do. We had no plans for such an eventuality. Our hopes rested on your success, were focussed on you."

Tears welled up in September's eyes. She held the Mordeyrn in her arms.

"I'm sorry," she cried, "I was ready for the Malevolence, but not for Malice. She overpowered me and I had to escape."

"Where?"

"Home."

"But you have come back. The end has not come yet. You still have the Maengolauseren?"

"Yes. Well, half of it."

"Half?"

"Mother has the other half."

"Your Mother? The Cludydd Breuddwyd?"

"Yes, she's here, downstairs, with Heulwen."

"Heulwen? She is still here?"

"She was. I'm afraid she's dead." If it was possible for Aurddolen to sink even more, he did so. His body seemed to shrink in September's arms. The brief resurgence when he realised that she was back with all her power, gone.

"Tell me what happened after the Conjunction," September urged. Aurddolen didn't answer for a few moments, absorbed in the misery of his loss. Then he spoke in a whisper.

"We met downstairs, all the cludyddau, but I felt impelled to check on Heulwen. I came up here and she was on her feet, her eyes open. I thought that somehow she had recovered, but she was radiating red light and I realised that it was not my daughter I was seeing. She had become a servant of the Malevolence, an acolyte of Malice. She didn't even speak to me but flung her bolts of energy as soon as I appeared. I barely fended them off with the power of aur. She threw more energy at me and I was trapped. I just about had the power to hold her energy at bay but a moment's loss of concentration, I knew, would result in my death or worse. It felt like I stood there for the age of the universe. I do not think I could have withstood her power for much longer. You have saved me, Cludydd."

"For now perhaps."

"But Heulwen is dead, you say. Take me to her." He tried to rise, but his exhausted muscles failed and he collapsed again into September's arms. He pleaded, "Tell me what happened to her."

"She met us when Mother and I arrived. She fought us but together we were able to beat her. She collapsed again into the coma she was in before, but then when I came up here and found you, Malice took her over. Mother told her who she was and Malice went wild, shook Heulwen's body and flung her onto the floor. Malice killed her, not us."

"I would not have blamed you, Cludydd if you had. She was not my daughter and I was a fool to think I could get her back. Where are the others?"

"The others? You mean the people and the cludydds?"

"Yes."

"There's no-one around. The town is deserted."

"What has happened? How long was I trapped for?"

"This is the third day since the Conjunction. Mother and I only got back this morning."

"So Heulwen had two days to wreak the vengeance of the Malevolence inside the dome."

"She bragged to us about making everyone run away."

"But the manifestations were outside the barrier – they can't have left."

September remembered how she and Cynwal and Ilar had set up the barrier as a sphere surrounding the town.

"There's only one place they can be," she said.

"Where?"

"In the mine. The dome is a sphere enclosing the shafts beneath the town."

For the first time a hint of a smile passed across the Mordeyrn's grey, lined face.

"Of course. Heulwen has never been to the mines. She wouldn't have known where the people ran to. They may still be safe if they haven't ventured beyond the barrier, and if it still holds."

"It's still there; there are no manifestations in the town. Malice could only reach inside through Heulwen. She couldn't get in herself."

"Help me. I must see my daughter's body and we must summon the people."

September hauled Aurddolen onto his feet, surprised at how light he felt. She put her arms around him and half-carried and half-supported him down the stairs, his golden staff still gripped in his right hand. In the meeting hall, Breuddwyd stood beside the crumpled body of Heulwen. September released the Mordeyrn when they reached her and he fell to his knees, sobbing.

"This is your Mordeyrn?" Breuddwyd said, with some doubt in her voice.

September knelt beside Aurddolen.

"Yes. He's exhausted. Heulwen had him trapped." She bent close to the Mordeyrn, whispering, "Aurddolen this is my mother, Breuddwyd."

He looked up, and September saw the sadness in his eyes but as he looked from September to Breuddwyd a light appeared and his skin took on a healthier hue.

"Two Cludyddau o Maengolauseren. Perhaps there is hope for us and the loss of my daughter can be assuaged," he murmured looking back down at the still form of the young woman. "Is her spirit amongst the Malevolence or has it returned to the centre of Daear for re-birth? I do not know but while I live and you are here, both of you bearers of the starstone, then we can resist the power of evil." He stood up, creakily, his back bent, an old man, but he gripped his staff firmly and it glowed with golden light."

"Yes, Mordeyrn, we can do it," September said, summoning all the strength and defiance in her voice that she could, "but time is short. Other settlements are exposed to the manifestations. From what we saw at Amaethaderyn the Malevolence is destroying everything and soon there won't be any people left in Gwlad or a land to live in."

Some of the sadness reappeared in Aurddolen's expression.

"You are right but first we must recall the people of Mwyngloddiau Dwfn, if they are indeed hiding in the tunnels. Tell them that Heulwen is no more and that their energy and skills are needed."

"I'll go," September said, "I can find my way around the mines I think. Mother, you and Aurddolen can get to know each other and find a way out of this mess."

September didn't run from the building but holding her piece of starstone aloft transported to the top of the mine workings.

She stood beside the vertical shaft. It was dark and empty. The cage must be at the bottom. There was just a ladder that descended into the depths. How was she to make contact with the people? The shaft was too narrow for her to fly down as the eagle. It would take too long to slither down as the cobra. She jumped. At first she fell swiftly but the starstone in her hand glowed and she slowed. The shaft descended hundreds of metres into the mountains well beyond the defensive dome so the people must be in the side shafts closer to the ground. The violet light from the stone hardly provided any illumination so September used her hope of finding the citizens of the town to summon the power of gold. Bright yellow light burst from her hand holding the Maengolauseren. Now she could see her surroundings. She noticed an opening in the side of the shaft and, slowing her fall, she stepped onto the floor of the adit. Her light lit up a hundred metres of the tunnel before a bend obscured her view.

"Hello, is anybody there?" she called, her voice reverberating off the rock walls. The echoes died and there was silence. Then a distant voice called out.

"Who is that? Announce yourself!"

"It's me, September, the Cludydd o Maengolauseren. It's safe to come back to the surface."

There was no reply but then there was the sound of many feet running over the rubble strewn floor of the shaft. People appeared in the distance and rushed towards her some carrying torches with tiny shards of starstone. With some difficulty the leaders of the crowd stopped metres from her and held their arms out to hold back the people behind them. Cynhaearn and Ilar were amongst the half dozen at the front. They stared at her.

"It is you," Cynhaearn said quietly.

"Yes, I'm back," September said.

"Is the Malevolence defeated?" Ilar asked, hope flickering in her care-worn face.

"No, but Heulwen is dead and the dome still protects the town. You can all come back to the surface."

"How can we trust you?" a voice behind Cynhaearn shouted.

"You let us down," another cried.

"You let the Malevolence fall on us," a third accused. Other voices agreed. September felt guilty and full of remorse but she knew she had to respond.

"You're right. I did let you down – once," she said, "I was not prepared to face the Malevolence and Malice. I couldn't stop the hateful spirits from coming down to the Land. But I am here now with the Cludydd Breuddwyd and together with Aurddolen and you we shall defeat the menace of evil." She was proud of her words but knew that they were empty until she and Mother found an answer.

"We don't doubt you," Cynhaearn said, "and we will fight the evil until there is not one of us left. We are the people of Mynydd Tywyll!" His voice carried back along the tunnel. The dissenters were overwhelmed by the cries of agreement. September could feel the hope and the anger of defiance radiating from them. She felt confident for the first time since she had returned to Gwlad.

"Let us return to our homes," Ilar urged and stepped forward. September turned and with her light led the people to the end of the tunnel. She stood on the edge looking down into the depths and up to the distant faint grey opening.

"Where is the cage to carry you to the surface?" September asked.

"Down there," Cynhaearn replied pointingdown the shaft, "We cut the ropes to stop anyone coming down after us – or up. Hordes of Tywyll teg, Coblynau, and Gwyllian fill the shafts and tunnel beyond the dome. We will have to climb the ladders."

"Is everyone with you?" September said.

"No. We're spread out on various levels," Ilar answered, "but we can send word to the others."

"Come on. We had better start climbing," Cynhaearn said,

staring up at the ladder.

"I'll meet you at the top," September said, "I must get back to Aurddolen and my mother."

"Did you really mean that the Cludydd Breuddwyd is with you?" Ilar asked.

"Yes. She's here to help." September lifted her hand and performed symudiad.

She was back with Breuddwyd, Aurddolen and the still form of Heulwen.

"You have found them?" Aurddolen asked eagerly, but still with fatigue in his voice.

"Yes. I've spoken to Cynhaearn and Ilar. They're starting to climb up the shaft. The lift is broken."

"In that case it will take them some time before they return."

"Some of the people were angry with me," September said forlornly, "they blamed me for the coming of the Malevolence."

"You must expect that, love," Breuddwyd said, "They had faith in you which you were unable to justify. We must do something quickly to restore that faith."

"I'm not interested in people worshipping me," September said, anger rising inside her, "I just want to get the job done – if we can. I want to see all my friends, the people I know, safe." She covered her face with a hand, suddenly. "What am I saying – my friends, Sieffre and Hedydd!"

"What about them?" Aurddolen asked.

"I left them on the ice. Hedydd guided me to the spot that you and Eryl had calculated. They left me there and started to walk back, but it was only hours before the Conjunction."

Aurddolen looked tired and sad.

"They must surely have perished when the Malevolence descended. They were so close to the vortex of spirits."

"No, they can't be dead," September cried, "they helped me. I can't have caused them to die. I must find them."

"September!" Breuddwyd said in the voice that September was familiar with when being scolded, "We have many more people to save. You haven't got time to go off to the polar regions."

"I must. Two people or millions. I must try to save them all." She didn't wait for any more arguments but closed her fingers around her piece of starstone and imagined herself at the site of the Conjunction.

18

It was dark; darker than she had ever known. Even when she had been outside the universe there had at least been the distant spark of the sphere of stars. Here there was no light whatsoever. Her feet rested on ice but she could barely keep her balance. Her head span with the voiceless cries of hate from the torrent of spirits that fell on and around her. September put her hands on her head and screamed to try and block out the piercing wails that filled her mind.

Here was the spot where the Malevolence came to Earth, the portal from beyond the stars. The stars themselves had been pushed aside, the Sun and all the planets still hidden by the bulk of the Earth. Spirits arrived in a ceaseless flow and soared away to spread their hate across the Land.

September sank to her knees, battered by the weight of hate, the agony in her hip spreading across her whole body. She could barely think, but a kernel of herself remained. You're the Cludydd o Maengolauseren. You have the powers of the seven planets and seven metals given to you by your control of the seven emotions. You can get out of this. Protection. Defence. That was what she needed. The thought of what was happening across Gwlad, to the people and the land itself made her sad. Sadness meant plwm. Plwm was security.

A grey shroud of virtual lead formed around her. At once the spirits were repelled. The drumming of their hate decreased. Her pain lessened but didn't fade completely. September breathed in. She could think again. She rose to her feet and stepped away from the focus of the stream of spirits. Direction didn't matter, just displacement from the descending Malevolence. The cloak of lead wrapped around her, shielding her from the hate and vengeance of the spirits.

One metre; ten; a hundred. There seemed no change to the darkness or the column of descending spirits. A thousand metres – was that a glow in the sky? Were the cries of the spirits weaker? Another kilometre and she was sure. She was emerging from the core of the Malevolence. Above she saw a faint segment of the circle of stars forced from their natural constellations. There was no other source of light but she could just make out the ice at her feet and the rough, cold plain stretching away from her into the polar night.

Where could Sieffre and Hedydd be? She couldn't work out directions. With the patterns of the stars distorted there was no Pole Star to point to the north. She didn't know which way to go to retrace the steps they had taken from the mountains to the Conjunction. How could she find them? She wanted to call but shouting would be no good. It was friendship and love which urged her. Love? That implied efyddyn, the metal of communication. Of course. She had the power to communicate through the power of copper. She let the feeling of love for Sieffre and Hedydd wash through her. She held it in her mind. There too were the hateful cries of the spirits; she ignored them as best she could. She called to Sieffre and Hedydd and waited for a reply. Was there one? Were they still alive or were they dead from cold or the manifestations or, a more horrifying thought, turned to evil? She called again and again, but no reply came out of the frozen wastes, until, yes, a faint whisper of response. She grabbed hold of it, concentrated and transported.

The landscape had barely changed. She was amongst cliffs and crevasses of ice and snow, but the stars in the sky were a little brighter and the cacophony of the spirits was a little less, though still hurtful. She must be further from the incoming Malevolence. Where were they? She felt Sieffre's character in her mind. She recognised him now but the call was still weak. She changed into the black panther and padded around trying to locate the source of Sieffre's signal. She raised her snout and sniffed the air for the odour of people. Yes, there it was – just a hint. She followed it and began to scrape with her paws in the snow.

A piece of grey cloth. She scraped more urgently. A leg. A body. Sieffre, and wrapped in his arms was Hedydd. They were cold. Were they dead? No, Sieffre's signal told her he was alive. September changed to her human self and touched

Hedydd. An even fainter call of life came from her. They were alive but close to perishing in the cold. She must revive them, restore them. Compassion. That was the key. Arian, the metal of healing. Her hand holding the starstone turned silver. She pressed it to Hedydd's head. She felt energy pass from her, the young woman warming. She began to stir. September moved her hand to Sieffre and in moments he too began to shiver.

They were waking, moving, sitting up, looking around. They saw her. Their eyes widened.

"Cludydd!"

"September!"

September felt such an overpowering feeling of joy that she flung her arms around both of them, pulling them to her, hugging them and enveloping them in her leaden cloak. Even through their clothes she could feel how cold they were. Nevertheless she felt hope at last for the future. Perhaps she could undo more of the evil caused by her failure to oppose the Malevolence. She felt the energy of aur flowing in her and she passed it to her friends as heat.

"What happened?" Sieffre asked.

"I failed," September said, "The Malevolence got through and is destroying the Earth."

"But you are here," Hedydd said.

"Yes. I came back. We must find a way to defeat Malice and send the Malevolence away. Then I remembered that you were still here on the ice. I had to find you."

"I'm glad you did. I fear we were close to death," Sieffre said, shaking his head.

"It was so dark and cold," Hedydd agreed.

"I felt sure that manifestations would get you," September said.

"We were afraid," Sieffre admitted, "When we left you we hurried as fast as we could to get away. We saw violet light and shafts of darkness."

"That was me and Malice fighting," September nodded, "I couldn't overpower her. I had to escape back home. I ran away."

"We understand," Hedydd said kindly, "Malice had the force of all the Malevolence with her."

"The light disappeared," Sieffre went on, "and then darkness spread across the sky and a countless number of spirits was all around us. Each one was speeding off to the ends of the Earth."

"Their cries of hate were unbearable," Hedydd said, "Sieffre suggested that we should bury ourselves in the snow to hide from manifestations. That's what we did, but it was so cold."

"But the spirits passed over you and rushed on to take on their forms elsewhere," September said, "I'm just so pleased that I have found you."

"How long were we buried for?" Sieffre asked, "I lost track of time and then we just drifted into the sleep of the dead."

"It is the morning of the third day since the Conjunction. The spirits have spread across the Land. Settlements are under siege and the country is being destroyed."

"Then why are you here?" Sieffre demanded to know, "There is a world to save."

"I know, but I couldn't do anything before I knew what had happened to you."

"We don't matter. The future of Gwlad does."

"I must get you back to Mwyngloddiau."

"How? Even on the back of your panther it would take days and your eagle cannot carry both of us. You cannot afford the time. We have seen the numbers of spirits that have come to lay waste to Daear." Indeed an endless procession of the screeching spirits continued to pass over their heads.

September stared at Sieffre. She hadn't thought how to rescue Sieffre and Hedydd once she had found them.

"Symudiad. I must transport you," September stated.

"You mean, from here to there in an instant," Hedydd said.

"Yes."

"But I thought only you could perform that miracle," Sieffre said doubtfully, "You alone of all the cludyddau have shown that skill. It is not mentioned in any of the tales."

"You're right, I know, it's never been done," September said, "I didn't think of it before but there is no other way. I have to try." She was thinking hard. How could she carry Sieffre and Hedydd with her when she teleported from one place to another? She needed a way of linking together, of reinforcing the bond between them, so that they stayed as one when she moved. Reinforcement. The quality of alcam. She was filled with joy. That was it. She turned her hand above her head and bands of silver-coloured tin formed a helix binding the three of them together. Sieffre and Hedydd looked around at the strips of metal winding around them.

"Cludydd?" Sieffre said, "Will this work?"

"I don't know but hold on tight. We're going." Sieffre and Hedydd flung their arms around her. September raised her hand with the starstone and thought of Mwyngloddiau Dwfn. Golden light fanned out from the stone enclosing them in a cone.

September staggered. Sieffre and Hedydd fell to the ground as the tin ribbons dissipated and they released their grip on her. They sprawled dazed on the floor of the Mordeyrn's meeting room. September looked around and saw an expression of delight appear on Aurddolen's face.

"I can scarce believe it, Cludydd," he said, "you found them and returned with them."

"How did you do it?" Mother asked looking astonished, "I never learnt this skill."

"I didn't know I could do it either," September admitted, "but I combined the power of tin with the starstone and just, sort of, brought them with me."

"Well, good, but you used up a good hour of the morning," Mother scolded, "We must get on and decide what we are going to do about disposing of the Malevolence."

September thought she sounded as if she was just going to do a spot of cleaning not dealing with the biggest threat to the existence of the universe.

"Yes, Mother, any ideas?"

Sieffre and Hedydd crawled onto cushions and sat staring at the two Cludyddau and the Mordeyrn in awe. The door opened and Ilar staggered in, panting hard. Behind her was Cari. As similar as twins with their white skin and black hair, now they both looked exhausted after their climb from the mines. For a moment they both stood leaning on the door and staring in wonder at the two Cludyddau, Aurddolen, Sieffre,

Hedydd and the body of Heulwen.

"Come in, come in," Aurddolen called, sounding more like his old, powerful self, "Join us, cludyddau, your knowledge will be invaluable."

"The people…?" September began.

"Climbing the ladders," Cari replied, "Cynhaern and Heulfryn are organising the queues, Cynwal and Isfoel are checking the tunnels."

"And Ariannell is caring for the sick," Ilar added.

"Good, good," the Mordeyrn, muttered, "Let us to business. We must hasten to devise a way of defeating Malice and of driving the Malevolence from the Land."

"It is a daunting task," Sieffre said, "The number of spirits coming from above the stars is too many to measure."

"More and more manifestations crowd around our defences," Ilar said, "We looked into the sky when we reached the surface and saw flocks of Adarllwchgwin covering the dome and Draig tân falling towards us one after the other. I'm not sure how much longer the barrier can absorb these energies."

"The Malevolence is here," Breuddwyd said, "but why? What does it need?"

"It has no needs," Aurddolen asserted, "Destruction is its sole ambition. It wants to destroy every living thing and every scrap of matter. It wants to eliminate the whole universe."

"Your universe," September corrected, "the structure and laws of your universe are different to mine."

Aurddolen looked confused.

"You're right, Cludydd. I cannot speak for your universe, but who knows what could happen if the Malevolence succeeds here."

"What can we do?" Cari asked.

"We must find Malice/Mairwen, and stop her from wielding her power," September announced.

"How?" Ilar asked.

"I'm not sure, but I think that is your job, Mother. She responded to you. OK, she killed Heulwen but you gave her something to think about."

"She is my daughter."

"Exactly, and that gives you some influence, although I'm not sure how you are going to use it."

"But even with Malice dealt with, the Malevolence remains amongst us," Aurddolen said.

"Yes, and it is my task, still, to send it back where it came from," September said firmly, "but before I can do anything I need answers to some questions that I have."

Aurddolen sat on one of the stone tables, still holding his staff upright.

"I'll try to help you," he said.

"We all will," Ilar insisted.

"You said that the Malevolence wants to eliminate the whole universe, not just this world. You mean the planets and stars as well?"

"The planets, yes. The evil spirits will spread out from Daear and devour all the planets."

"That's because the planets and Daear are basically made of the same stuff?"

"Yes." Aurddolen nodded.

"So the seven metals and the four elements are the same thing?"

"The four elements make up each of the metals in different proportions. That is correct."

"But the stars are different aren't they?"

There was a hush as everyone looked to Aurddolen to answer.

"Yes." Aurddolen's eyes had a look of expectation as if he knew that September had an insight.

"The stars and the Maengolauseren are made of a fifth element that's called quintessence in my home. Is that right?" September recalled the information she had gleaned from the internet.

"Yes. In the old tongue it is called egwyddorpum."

"Nothing else on Daear or the planets is made of this quintessence."

"It may be at the centre of Daear but out of our reach" Cari explained, "We just find tiny fragments of starstone that we use for lighting but they are hardly bigger than particles of dust."

"Nevertheless, without egwyddorpum the universe would

not exist," Aurddolen said, "The emanation of egwyddorpum fills the universe from the centre of Daear to the sphere of stars. It is what makes time and space. Outside our universe there is neither."

"But the Malevolence cannot control it like it does the other elements?"

"You are right., The spirits of the Malevolence are from above the stars. Until the Cysylltiad they could only exist here by moulding the elements to their forms and still they must do that to exert their hate. They cannot use egwyddorpum but they can imprison it, nullify its life-giving power. That is the ultimate aim of the Malevolence," Aurddolen said with a tone of great sadness.

"The end of everything," Hedydd sighed.

"The destruction of space and time and all that is within it." Sieffre shook his head in disbelief.

"But the Maengolauseren opposes the Malevolence and can defeat it?" September asked, needing reassurance.

"Oppose yes. Defeat no. All that can be done is to push the Malevolence from within the sphere of stars. Usually the forces of the planets are enough to hold it at bay but as you know at a Conjunction that defence fails and then only the power of the Maengolauseren can push it back. That has been the pattern until this cycle and the appearance of Malice."

"That is my task and I must succeed." September slammed the fist holding her piece of starstone into her other palm.

"If Cludydd Breuddwyd can subdue Malice, perhaps your power can force the Malevolence back above the stars," Aurddolen stated, looking worried as if he was not certain that she could do it.

"The Malevolence has spread across Daear. It will be harder for me to round up all the spirits and send them back," September said.

"The power of the planets and the cludyddau can help," Ilar said.

"But the cludyddau are spread out across the Land. Most of them don't even know that Mother and me are here," September said.

Aurddolen sagged again. "That is true. The spirits have brought chaos to our community."

"My mind is filled with their hate," Cari said, holding her head in her hands, "I cannot hear my fellows."

"But perhaps there's another way." An idea had come to September. Aurddolen looked interested. "The seven metals are each mixtures of the four elements. So they're all the same really. Lead is made of the same stuff as gold."

"That is true but…" Aurddolen looked perplexed.

"Back home when people believed all this stuff about four elements, some of them thought that other metals could be turned to gold."

Aurddolen's mouth dropped open.

"That is heresy!" he thundered.

"How can you shout heresy when you don't believe in God the Father and Christ his Son," Breuddwyd cried, her eyes blazing.

"Mother, calm down," September urged, "This isn't about religion."

"I don't know who your God or this Christ you call on, are," the Mordeyrn said in a more controlled voice, "but to suggest that one metal can be converted into another goes against all our understanding. Cludydd, you know yourself that each metal is associated with a single planet; Aur with Haul, Arian with Lleuad and so on. How can the metals of one planet be converted into the metal of another?"

"But you agreed that each of the planets are themselves made of the four elements," September replied, convinced she was onto something.

"Yes," Aurddolen nodded, "but even so…"

"Mordeyrn, you are ignoring the tales," Cari said.

"Tales?"

"Yes. You know the stories of the Cemegwr."

Aurddolen waved his hands dismissively.

"Mere myths told to children."

"They are not children's stories," Cari insisted, "They are passed from one cludydd o efyddyn to another."

"I too have heard tales of the Cemegwr, on my journeys," Sieffre said, "but they seemed like strange fantasies."

Aurddolen sighed and seemed to shrink.

"The Cemegwr are a fabled people who claimed to have created the world," he explained, "It is said they live apart from the rest of our communities and have nothing to do with cludyddau or their powers. It is claimed they are able to mix water, earth, air and fire to make strange materials and metals, especially gold. But they are stories told by people who have no knowledge of the powers of the metals or planets."

"Why gold?" September asked, "It doesn't have the same value here as at home. You don't use money."

"You are right. All the metals have their powers and uses that are invaluable but the Sun is the greatest of the planets as it provides warmth for all living things on Earth, so Aur is the first among the metals. It is why I, the Prif-cludydd o aur, am considered the Mordeyrn of all the peoples of the Land, though I am hardly worthy of such prominence. In the absence of the Cludydd o Maengolauseren the cludyddau o aur wield the greatest force opposing the Malevolence."

"Perhaps these Cemegwr have skills that I could use," September wondered.

Aurddolen's cheeks turned red and he looked as though he was about to explode.

"They do not exist, I tell you. Their powers are mere myths."

"You do not know that that they don't exist," Breuddwyd said gently but firmly, "you may deny the stories but if you have made no attempt to disprove the legends then how can you be sure?"

"But they claim to control the power of the metals without the authority of the planets given to cludyddau. They contradict all that has been revealed to us." Aurddolen was defensive now rather than angry.

"You seem to know quite a bit about them," September said.

"Of course I have heard the rumours, but there is nothing written about them in any of the books. Heulyn wrote nothing about them."

"I don't remember hearing anything about them," Breuddwyd agreed.

"Nevertheless, the stories go on," Cari insisted, "Perhaps it is the same one circulating over and over again, or perhaps there are occasional contacts with the Cemegwr that keep the rumours alive."

"I think they could have something to offer us," Ilar said soothingly, "we must not reject their ideas because they differ from ours."

"But how are you going to find them if so little is known about them?" Sieffre asked.

"We have no time for pointless quests," Aurddolen said, "Our priority must be to find a way of assisting the Cludydd in opposing the Malevolence."

"I think the Cemegwr are the only lead we've got," September said, "but Sieffre's right. Where are they?"

No one spoke for a while but September could see that Cari was thinking hard. Eventually she spoke.

"From what I recall, some tales of the Cemegwr mention Coedwig Fawr."

"Coy what?" September asked.

"Coedwig Fawr, The Great Forest," Ilar explained, "It stretches from the foothills of Mynydd Tywyll to the Northern River."

"I remember flying across it," September said, "It's vast."

"And dense," Sieffre said, "many parts are impenetrable. There are few tracks or paths that cross it."

"Perhaps that's how the Cemegwr, like it," September noted, "Stop people blundering in on them."

Cari had more to say, "The tales come from woodsmen and charcoal burners who supply the mines and foundries here in the mountains. Just once in a lifetime perhaps they come across these people who act differently."

"Differently?" Breuddwyd queried, raising an eyebrow.

"They are just normal people who for some reason have been cut off, probably because they have no cludydd o efyddyn," Aurddolen said.

"Perhaps, but these people shun contact, and are hostile to cludyddau," Cari explained.

"I'm not surprised if the cludyddau consider them to be heretics," Breuddwyd said.

"Right, so I need to go to this Coedwig Fawr, and listen out for secretive people who are different," September said, determined to make a start on something, "I'd better go."

"Wait," Aurddolen said, "Even if these people, these so-called Cemegwr exist, even if you find them, they may be servants of the Malevolence."

"In which case I have wasted time as they won't have the answer to my problem but until someone comes up with a better idea, I'm going."

"I'll help you," Breuddwyd said.

"No Mother, you must track down Malice, find out from where she is controlling the Malevolence and think of ways of stopping her."

Breuddwyd nodded.

"So first I need to get into the forest. Cari, give me an image of the most remote and apparently unpopulated place you know."

The young cludydd o efyddyn closed her eyes. September saw in her mind a dark place under immensely tall trees so close together that their branches intertwined. September closed her hand around her starstone and moved.

19

She was standing ankle deep in dry, fragrant pine needles. It was dark, but not the darkness of the Malevolence in the polar night but because the thick foliage far overhead blocked out the rays of the Sun. Just a dim green illumination reached the ground. In each direction September saw tree trunks, crowding together, straight and tall, reaching upwards for the light.

There was less noise in her head from the spirits of hate. The spirits must be well above her in the sky above the forest. For some reason they had not descended between the trees. Then she noticed that the pain in her hip, a constant companion since she had returned to the Land, had lessened to an irritation. Something in this forest was resisting the Malevolence, keeping it at bay. September summoned the power of efyddyn to listen for mental chatter. There was less interference from the hate of the spirits but at first there was nothing else. She concentrated, amplifying the soundless voices in her head as much as she could bear. Yes, there was a hint of something else, different in quality to any cludydd or person that she had hitherto had contact with. It was self-contained and confident but it seemed distant, very distant and difficult to pin down.

September changed into the panther and set off in the direction she thought the mind signals came from. She loped through the trees, their closeness preventing any attempt to move in a straight line or at speed. She made a few false starts, the signal weakening as she moved. At last she found a direction where the thoughts became stronger although they were still incomprehensible. She padded carefully through the forest using all her feline senses to detect her quarry. She picked up a strange scent. It contained wood smoke but there were other components. Sulfur and chlorine she recognised from home, school and swimming pools, but others were unfamiliar. There were sounds now as well; the crackling of fires, of hammers falling on metal. Still, though, the projections of the mind were weak and more like a shaft of light leaking from around a closed door than the bright beacons that were the cludyddau or the flaming torches that were the minds of normal people.

The trunks of the trees became more widely spaced but still close enough for their branches to overlap. She froze when she stumbled in to the clearing. There was a space where no trees grew although the foliage of the trees at the edge of the circle still formed a canopy high above.

At first she thought the clearing was empty but as she looked around she caught sight of a different image like looking at the myriad broken shards of a mirror. If she looked straight ahead she saw nothing, but at the edge of her vision she had glimpses of a different scene. She turned her head away and tried to see without looking directly.

At the centre of the clearing was a forge. There were four people working at the furnaces tending the fires, stirring the contents of ceramic pots and hammering on an anvil. They wore identical clothes of rough brown tunics and trousers and all had light brown hair. Only the men's beards and the women's bosoms revealed that there were two of each gender.

September returned to her normal form.

"Ah, so you have found us at last." The woman stirring the pot paused in her action and, looking directly at September, called out "Join us, holder of egwyddorpum." The image seemed to crystallise in front of her as if all the pieces of the mirror were coming together to form one. She saw clearly at last.

"You expected me?" September took a step forward. Each of the people had stopped in their tasks to look at her.

"Of course. We felt your arrival in the forest and followed your attempts to locate us." The woman looked young, with long hair tied back.

"You didn't give me a signal to find you easily."

"It was not for us to guide you but for you to find us. You have succeeded."

"You are the Cemegwr?"

"So we are called." The woman stepped out from the forge and a man who had been hammering took her place, taking over the stirring. The other two resumed their work. The woman directed September to a pair of wooden chairs. She sat in one and indicated that September should sit in the other.

"Show me your egwyddorpum," the woman said in a voice that expected to be obeyed. September found herself opening her hand to reveal the half of the Maengolauseren lying on her palm. The woman's eyes were drawn to it. She seemed to be examining it.

"Ah, but this is but one half of the carregmam. Where is the rest of the Maengolauseren?"

"My mother has it," September replied, surprised that this woman should be able to identify the starstone so clearly. No cludydd, not even Aurddolen, had looked at it as closely.

"Ah, your mother. The previous Cludydd. She has returned to the Land with you." It wasn't a question but a statement of fact.

"Yes. How do you know these things?"

"We listen and we feel the currents in the substance of Daear."

"But you have no contact with the People or with the cludyddau."

The woman waved her hand dismissively.

"Mere children and dabblers in the power of materials."

"You know more than Aurddolen, or Arianrhod or Cynhaearn or any of the cludydd? You don't seem old enough."

"How old do you think I am?"

September looked closely at the woman's unlined face, her glowing skin, long shining hair and smooth hands.

"I'm not sure. You look less than thirty years old but you act as if you are older."

"If you had seen me when your mother came to the Land, I would have looked the same."

"But that is a thousand years ago. Here that is." September was confused and astonished.

"Time does not age me."

"I don't understand." September wanted to know more but

she remembered that she was in a hurry to find a solution to the crisis facing the universe. "But you won't have time at all if we don't stop the Malevolence."

"The evil cannot harm us," the woman said dismissively.

"Why not? I can see that manifestations do not seem to be threatening you. How do you do it without the protection of lead and tin?" September looked up to check that there was no sign of a dome of plwm.

"Because they are no protection. Your powers and those of the cludyddau," she said the word derisively, "attract the evil and can only hold the spirits at bay for a limited time." September recalled the hordes of manifestations besieging Amaethaderyn, Mwyngloddiau and other settlements that used the powers of the metals for defence.

"So you have a better way?"

"The evil cannot harm us," she repeated.

"Is that because the bearers of the starstone before me, such as my mother, kept the spirits from you?"

"They had their little triumphs," the woman shrugged.

"But it's all gone wrong now. I failed. My twin sister, Malice stopped me. Now the Malevolence is pouring down and it will destroy everything. Aurddolen says that the Malevolence won't stop until it has destroyed everything in this universe."

"So space and time will come to an end."

"Yes. Doesn't that worry you?"

"It is an inconvenience but it will not affect us."

"Why not?"

"Because with the power of egwyddorpum we can create a new universe. You know there are many as you come from another yourself."

September was shocked by the assertion but it meant little to her. What did concern her were the people of the Land who she knew and those she didn't.

"Yes, but what about all the people who will die or become spirits of hate?"

"They are no concern of ours nor we of them."

September was disgusted and angry.

"What do you care about?"

"You can have no conception of where our interests lie."

September was annoyed by her haughtiness but she dismissed it.

"I don't care. It's what's happening here that worries me."

"Why do you feel such an attachment for these people? How long have you been on Daear?"

"A few months. It was autumn when I was first called. I know it's been less than one night at home."

"So in a quarter of one year taken out of your lifetime you have come to think of yourself as the saviour of the whole population of Gwlad and everything in it."

"That was my task. Aurddolen told me. Everyone expected me to stop the Malevolence." September was confused. Tears came into her eyes and a sob was growing in her chest.

"And you thought it would be easy?"

"No, I didn't, but once I'd been to the planets and learnt how to use the power of the metals I thought I could do it. Until, until…"

"You failed."

"Yes, because of Malice."

"Partly but not solely. You don't understand do you?"

"What?"

"Who you are and why you are here."

"I'm the Cludydd o Maengolauseren. I have to send the Malevolence back above the stars."

"That's what you've been told. Who are you really?"

September remembered. She was a fat, stupid, silly teenager. She buried her head in her arms and cried.

"I'm September Weekes and I'm useless."

"There's no need to be so hard on yourself."

September peered through her hands at the woman who was looking at her with an inscrutable expression.

"But you said…"

"I asked who you were. I didn't say you were good for nothing. Since you have been here you have been strong and fearless. You have defeated countless manifestations of evil and helped thousands of people. You are who you are and you can be whatever you have the power to be."

"I don't understand."

"That's better. You have admitted the one truth that is important."

"But Aurddolen has explained things to me. I've visited each of the planets."

"And who did you meet there?"

"The spirits of cludyddau who are alive now and who were alive in the past."

"Exactly. All your contact has been with cludyddau who have told you what they think they know and nothing else."

"But their powers are like magic. They do things with metals that would be miracles at home. They understand how this universe works."

"They think they do but they themselves are of this universe and only see part of it. A person standing on a beach can only see a short distance out to sea. A leaf on a tree has no experience of what it is to be a root or the bark of the tree trunk."

September thought she understood the analogies.

"So you're different. You can see and understand more."

"Yes. As I said, we create universes. We made this one. We experiment with modes of existence and this was one."

"You're gods?"

"What does that mean?"

"Creators, all powerful beings."

"No, gods is too grand a term. We inhabit the dimensions from which universes emerge. We are scientists, experimenting, observing, analysing, evaluating."

"Why are you here?" September looked around at the forest clearing, the open fires, the people in the simple clothes. "Why aren't you outside looking at us through some cosmic microscope?"

"Because to truly experience our construct part of us has to live within it."

"But what about the Malevolence?"

"What about it?"

"It's destroying this universe you say you created."

"The Malevolence is everywhere and attacks all the universes."

"Even mine?"

"Even yours. The black holes at the centre of galaxies, gobbling matter – a manifestation of the Malevolence. The cancers that consume your bodies – the same. Viruses neither dead nor alive – yet another.”

September wasn't sure what she was talking about. She wasn't even sure she was following any of this conversation.

“But why let the Malevolence destroy this place?”

“Because it's reached the end of its lifetime. A little soon to be sure but it's degraded so its time has come.”

“What do you mean?”

The woman took a deep breath.

“Let me try to explain. Why are you the Cludydd o Maengolauseren?”

“Why me? Aurddolen told me that it was because I was the seventh child.”

“Good; and how many Cludyddau have there been?”

“People don't seem sure but they think Breuddwyd, my mother was the sixth. So I'm the seventh.”

“And how many metals, planets and principal emotions are there?”

“Seven.”

“Do you see?”

“No. Yes, I see that seven is important but why?”

“We designed it that way. It amused us to set up a universe governed by the principles dreamt up by thinkers from your universe. They believed that the number seven plays a significant role in the workings of your universe. That was before your modern scientists discovered some different truths. It was our intention to run this universe for seven cycles, seven conjunctions using seven Cludyddau to hold back the Malevolence.”

“What went wrong? Why couldn't I do the job.”

“Well things do go wrong. Entropy, chaos. Things wear out. Your twin died.”

“Are you saying that Malice has mucked up your experiment?”

The woman bit her lip and for the first time showed some emotion.

“There was some interference when you were born and your sister's spirit became merged with the Malevolence. It is complicated.”

“I don't understand. What's the connection between my family and this place? Why are Mother and I the Cludydds?”

"Is that all you've noticed. Haven't you wondered why the people speak the same language as you or why they have these quaint old names for themselves and things?"

"Uh, well no. It was just one of the things I took for granted."

September wondered why she hadn't thought about these things before.

"You take a lot for granted don't you."

"Well, there's been quite a lot to take in."

"I suppose there has. I shall try to explain it to you. Since this universe is linked to your own by the beliefs on which it is based we made your family the conduit. Do you know anything about your ancestors?"

"Not a lot. Mother comes from Wales. She's still got family there."

"That's correct, an old people, celts. Celtic was the root of the old language the people here were given and the language of the first Cludydd o Maengolauseren; later it became English as your ancestors acquired the language."

"So all the Cludyddau have been my ancestors?"

"Of course. Daughters who were the seventh child."

The sudden noise of rending wood and falling trees caught September's attention and she noticed the woman look into the forest anxiously. The tall trees swayed and branches crashed to the forest floor. Shadows moved and then at the edge of the clearing appeared a huge lizard. When it raised itself up on its rear legs, ten metres tall or more, it resembled a tyrannosaur. September leapt to her feet. She hadn't seen dinosaurs on Daear before but she knew what this was.

"It's a Pwca," she said, raising the Maengolauseren.

"Calm yourself," the woman said, still seated, "It's only a manifestation."

The monster lurched forward, its red fiery eyes fixed on September.

"It's after me," September said, feeling the fear she needed to activate the starstone.

"Of course," the woman said, "You attract them." She raised her hand. As far as September could tell she held no starstone or metal or any other object. She merely flicked her fingers. There was no beam of light, no explosion of energy, the giant reptile simply vanished.

"It's gone," September said, open mouthed.

"Returned to the dark," the woman said off-handedly.

"You just made it go."

"I manipulated the dimensions of the omniverse, dispersed its elements and relocated the spirit."

"But if you could do that so easily, why not get rid of the rest?"

"Why should I? The experiment is over. The Malevolence can have this paltry little universe."

"But the people…"

"They're part of it, a combination of four elements."

"And a spirit."

"Hmm. That is true."

September stood in front of the woman and glared at her.

"I'm not sure I understand any of this but I have learnt that the people here have their lives. If they are overcome by the Malevolence they lose all their individuality and become spirits of hate. That's not a fate that they want."

"It *is* a waste." The woman looked pensive.

September was frustrated and angry.

"Is that all you can say? Look, I don't know whether I believe all this stuff about creating whole worlds but you seem to have a power which could save the people of this planet, perhaps save the whole universe. Help me push the Malevolence away and let these people live."

The woman chewed her lip and looked at her three fellows. They had stopped their work and were looking at September.

"The girl has a point," the man who had been stirring the cauldron said.

"You know it has been amusing seeing how the intelligences have coped with the limitations of this world," the other woman said.

"Why allow it to destabilise now before we've wound it up?" the other man added.

"It is a little annoying allowing the Malevolence to have its way," the woman sitting in front of September said.

"So help me," September insisted, "show me how I can drive the spirits back to the dark."

"It will require more than your little bit of egwyddorpum,"

the woman said.

"I realise that. Why can't the power you used against the Pwca be directed at all the spirits of the Malevolence?"

"Oh, that was nothing, just a local distortion of the dimensions. To specifically exclude all the parts of the Malevolence from this universe while leaving its occupants untouched; now that is a more difficult task. It would be easier for us to dismantle the whole system."

"How can you help me then?" September cried.

"She will have to work within the confines of this universe," the other woman said.

"Yes, using the principles we built into it," the cauldron man agreed.

September looked anxiously from one to the other. Did they mean that she had to work with the four elements and seven metals? She remembered Aurddolen's accusations of heresy.

"Aurddolen said that there were rumours that the Cemegwr had powers over the elements that no cludydd had, powers that it was forbidden to even suggest," September said.

"That is true. We spread those stories to keep our presence here a mystery."

"Well is it true? Do you have those powers?"

"Of course. They are ideas that came from your world. The secrets of the alchemists."

"Turning lead into gold. The Philosophers' Stone. The Secret of Eternal Youth," September cried excitedly. It all tied in with what she had read on the internet.

"Yes. The Maengolauseren, a piece of egwyddorpum, is a sort of philosophers' stone. Our recipes can use the stone to bind all the metals together as one and through the emanations of egwyddorpum spread their power throughout the universe to the sphere of stars."

The woman had grown excited. She got up from her chair and went to the man by the cauldron. The other man and woman joined her. They muttered together.

"Give us the Maengolauseren," the woman said.

There was more crashing in the forest, this time from all directions. September glanced at the stone in her hand. It was pulsing with violet light. Pain shot through her hip.

"Manifestations," she said.

"Yes, I know, more are coming," the woman said, "I told you that you attracted them. Give me the stone."

September looked around at the swaying trees and deafening sound of splintering wood.

"But…"

"We'll deal with the manifestations. Give me the starstone."

One man and the other woman moved away from the forge and came and stood between September and the forest. They looked into the trees. September made a decision, reached out her hand and passed the starstone from the palm of her hand into the woman's. She felt naked, powerless. The Maengolauseren had not been parted from her in the Land except when Tudfwlch had torn it from her. She recalled the loss she had felt when that happened and her response – she had killed him. She trembled. The woman dropped the stone into the pot and stirred it with a long wooden spoon. The liquid churned and smoked and glowed violet and red and green. There were smells; some sweet, some acrid.

Behind her there were screams and roars and the thunder of falling timber. She turned and saw a horde of manifestations pouring into the clearing. There were all sorts, Adarllwchgwin, Llamhigwyn y dwr, Tylwyth teg, Coblynau, Cefyll dwr, Gwyllian, Cwn annwn, and Pwca in grotesque imitations of animals. Overhead was the glow of falling Draig tân and, despite the noise, above it all she heard the chilling moan of Cyhyraeth.

She shook with fear, defenceless, petrified.

The man and woman in front of her stood unflinching and like the woman earlier, simply raised their hands and flicked their fingers.

There was silence. No, not quite. There was a light breeze that made the branches in the treetops rustle. The manifestations were gone, every last one of them.

September drew air into her lungs. She had forgotten to breathe.

"There will be more," the man in front of her said calmly, "There is a powerful attraction between the Malevolence and the Maengolauseren, but do not be afraid. You are safe."

September turned back to the cauldron. The other man and woman were still stirring and adding powders and crystals both orange and purple. The liquid shimmered and steamed and then quite suddenly settled and cleared.

The woman put a spoon into the liquid and lifted out the Maengolauseren.

"Take it," she said to September.

"Is it hot?

"No."

September took it from the bowl of the spoon. Its violet light had dulled but otherwise it looked unchanged by its immersion in the chemical mixture. It was its normal temperature, a little cold against her skin. The man took a flask made from a material like clear glass about the size of a perfume bottle, dipped it into the cauldron and drew it out filled with a colourless, clear liquid which moved like syrup. He fixed a glass stopper in the top of the flask and handed it to September. She held the stone in one hand and the flask in the other.

"What do I do with it?" she asked.

"Ask your cludyddau friends to gather samples of each of the seven metals," the woman said, "Melt them together with your starstone and add the Alkahest. You will be enveloped in the fundamental energy of this universe and reborn as the union of all the elements with the power to eliminate the Malevolence from within its dimensions."

"Oh."

"But you will need Malice."

"Malice? Why?"

"She is the cause of the disturbance. She has given the Malevolence leadership, directed the spirits to achieve the greatest destruction. You must pull her from the darkness that has been her only experience till now. She and you are more than just twins. Your spirits are one. The Alkahest we have given you will rejoin your two parts, make you complete and give you the power you should have had to overcome the Malevolence."

"What must I do?"

"We can't know the thoughts and feelings of every spirit in the multiverse. You and your mother must find a way of drawing Malice to you when you perform the transformation."

September felt frustrated. It seemed that she had been given the key to fulfilling her task but then it had been taken away and replaced with this further problem – how to win over Malice.

"The future of this universe is in your hands, September Weekes. We will observe whether you can save it."

"What? Can't you help anymore?" September cried. Her head was full of confused ideas, questions. "I don't even understand who you are."

The woman did not reply but simply gave an enigmatic smile. The image of the woman and her companions began to break up, the mirror splitting into shards again. They didn't disappear in a flash of light as September did when she performed symudiad nor did they depart in a puff of wind or water or dust or flame. The pieces turned and broke into smaller and smaller fragments until they weren't there anymore.

September was alone, in an empty clearing carpeted with leaf litter.

There was a roar from the forest. September turned to look and saw another army of manifestations emerging from between the trees. They were crawling, staggering, running, flying towards her. Each set of flame-red eyes focussed on her. September didn't think to destroy them; she just thought of Aurddolen in Mwyngloddiau.

20

Aurddolen and his companions recoiled as September materialised amongst them.

"You were not long, Cludydd," Aurddolen said pulling himself upright, "the sun is still rising in the sky although it cannot be seen behind the dark clouds of abomination and the hordes of manifestations that besiege us."

Sieffre held Hedydd in a protective hug while Ilar held onto a table for support.

"That's good," September said, "perhaps we still have time."

"Your quest was successful?" Cari asked, picking herself up from the stone floor, "You have a container in your hand that you did not have before."

September looked at the flask that she grasped in her right hand.

"Yes, I found the Cemegwr," she replied, wondering if indeed she had located them or they had drawn her to them, "They gave me this. They called it the Alkahest."

Aurddolen looked sceptical.

"And what does this Alkahest do?"

"They say it will unite all the metals with the egwyddorpum of the stars and enable me to push the Malevolence from the universe."

"Ah, it is a Toddfa Penbaladr."

"A what?"

"A liquid that can dissolve everything, that can be contained only by a material that we have no power to devise."

"It looks like glass," September said, peering at the small clear container.

"So these Cemegwr have decided that they are on the same side as us," Aurddolen said.

"Well, I think it's a bit more complicated than that,"

September replied, unsure how much she should say about what the Cemegwr were, not that she was certain herself. Aurddolen was however looking at her quizzically.

"More complicated? What can be complicated about being for or against the Malevolence?"

September was trying to think of an answer when a blast of air almost knocked her from her feet and Aurddolen and Cari and the others were again blown to the ground.

Breuddwyd appeared, in a heap on the floor.

"Mother, what happened?" September knelt, confused because her hands were full but wanting to reach out to her mother. Breuddwyd stirred and heaved herself up, pushing on the floor with the hand grasping her half of the Maengolauseren. She pressed her free hand to her forehead.

"I found her. I found Mairwen," she gasped.

"Where? What is she doing?"

Breuddwyd sat up, looked around a little dazed, then looked back at September.

"She's at the observatory, the Ars…"

"Arsyllfa," September filled in.

"That's it. She's brooding. Angry at losing Heulwen and her power here. Anxious about what our return means to her plans. Impatient for the final destruction of this universe."

"You talked to her?"

"No, I wouldn't say that."

"How do you know all those things then?"

"I'm her mother, September. I understood what she was feeling from the insults she screamed, the bolts of darkness she threw at me and the expression on her face."

"Oh. She didn't listen to you then."

"She never gave me the chance." Breuddwyd hauled herself to her feet and looked at Aurddolen. "I'm sorry about your daughter, Mordeyrn. Mairwen was just using her."

Aurddolen looked at the body of the young woman, still lying amongst them.

"She was lost, like the Arsyllfa, weeks ago. Cari, Sieffre do you think you could remove her body to the House of the Dead? Then we can get on with what we must do."

Sieffre and Cari nodded and with help from Hedydd and Ilar, lifted up the body of Heulwen. As they passed through the doorway, September called after them.

"Oh, and please find all the other cludyddau. We all need to meet as soon as we can."

"All the cludyddau?" Aurddolen asked, "What is your intention, Cludydd?"

September brandished the flask.

"The Cemegwr said that I needed samples of all the metals from each of the cludyddau. They have to be melted together and then I add the Alkahest."

Aurddolen shrugged.

"I know nothing of this Alkahest, the Toddfa Penbaladr, or the ritual you describe, but if you think these Cemegwr can be trusted it shall be done."

"I am not sure that I trust them but I think this is our only chance of defeating the Malevolence," September said. "There's one more thing."

"What's that?" Breuddwyd and Aurddolen said simultaneously.

"Malice must be with me when I do it."

"This 'union' of the metals involves you and her?" the Mordeyrn asked.

"Yes. It will end her power and give me control over the Malevolence."

"So the Cemegwr say."

"So they say," September agreed.

"They seem to have been able to convince you of their skills and their good intentions in a short time, Cludydd."

"They did."

"You found them? They helped you?" Breuddwyd said excitedly.

"Yes, Mother. I'll tell you all about it later." There were many things that September wanted to discuss with her mother but she wasn't sure that Aurddolen should find out who the Cemegwr really were. How would someone like the Mordeyrn react to being told that she had met the creators of his world and that they didn't really care much about its inhabitants?

"How are you going to get Malice to join you in this ceremony?" Aurddolen said sceptically.

"I don't know," September admitted.

"You can't bring her here without lowering the dome you created," the Mordeyrn continued, "and as soon as you do that the manifestations will destroy us all."

"Aurddolen's right," Breuddwyd said, "Mairwen is very powerful. I discovered that just now. Neither I nor you can overpower her and make her go somewhere she doesn't want to go."

"Well, that's it. We must lure her to the place where we carry out the union. Make her follow us there. Let her think she is chasing us."

"That's a good idea," Breuddwyd agreed, "but where? If we choose any settlement there will be people who might get in the way and they will be killed or turned to evil."

"We need somewhere we can protect where there aren't any people," September said. They were silent.

"There is a place," Aurddolen said, "a place where no people go; far away from any community and far away from the greatest concentration of the spirits of the Malevolence."

"Where?" September and Breuddwyd asked.

"Diffaithmawr."

"Where?" they both asked again.

"The great desert beyond the southern plains."

"Where I defeated the Malevolence," Breuddwyd said.

"Yes. That's right. Not even the nomads travel to where you threw back the evil."

"Tudfwlch told me the story about how you defeated the Malevolence and I read Heulyn's account of it," September said, thinking back all those weeks to when she was new to the Land.

"I think it would be the ideal place for us to meet Mairwen and finish this for good and all," Breuddwyd said.

"I hope the Cemegwr have spoken true and that this Alkahest is the solution we seek," Aurddolen said. He pulled himself erect, "I must go to see that my daughter's body is accorded the care she deserves, and I'll help collect the cludyddau for you." He nodded to both of them and left.

September was relieved that she and Breuddwyd were alone for a while. She quickly recounted what she could recall of her conversation with the Cemegwr. Breuddwyd was confused.

"Were they angels?"

"I don't think so. They didn't wear white or have wings and halos and things."

"And they didn't mention the Holy Father?"

"No Mother. There was no mention of anything religious at all. She even denied being a god of any sort. I don't get it but she seemed to suggest that they inhabit a greater universe. I don't think I saw them as they really are or even the whole of whatever they are. They were like the manifestations of the Malevolence. They had adopted human bodies to be part of this place."

"Are you sure they were not the Malevolence? Your Mordeyrn seems suspicious of them."

"He doesn't like having his beliefs questioned, but I'm sure that what the Cemegwr told me was true. They weren't like anything to do with the Malevolence, and they weren't filled with hate."

"They seem very strange beings and I don't know what to make of their warnings that our home is being attacked by the Malevolence."

"Neither do I, but first we must hope that we can protect this universe."

"So my love, how do we get Mairwen to come with us to the desert?"

"I think she'll come if she thinks she has a chance of getting hold of the starstone. We must get everything ready in secret and then draw her to us."

Cari burst through the door followed by Cynhaearn and Heulfryn, the young cludydd o aur.

"You have a way of fighting the Malevolence?" Cynhaearn was barely through the door and breathless from his climb from the mine but he launched into his query.

"I hope so," September replied, "but we need your help. We need help from all the cludyddau."

"The others are on their way," Cari said, "Isfoel is still in the mines, but he won't be long."

"Cari told us that you need our metals," Heulfryn said, "here is mine." He held out a gold amulet, the twin of one that he wore on his right arm. It was covered with symbols of the Sun. September realised that she already had her hands full with the starstone in one and the flask of Alkahest in the other. Breuddwyd took the amulet from the young man.

"We will need something to collect all the metals in," she said.

"I know what you need," Cynhaearn said, rushing out again.

"Here is mine," Cari said, holding out a bracelet of thick copper wire. Breuddwyd took it from her.

The door opened again and Cynwal and Ariannell entered. They held out objects of lead and silver, which Breuddwyd gathered. Then Cynhaearn crashed in carrying a small black cauldron.

"Here," he gasped through panting breaths, "You can carry all the metals in this and it will be my gift of haearn."

"Thank you," September said. Breuddwyd dropped the gold, copper, silver and lead in the pot.

"I'm not sure this will be what we need," Breuddwyd said, "If all the metals have to be melted and mixed before the Alkahest is added, the pot will itself melt and leak."

Cynhaearn looked dejected, his broad shoulders slumped.

"How stupid am I?" he said, "You need a material that can take all the metals and stand up to the heat of melting."

"What can withstand such heat that even iron will turn to liquid?" Cari said shaking her head.

September wondered why they were all puzzled. Surely the people of the Land had materials that could stand such temperatures. Then she recalled that glass was not used in the Land, that buildings were made from wood, reeds, stone or baked mud. They wielded the seven metals but apparently had not discovered the qualities of clay.

Cynwal spoke, "Only the rock in the depths of Daear can withstand such heat, the stone we used to build Mwyngloddiau Dwfn." The town was built from the hard dark rock through which the miners tunnelled. The others agreed that the rock could indeed stand up to great heat. Cynwal turned towards the door, "I shall find a piece," he said, "that has been fashioned into a bowl." He departed just as Ilar returned with the old, wiry bearer of mercury.

"Here is alcam," Ilar said, passing over a folded sheet of the silver-grey metal.

"And Arian byw," Isfoel added, handing to Breuddwyd a small vial made of dark, polished wood

"It is like what Eluned gave me," September observed, feeling a sadness and regret that surprised her, "I left it at the Arsyllfa when I no longer needed it to transform."

"That is all the metals," Breuddwyd said, "Thank you, all of you."

"But you won't be needing a heavy old pot," Cynhaearn said, "Not when Cynwal brings the bowl of stone." He reached to his belt and drew out a short iron dagger. It was undecorated but its blade was a highly polished blue-grey "You must have this as your piece of haearn."

Aurddolen rejoined the company, his face white and drawn.

"Ah, you are all here," he said in a soft, sad voice. Ariannell went to his side and placed a hand gently on his arm.

"We feel your loss, Mordeyrn," she said, "We all know of your love for your daughter. Her death pains us all, but at least she is now free of the Malevolence."

"But is she?" Aurddolen looked at Ariannell with deep lines of anguish in his face, "She died in the power of Malice. I don't know whether her spirit has returned to the centre of Daear to be reborn or has joined the hate-filled ranks of the evil."

"Let us have hope," Ariannell insisted. Aurddolen took a deep breath and seemed to draw strength from Ariannell's grip. September knew she was passing her healing compassion into him. He drew himself up to his full height and seemed to shed a number of years. He looked at September.

"You have all that you need?"

September looked at the small heap of various shapes and colours of metal in the pot at Breuddwyd's feet.

"Yes," September replied, "We have all seven metals. Cynwal has gone to find a bowl that they can be melted in." A thought came into her head, something that she hadn't considered. "But how will we heat it? Will we have to build a furnace like you have in your workshops and carry wood to burn?"

"You have no need of fuels and fire," Aurddolen said,

"You control the power of Haul. That is power enough to melt the mountains if necessary."

"Oh, yes, the energy of the Sun," September said sheepishly, having forgotten the powers that she had at her disposal.

"And that in turn will give you the hope that your experiment will be successful," Aurddolen went on, "Our hopes rest with you as I fear we have little time left."

"That is my fear too," Isfoel said, "The manifestations of earth are reducing the rock at the town's foundations to dust. The protective sphere will not prevent us sinking into the heart of Daear."

"The manifestations of fire, air and water crowd around the town biting into our defences," Aurddolen added, "Soon it will dissolve and we will be lost."

Cynwal staggered through the door bearing a lump of black rock. He placed it at September's feet. It was a seven sided bowl, carved and polished so that the surface shone. Tiny crystals in the rock glinted and sparkled. September thought it looked beautiful.

"Where did you find it?" she asked.

"It is used as a bowl for washing hands in the Meeting Hall," Cynwal said, "It was made by one of the miners long ago. Will it do?"

"I am sure it will," Breuddwyd said, bending to place the seven metal items into it. She placed her hands under the broad rim and, with an effort that tensed the muscles in her arm, heaved it up.

"Thank you, all," September said, "Now we must go to the desert and make our preparations to end Malice's power."

"You must hide yourself from the Malevolence," Aurddolen warned, "or else your plan will be discovered."

"Of course," September said, again feeling foolish. She raised the Maengolauseren above her head and moved it in a circle thinking the now familiar mantra of sadness and joy. Ribbons of silver grey wound around her and her mother, enveloping them in the protective and concealing metals.

She looked to Breuddwyd, wrapping her hand that grasped the flask around her arm.

"Take us to Diffaithmawr, Mother," she said, raising her

starstone above her head.

"Farewell," Aurddolen called, and the others added their best wishes as golden light swirled around September and Breuddwyd, obscuring the cludyddau from view.

21

They stood on a plain of glass. The air shimmered in the heat of the Sun shining from its zenith. The pale beige surface stretched in every direction reflecting the cloudless blue sky. September looked all around her, astounded by the desolation.

"Was it like this when you were here before?" she asked.

Breuddwyd bent to place the black bowl on the hard surface.

"No, it was desert covered in sand. There were dunes."

"It's like a nuclear bombsite. The sand has been melted." September knelt to place the flask beside the bowl and then slid her hand over the vitreous surface.

"I suppose it was. Of course I wasn't here when it was all over so I didn't see what had happened," Breuddwyd said, looking thoughtful, "The Malevolence was starting to descend from the black sky. I lifted the Maengolauseren and commanded it to go. There was a blast of light and that was it. I was back home."

"You completed your task. The power of the starstone threw the spirits of the Malevolence back beyond the stars. You cleared Daear of manifestations. Your job was done." September felt weighed down by the knowledge that was what she had failed to do on the night of the Conjunction. Now she had to make this second chance work.

"I didn't have Mairwen to oppose me," Breuddwyd said, placing an arm around September's shoulder, "Now I have met her I understand how difficult your task has been."

Her mother's words cheered September.

"Well, let's hope this plan works and that Malice and all the Malevolence are thrown off this planet. Do you think she'll come?"

"I am sure of it. The bond between you twins is strong despite your separation and your different lives." Breuddwyd was thoughtful. "Her hate is powerful and consumes her but she is also envious of you and covets the starstone. Now that we are out of the shield that you erected she will soon come after you. I think it would be better if you went to her and led her here rather than waiting for her to turn up."

September could feel spirits of evil around them, not as many as in the north but growing in number as the Malevolence spread over the whole Earth. She looked again at the barren wasteland.

"You're right. There was nothing here for the Malevolence until we arrived, but we will attract them - these thin ribbons of lead and tin will not hide us for long."

"Take care my love. Mairwen is strong."

"I know." September raised the stone above her head and thought of the valley below the Arsyllfa. Light enveloped her.

She was there, standing on the grass at the base of the pinnacle of rock that bore the observatory. The last time she had stood here had been with Sieffre shortly after his escape from Malice's attack. Spirits swarmed around her, unseen, but their hate battered against her and aggravated the pain in her birthmark. The spirits flocked down the valley and around the outcrop but they seemed to avoid the summit and the Arsyllfa itself, like the hole at the centre of the vortex of water flowing down a plughole. Perhaps Malice keeps some space around her, September wondered.

She transformed into her eagle and leapt into the sky. Her wings beat at the air and she surged into the heights above the ruined observatory. She looked down and saw Malice standing on the cracked paving of the rooftop from which the astronomers had followed the movement of the planets. Malice was staring up at her.

September circled down and as her feet touched the marble she transformed into the panther.

"You've returned then," Malice said in a matter of fact tone, "I thought I had flung you out of this universe for good."

"You flung me nowhere," September growled, stalking her twin, watching her warily, "The Maengolauseren protected me. It took me back home. Home to our world. Home to Mother, our mother."

"The Maengolauseren," Malice said repeating her words almost absentmindedly, but September sensed her desire for the starstone.

"Yes, the stone that gives me power over all the elements of this universe."

"It's just a pebble. I have all the power I need from the Malevolence."

"Do you? You thought you had defeated me but now you can see that you did not."

"But you failed your task. The Malevolence possesses this world now and all that are in it will die."

"Are you sure of that? While Mother and I are here, each with our pieces of the starstone, you suspect we could overpower you." September's careful goading was having success. She saw Malice's face turn a shade of red that resembled the planet Mars. September returned to her human shape and thrust out the stone in front of her. It glowed a bright violet.

"No, I have the power," Malice screeched, "The Maengolauseren shall be mine and I shall rule this universe for the Malevolence." Malice reached for the stone with a hand and a shaft of black light.

September fended off the beam of darkness with a twitch of the stone. Its light grew brighter.

"You'll have to defeat me to get the starstone," September taunted, and went.

She stood on a beach. There was dry, loose sand beneath her feet, grass-topped dunes behind her, breaking rollers in front of her. The beach extended north and south as far as the eye could see. She'd been here just once before when the people of the eastern coast had needed her help. Now there was no sign of anyone, just the ever-present cries of the spirits that filled the overcast brown sky. She transformed into the iridescent blue cobra and slithered through the sand. She knew that Malice would not be long in following her.

"You can't get away," Malice cried, appearing in front of her, "I can feel you, you know."

September became herself and stepped towards Malice, stopping just out of arms's reach.

"I know. It doesn't have to be like this."

"What do you mean?"

"We don't have to be enemies. We are sisters. Mother still loves you, she loves both of us."

Malice looked mystified.

"I don't understand your words. I have no mother."

"She gave birth to you."

"I was born in darkness, alone; alone among the spirits of the Malevolence."

"Your body was without life. Mother would have cared for you if you had lived. She would have fed you like she fed me."

"I was fed by the hate of the spirits. They gave me power. Now I control them."

"We can give you more; love, peace, happiness."

"I do not understand those words. They mean nothing to me so I have no need of them. The Maengolauseren is all that you have that I want. Give it to me." Again she reached out her hand, grasping and firing a blast of coal-black darkness at September. The force of it made September stagger back, but she recovered her footing, held her ground and opposed the light-devouring beam with her own violet light.

"No, I shall not," September screamed into the maelstrom of clashing light and dark. Malice's force was indeed stronger than hers. She could feel her wall of shimmering light being forced backwards. She moved.

She was standing among the ruins of Amaethaderyn. Around her the dust of mud walls and splinters of thatch swirled in little eddies. At the edge of the dried out lake, the reeds lay flat and desiccated. Dry soil blew off the bare allotments and the trees at the edge of the forest were grey and dead. Were the people still huddling under their shelter among the trees, September wondered? Was it really just a few hours since she had been with them?

"I told you. You can't escape," Malice bellowed, appearing in front of her, leering and renewing her onslaught of jet-black power.

September fended off the energies of hate and fired one or two blasts of her own at her sister, but she was driven back step-by-step.

"You will not win," she shouted at her twin.

"And you cannot keep running away," Malice replied, "Soon every spirit on this world will be of the Malevolence. You will have nothing left to fight for and I will have the Maengolauseren."

"No!" September screamed, launching a lightning bolt at Malice. It guttered uselessly and Malice answered it with her own shadow beam. September was battered to the ground. She held the starstone above her, defending herself. Was now the time? Was Mother ready with the bowl of metals and the Alkahest?

"You will be no more and all of this Universe will be mine," Malice roared, stepping forward to stand over September binding her with fingers of ebony. She reached down to grasp the starstone from September's hand.

September moved.

22

September sprawled on the glazed ground, the black stone bowl beside her and Breuddwyd standing over her.

"She'll be here. We must melt the metals," September cried, scrambling to her feet.

"It's alright love, I have hope." Breuddwyd held her half of the stone over the bowl. Brilliant yellow light, the colour and intensity of the Sun, shone on the heap of metals. Instantly the wooden vial containing the mercury disappeared in a puff of smoke and the silver droplets trickled into the bowl. The sheets of tin and lead, the copper bracelet, golden amulet, silver brooch, and lastly the iron dagger, softened, slumped and melted into liquid. The fluids swirled together mixing and merging into one. September grasped the flask of the Alkahest and pulled out the stopper.

Malice appeared on the opposite side of the bowl from Breuddwyd's beam of energy. She advanced towards September then stopped as if noticing where she was and what Breuddwyd was doing.

"I know this place," she said, a note of uncertainty in her voice.

"So you should if you and the Malevolence are one," September called.

"Why?" Malice asked.

"This was where I faced the Malevolence at the last Conjunction," Breuddwyd said, still focussing the beam of sunlight on the bowl. The liquid metals churned and glowed red-hot.

"The last time that the Maengolauseren defeated the Malevolence," September taunted.

"It will be the last time," Malice sneered, "Now the starstone will be mine."

Malice stepped forward then stopped and looked at the bowl.

"What are you doing?"

"Cooking up something for you," September said, indicating to her mother to move away. Breuddwyd's beam of fire cut out and she stepped back. September stood up holding both the starstone and the flask directly over the bowl of glowing, molten metals.

Malice moved forward; now she was just a pace from September. September dropped her stone. It sank into the mixture and disappeared into the liquid. The surface boiled and violet vapours rose from it.

"No!" Malice screamed and leapt at September. Malice's arms closed around her as she tipped the contents of the flask into the bowl. The colourless drops of liquid disappeared into the swirling mixture. September felt Malice's claw-like fingers on her shoulders as cold as liquid nitrogen, the cold of space. She dropped the flask and grabbed Malice around the waist. Malice's chill spread from her shoulder into her arms and down her body. They were locked together over the churning, smoking bowl. A vortex of rainbow coloured light rose from the liquid, engulfing them, expanding, rising. September's eyes were locked on Malice's hate-twisted face.

"What have you done?" Malice said, her words stretching out as if time was slowing down.

"I don't know," September said, her feet no longer resting on firm ground. She was floating. "But I hope it will rid the world of the Malevolence."

The light twisted around them and through them and seemed to turn in on itself through a dimension of space that wasn't there. Forces pulled her in every direction, stretching and compressing her as if she was made of rubber. Still she kept hold of Malice.

"What is happening?" Malice cried in deep, ponderous tones. They were no longer in the desert. The stone bowl had disappeared and beneath their feet was the same whirling mixture of rainbow colours as was all around them. Breuddwyd and the whole of the Land had gone.

"I don't know," September repeated, feeling as though her voice came from outside of her. She was being turned inside out but there was nothing to see other than the writhing bands of orange, blue, red, green, violet, yellow, indigo and white.

Then she noted black spots appearing in the light around them like the reverse of stars in the night sky. Their number grew, galaxies of them formed, swirled around them then winked out to be replaced by more.

"My spirits!" Malice's cry dragged on and on.

"What's happening to them?" September asked, her question taking an eon to express.

"I'm losing them!" Malice's voice was an eternal sob but September was cheered. Were the spirits of the Malevolence being drawn from the Land and flung out into the darkness? She hoped that was what she was seeing, that the plan was working and the people would be freed from the terror of the Malevolence.

Malice's cold grip on her shoulders weakened. September looked at her; she was fading to grey, losing her solidity, ceasing to be real, becoming a wraith. Malice looked at her, her face contorted in fear.

"No! I don't want to go back to the dark," her voice was that of a young child, "Save me! Please!"

September didn't know what to do. She tightened her grip on what substance was left of her twin. This was what she wanted wasn't it? Victory over Malice; if not to destroy her then force her back into exile beyond the stars; but, after all, she was her sister though they had never known each other. She remembered Mother's continued love for her dead daughter, how she always referred to her by her given name, Mairwen, rather than the label she had taken for herself. She recalled the years of growing up feeling incomplete, only half there, as if she was missing something. She had thought she was stupid and careless but perhaps what she really lacked was her other half, her twin.

With the swirling streamers of light of the seven colours originating from the seven metals plus the Maengolauseren, the egwyddorpum, and the Cemegwr's unifying Alkahest she felt all the emotions competing within her – fear, sorrow and joy, anger and love, hope and surprise, and compassion. She hugged the remnants of Malice to her.

"You will always be with me, Mairwen," she said. Malice's face took on an expression of calm as her form faded away but rather than being blown away by the vortex it seemed to

September that she hadn't gone but had merged with her. Now though she was alone, tossed by the maelstrom of light. There was no space, no time, just energy. Where was she? She was nowhere and everywhere. The flickering lights made her dizzy, her head was spinning on her neck. She closed her eyes. She was falling.

23

The floor hit her. It was reassuringly solid rather than painful. September sprawled, arms and legs flailing. Then there were hands on her.

"September! Are you alright?"

She opened her eyes to find herself cradled by her mother, kneeling on the floor of her bedroom.

"We're home?" she said, almost unable to believe her own eyes.

"Yes, we're back."

"What happened? Where did you go?"

"I could ask you the same thing. When I stepped back from the bowl I flicked back here. That was just a moment ago. You fell into my arms."

"But it seemed a … No I can't say how long it was. It just was me and Malice and the light." September described what had happened after Malice had appeared and she had dropped the starstone and the Alkahest into the cauldron of molten metal.

"So you think it worked as the Cemegwr described? The Malevolence was pushed back into space?"

"I think so, Mother. Malice certainly seemed to feel that the spirits were being pulled away from her and then she faded."

"And she went with them."

"I'm not sure. I think she may be here." September tapped her head.

"Hmm. Well let us hope that the Malevolence is dealt with."

"What about your piece of the Maengolauseren?"

Breuddwyd held up her hands to show that they were empty.

"Gone. Just like the last time. I presume it means that our task, your task, is complete."

"Gone? We have no way of getting back, of finding out

who has survived or how they are getting on?"

"No, my love. After my experience I began to wonder whether it had actually happened. I had no souvenirs to prove it and of course I had spent no time out of our own world."

There was a tap on the door.

"Are you alright in there?" Julie called.

"Yes, we're fine, love," Breuddwyd replied, "Give us a moment. September's a lot better."

Footsteps retreated along the landing.

"There, you see, September, it's still the night of your birthday. No one will have any idea that you've spent a quarter of a year on another world, fighting evil."

September looked down at her nightie, examined her hands and arms, felt her face and hair. She was back to her old self – short hair, too much flab around her middle and her thighs; the silly, old September.

"No one will know that I'm not the stupid little girl that I used to be. They won't see any difference."

"Not at first, my love, but your experiences have changed you, will continue to change you. People will just think you're growing up, but I know it's because you are a hero."

September felt a glow inside her. She smiled.

"I'm glad you were there too, Mum. I couldn't have finished it without you."

Her mother hugged her.

"And perhaps if Mairwen is part of you too she can at last feel at peace, away from the hateful Malevolence."

The mention of the evil reminded September of the Cemegwr's words. She felt a sudden fear grip her.

"Do you think the Cemegwr was right and the Malevolence is here too?"

"Who knows, love. Our universe is different isn't it? I don't know much about astronomy and all that but even I can see that our universe is a lot bigger and more complicated than Daear and its seven planets and stars."

"Can we find out?"

"I don't know. There is evil all around us; and good too. Perhaps a Cludydd will be called to protect us if the Malevolence becomes powerful, but I don't think it will be us."

September didn't reply. She was wondering what form the powers of a Cludydd would take in her own world.

"Let's pretend that nothing special and fantastic has happened," Breuddwyd went on, "You know Julie and everyone else couldn't understand what we've been through, what you've seen and done. Let's just say you had a bad dream and we can all settle down again now."

September nodded and got up. She climbed into the bottom bunk and her mother tucked her in like she used to do.

"We'll talk about it all again when Julie has gone. For now, sleep well my brave and resourceful daughter, the Cludydd o Maengolauseren."

THE END

Although September will be back in

Volume 3 of Evil Above the Stars

Unity of Seven

Acknowledgement

Writing is largely a solo activity but being a writer requires support and assistance from a lot of people. I couldn't cope without my wife, partner, best friend and chief critic, Alison, who encourages me with all my writing projects.

The idea for *Evil Above the Stars* grew out of a short assignment for Ludlow Writers' Group and I must thank all the members, but particularly Sally, for encouraging me to go on to develop it. All the comments have been much appreciated.

Then there are the folk at Elsewhen Press. It is a joy to find a company as enthusiastic about their business as Peter and Alison are. Their mixture of astuteness, skill and excitement is both reassuring and invigorating. I was delighted when they took on *EAtS* and have been proud to become a part of their publishing family. Then there is Deirdre who had the unenviable job of finding all my typographic, punctuation and grammatical errors and make patient and sensible suggestions for improvements. Thank you Deirdre. Another thank you goes to Sofia for the proofreading. Any errors that remain are all mine.

Finally I would like to thank you the reader. Nothing gives me more pleasure than knowing people are reading my work (the royalties are useful but secondary). If you are reading this before launching into the novel, then I hope you enjoy it. If you have completed it then I hope it was a pleasurable experience and that you look forward to further tales of September Weekes.

Elsewhen Press
an independent publisher specialising in Speculative Fiction

Visit the Elsewhen Press website at elsewhen.press for the latest information on all of our titles, authors and events; to read our blog; find out where to buy our books and ebooks; or to place an order.

Elsewhen Press

an independent publisher specialising in Speculative Fiction

Volume 1 of Evil Above the Stars

Seventh Child

Peter R. Ellis

September Weekes is accustomed to facing teasing and bullying because of her white hair, tubby figure and silly name, but the discovery of a clear, smooth stone at her home casts her into a struggle between good and evil that will present her with sterner challenges.

The stone takes her to *Gwlad*, the Land, where the people hail her as the *Cludydd o Maengolauseren*, the bearer of the starstone, with the power to defend them against the evil known as the Malevolence. September meets the people's leader, the *Mordeyrn Aurddolen*, and the bearers of the seven metals linked to the seven 'planets'. Each metal gives the bearer specialised powers to resist the manifestations of the Malevolence, formed from the four elements of earth, air, fire and water, such as the comets known as *Draig tân*, fire dragons.

She returns to her home, but is drawn back to *Gwlad* a fortnight later to find that two years have passed and the villagers have experienced more destructive attacks by manifestations. September must now help defend *Gwlad* against the Malevolence.

Seventh Child is the first volume in the thrilling fantasy series, *Evil Above the Stars*, by Peter R. Ellis, that appeals to readers of all ages of fantasy or science fiction, especially fans of JRR Tolkien and Stephen Donaldson. If old theories are correct until a new idea comes along, does the universe change with our perception of it? Were the ideas embodied in alchemy ever right? What realities were the basis of Celtic mythology?

ISBN: 9781908168702 (epub, kindle)
ISBN: 9781908168603 (256pp paperback)

Visit bit.ly/EvilAbove

Elsewhen Press

an independent publisher specialising in Speculative Fiction

Volume 2 of Evil Above the Stars

The Power of Seven

Peter R. Ellis

September Weekes found a smooth stone which took her to *Gwlad*, the Land, where the people hailed her as the *Cludydd o Maengolauseren*, the bearer of the starstone, with the power to defend them against the evil known as the Malevolence. Now, having reached Arsyllfa she is re-united with the *Mordeyrn Aurddolen* with whom, together with the other senior metal bearers that make up the Council of *Gwlad*, she must plan the defence of the Land.

The time of the next Conjunction will soon be at hand. The planets, the Sun and the Moon will all be together in the sky. At that point the protection of the heavenly bodies will be at its weakest and *Gwlad* will be more dependent than ever on September. But now it seems that she must defeat Malice, the guiding force behind the Malevolence, if she is to save the Land and all its people. Will she be strong enough; and, if not, to whom can she turn for help?

The Power of Seven is the second volume in the thrilling fantasy series, *Evil Above the Stars*, by Peter R. Ellis, that appeals to readers, of all ages, of fantasy or science fiction, especially fans of JRR Tolkien and Stephen Donaldson. If old theories are correct until a new idea comes along, does the universe change with our perception of it? Were the ideas embodied in alchemy ever right? What realities were the basis of Celtic mythology?

ISBN: 9781908168719 (epub, kindle)
ISBN: 9781908168610 (288pp paperback)

Visit bit.ly/EvilAbove

Elsewhen Press

an independent publisher specialising in Speculative Fiction

GHOSTS ON THE PRAIRIES

A SACRED LAND STORY

TANYA REIMER

Some things are worth a fight. Strong words that Antoine's father drilled into him. After his father mysteriously vanishes one night, Antoine must find another income or he risks losing the Sacred Land that his father swore to protect.

On a well-paying ranch, Antoine meets Emma, a victim of underground slavery. Fighting for her freedom costs him his home, his sister, his best friend, and puts in question all of his values. If he succeeds, will she and her son fit into his world?

The prairies of 1916-19 come alive with bootleggers, slavery, fools in sheets, haunting spirits, shifty tunnel runners, and even exploding churches. *Ghosts on the Prairies* is alternative history suspense incorporating the paranormal and infused with romance.

Born and raised in Saskatchewan, Tanya enjoys using the tranquil prairies as a setting to her not-so-peaceful speculative fiction. She is married with two children which means among her accomplishments are the necessary magical abilities to find a lost tooth in a park of sand and whisper away monsters from under the bed.

Tanya was fifteen when she wrote her first column. She has a diploma in Journalism/Short Story Writing. Today, she actively submits to various newspapers, writes and publishes the local Francophone newsletter for her community, and maintains a blog at Life's Like That.

Ghosts on the Prairies, a Sacred Land Story for adults, is her debut novel.

ISBN: 9781908168535 (epub, kindle)
ISBN: 9781908168436 (356pp paperback)

Visit bit.ly/GhostsPrairies

Elsewhen Press

an independent publisher specialising in Speculative Fiction

Bookworm series by Christopher Nuttall

Bookworm

Elaine, an inexperienced witch in Golden City, has her life turned upside down when she triggers a magical trap to end up with all the knowledge in the Great Library stuffed inside her head. Avoiding the Inquisition she tries to understand what has happened to her. But she is a pawn in the dark plans of one who wants the Grand Sorcerer's power.

Bookworm won the Gold Award in the Adult Fiction category of the 2013 Wishing Shelf Independent Book Awards.

ISBN: 9781908168320 (epub, kindle) / 9781908168221 (368pp, paperback)
Visit bit.ly/Bookworm-Nuttall

Bookworm II – The Very Ugly Duckling

Not every ugly duckling becomes a swan ...

In the wake of the disastrous attack on the Golden City, Lady Light Spinner has become Grand Sorceress and Elaine, the Bookworm, has been settling into her positions as Head Librarian and Privy Councillor.   But any hope of vanishing into her books is negated when a new magician of staggering power appears in the city, one whose abilities seem to defy the known laws of magic.

ISBN: 9781908168382 (epub, kindle) / 9781908168283 (432pp, paperback)
Visit bit.ly/Bookworm2-Nuttall

Bookworm III – The Best Laid Plans

Elaine and Johan prepare to leave Golden City, with Daria and Cass, to search for the Witch-King. But Elaine is arrested on the orders of a new Emperor, puppet of the Witch-King. She must escape and destroy him. Privy Councillors and Heads of the Great Houses have bowed to the Emperor. Only Elaine and her friends can prevent an all-out war.

ISBN: 9781908168764 (epub, kindle) / 9781908168665 (400pp, paperback)
Visit bit.ly/Bookworm3

About the author

Peter R. Ellis would like to say he's been a writer all his life but it is only since retiring as a teacher in 2010 that he has been able to devote enough time to writing to call it a career. Brought up in Cardiff, he studied Chemical Physics at the University of Kent at Canterbury, then taught chemistry (and a bit of physics) in Norwich, the Isle of Wight and Thames Valley. His first experience of publishing was in writing educational materials, which he has continued to do since retiring. Of his fictional writing, *Evil Above the Stars* is his first published speculative fiction series.

Peter has been a fan of science fiction and fantasy since he was young, has an (almost) complete collection of classic SF by Asimov, Ballard, Clarke, Heinlein and Niven, among others, while also enjoying fantasy by Tolkien, Donaldson and Ursula Le Guin. Of more recent authors Iain M Banks, Alastair Reynolds and China Mieville have his greatest respect. His Welsh upbringing also engendered a love of the language (even though he can't speak it) and of Welsh mythology like the *Mabinogion*. All these strands come together in the *Evil Above the Stars* series. He lives in Herefordshire with his wife, Alison, who is a great supporter.